In Our Veins

Lynne M. Smelser

DEDICATION

This is dedicated to my two wonderful children, Rebecca and Megan, who make me believe in myself and to all of my wonderful family and friends. But I would especially like to dedicate this book to the memory of my grandmother, Pearl Smelser, who lost two children and a husband during a horrible flu epidemic and through her strength lived on with grace and dignity.

CONTENTS

Acknowledgments   I

Chapters 1-55   Pg. 1-259

About the auhtor2   Pg 260

ACKNOWLEDGMENTS

This book would not be possible without the guidance and support of my friends and family. I am a very blessed writer to have so many wonderful people in my life who believe in me and my work. It also would not be possible without the steady guidance of Rivka Kawano, who kept me on track and moving forward.

CHAPTER 1

Silently Weston Anderson sat and stared at the dark laptop monitor in front of him. *It's time*, he thought. He sighed as he stared at the obituary taped to his wall. Five years and it still looked like it did the day after his grandfather died. "Accused of unethical human experimentation," Weston read aloud as he pulled the clip from the wall. "Unethical human experimentation," he repeated slowly and morbidly enunciating each word. For a moment he sat and stared. Then carefully he picked up a pen, he marked through his grandfather's name. With a shaking hand he held it up and looked at the newsprint with new eyes. Then slowly, meticulously his pen wrote WESTON ANDERSON at the top and then he returned the scrap of newspaper to the otherwise barren wall.

Weston ran a blistered hand through the wave of gray and black hair that fell across his forehead and then turned back to the laptop. "Confession—good for the soul," he whispered. The words hung in the air. In high school he had dated a Catholic girl and confession seemed to be all she ever wanted to do after sex.

The thought made him smile for just a moment.

Then he focused on the monitor, so empty, so non-judgmental about the figures, numbers, charts, and symbols that the 57-year-old scientist had filled it with for more than four years; four years in which every passing minute taunted him with possibility that was always out of reach. What was it that Beeman always said? "Every human act revolves around power," Weston whispered. Then he looked at the summons to appear before a Senate panel in January. "Every human act revolves around power," he whispered again.

Weston leaned back in his chair and rested his elbows on the arms. As he tapped the tips of his fingers together he thought back to the day he met Beeman and his fat, slimy assistant....what was his name? Oh, yeah, Michael Jameson. Closing his eyes, Weston saw that first conversation so clearly.

"We're so pleased you agreed to join our project," Beeman had said as he thrust his hand out awkwardly.

"Pleased to be here and ready for work," Weston responded as he shook Beeman's hand. Briefly he looked up and down the tall thin man. Noting Beeman's pale appearance he was tempted to ask if the man had been ill, but something about the way he sniffed at the air and stepped backwards as if Weston were contagious made him think better of such a personal remark.

Jameson cleared his throat and quickly added, "Everything you asked for is here. It's all here. It's all here."

"I can see that," Weston replied as he looked around trying to stifle a chuck at the chubby little man's over eager response. "Wow! Back at the university I had to fill out a thousand forms to get any new equipment and it was nothing like this."

Beeman ran his index finger along a countertop as if checking for dirt as he responded, "Pharmaceutical companies have deep pockets and there are many parties interested in your work."

"I would think the entire world would be. After all, containing flu mutations would mean no more pandemics, no more epidemics, and in time…"

"…no more flu," said Beeman sharply. "Yes, there are many parties interested." Beeman walked briskly to the door as he motioned for Jameson to follow. "Do your work, Dr. Anderson. We'll be in touch."

Weston opened his eyes and returned to the moment. As he placed his fingers on the keyboard, he swallowed hard. His fingers momentarily curled into fists leaving the power button untouched.

He turned to his left to see the whiskey bottle that sat waiting for him in the middle of the piles of lab reports, data from clinical trials, and memos neatly stacked on his desk. "Never any time for filing," he mumbled. Looking up briefly to see that the front door to his one bedroom apartment was locked, he reached for the bottle, displacing a tiny square of paper that had been propped up behind it. He took a drink from the bottle and as he lowered it, he eyed the paper that was now lying flat on his desk. Slowly as if he were approaching something hot or dangerous, Weston reached for it. As if somehow hypnotized by it, he brought the black and white ultra sound picture closer to himself. For a moment his index finger traced the tiny figure, and then he turned it over. He saw the thumb print in blood pressed onto the back and

2

he held his breath as he closed his eyes momentarily. Then reluctantly he dropped it into the waste basket near his leg and took another drink. Wiping his mouth with the back of his hand, he kicked over the waste basket sending its contents sprawling out across the pale blue carpet. He turned back to the laptop and hit the power button. After hitting a few more keys he stared into the webcam at the top of the monitor. Weston felt ill. He put his hand to his mouth for a moment and then lowered it as he cleared this throat.

"November 8th. I am...I am..." he cleared this throat again and out of the corner of his eye looked at the bottle. "This will be one of my...no this will be my last entry. My last piece of puzzle that I can provide as to what has happened these past few years, months. Hell, hours," Weston paused again. He looked up startled at what he thought was the sound of the door knob jiggling. "Who's there?" he shouted across the room. He caught his breath and listened. Nothing. After a moment of listening to himself breathe and staring intently at the gold knob, he continued. "RCG35-98. If you've been listening to my other entries and the tape recordings I plan to include with this you know I created it. Yes. I created a strain of virus. I....I," Weston couldn't breath as he felt the weight of his words. Finally, after several minutes he continued. "RCG35-98 is no longer in my possession. No matter what they say."

Weston grabbed the bottle as he turned and then he slumped back into his leather chair and swiveled around to face the window. Pulling back the dusty, gray curtains he stared somberly at the darkness.

At his feet sat piles of newspapers. The top headlines read: *Flu Pandemic Certain. Vaccines Not Working.*

One last time he turned towards the camera. "Erica, I need you to do the right thing and get this evidence into the right hands because if you're watching this I'm dead." Weston took a deep breath and whispered, "I'm dead." He rubbed the back of his neck as he slowly turned again to the pile of newspaper briefly. His lips quivered slightly. Then looking into the camera one last time he said, "I didn't do this. Just know that whatever happens, whatever is said I didn't do this."

Weston fumbled with a flash drive he pulled from his top desk drawer. Inserting it into the laptop he downloaded the video then turned off the computer. Carefully he placed the flash drive in a box and addressed it. Then placing it in the zipper pocket of his Italian leather laptop case, Weston returned to his bottle. As he eyed the ultra sound picture in the midst of snickers wrappers and fast food bags he bowed his head for a moment and then took another drink.

CHAPTER 2

Erica blinked as the sun began to appear between the pink window shade and the Winnie-the-Pooh figures lined up on the window sill. "Had enough?" she asked as she looked down at baby in her arms. The tiny, brown eyes stared intently into Erica's. Erica smiled, placed the baby bottle on the nearby dresser, and then moved her daughter up to her shoulder. She began to pat the baby's back tenderly. "Tomorrow you're eight months old!" she whispered. Erica shook her head and repeated the words. "Eight months!"

Her eyes immediately went to the photographs on the white and pink dresser across the room. "That means your Grandma Ann has been gone for almost one month," she said as she looked at the photograph of a smiling woman with graying hair whose arms were wrapped tightly around Erica. "She really loved you, Reilly," Erica said as she moved the infant back onto her lap. "You have her eyes." Reilly smiled. "And you have your fa..." she paused for several seconds before continuing. "You have *his* smile."

Erica shifted Reilly into her arms and stood up. "It's time to get going, Reilly. Mommy has to get to work."

Reilly cooed and began to suck her fist. Erica walked briskly to her bedroom and placed Reilly in her pink bouncy seat on the floor next to the bed. Immediately Reilly began to play with the white, lacy edge of the bedspread. Erica bent down to move the seat and spotted the edge of a bridal magazine. Her eyes focused on the date. "Your grandma brought this over the very last time I saw her alive...just before the accident," she whispered. Her whole body tightened. Dropping to her knees, Erica pulled out the magazine revealing two more beneath it.

Slowly she opened one of the magazines and turned to the petite section where she had circled an A-line ivory dress. "Grandma thought this one was too fancy. What do you say?" she said turning the page towards Reilly who was still trying to put the lacy edge into her mouth. Then picking up all three magazines Erica shook her head. "I guess I guess I forgot to throw these away. She looked at the wastebasket for a moment and then silently shoved them back under the bed. *I can always throw them away tomorrow*, she thought.

Abruptly the doorbell shattered the moment. Startled, Erica

looked up at the clock on the night stand. Then she picked up Reilly and quickly headed out of the bedroom and down the stairs towards the front door of her condo. As she approached the door she knocked over an orchid in a decorative pot. The doorbell continued rapidly ringing, but Erica paused and looked down at the delicate flower lying on the floor. "We'll get that in a minute," she said to Reilly. Then she turned her attention back to the front door.

"Who is it?" she asked standing on her tiptoes looking through the peep hole.

"Dr. Anderson sent us," a deep gruff voice said.

"Weston?" asked Erica surprised.

"Yes, Weston. We work for him," the voice shot back quickly.

Erica shifted Reilly around as she fumbled to unlock the door. "Weston sent you?" she asked again as she opened the door. Two men stood in front of her. The shorter man huffed slightly and wiped the sweat from his forehead. Erica noticed his hands shaking slightly. While she had never seen this odd man before, she did indeed know the taller gentlemen. Weston called him the "walking corpse" because he was so pale and stiff. Arrogance still filled the air around him, just as it had the day Erica met him in Weston's office.

"Dr. Beeman," she said extending her free hand towards the taller man. He briefly touched her hand and then let it drop.

"Erica," he said curtly nodding. "And this is my associate, Mr. Jameson." Upon being acknowledged, the shorter man held up a black medical bag briefly.

"Yes, ma'am, we're from his lab," he replied.

Abruptly, Beeman pushed past Erica almost knocking her and Reilly over. Mr. Jameson grabbed her elbow to help steady her.

"Allow me," he said through a yellow crooked smile.

Erica stared at his mouth for a moment and cringed. Then Dr. Beeman spoke and she turned towards him.

"Dr. Anderson asked us to stop by and ensure that you and Reilly have had your flu shots."

6

"He talks about her non-stop," mumbled the short man nervously as he nodded towards Reilly. Beeman shot him an angry look.

Erica stopped and looked at the men for a moment. "Weston hasn't really been hands on when it comes to Reilly," she said. "Which I guess is why he sent you instead of coming here himself," she added with a touch of anger.

Beeman paused as if in thought. "He doesn't come here often?"

"Uh, yes, it's been quite awhile. Why?" Erica asked surprised.

Beeman shook himself and then his mouth twisted into a smile. "Oh, nothing." Then he walked over to the sofa and sat down. Erica remained standing near the door. "Why is it that you're here?" she asked. "I'm just on my way to work."

"Ah yes," replied Mr. Beeman as he straightened his tie. "How are things in public relations these days?"

"Fine. I understand that soon we'll be announcing something from your department," she replied.

"Oh, that's nice," Mr. Jameson squeaked. Mr. Beeman shot him yet another angry glare as he cleared his throat. "Sorry," he said. "Dry throat."

Mr. Beeman rolled his eyes and then turned back to Erica. "I'm sorry, Ms. Schmidt, but we haven't a lot of time," he said with each word coming out of his mouth as stiff as the stick that Erica always thought was up his ass. "We agreed to do this favor for Dr. An...I mean Weston and we have other places we need to be."

For a moment no one spoke. Mr. Jameson looked down at his feet as Erica studied both men. Finally Beeman spoke. "So would you like a flu shot as well, Ms, Schmidt?" he asked.

"Um, I've already had one...but Reilly hasn't yet. It's nice that Weston wants to do this for her, but I wish he would've called. But isn't that the way he is," she snapped.

With great effort Mr. Jameson struggled to get off of the couch and then waddled over to Erica. He motioned with his stubby fingers to the beige Queen Ann chair behind Erica and she moved towards it and

7

sat down. He stumbled down onto his knees, steadied himself by holding onto her mahogany coffee table for support, and then opened the black bag. Can you undress her a bit?" he asked.

Erica unbuttoned the sleeper slightly and removed Reilly's leg. In a flash Mr. Jameson had swabbed Reilly's thigh and completed the injection. As Erica comforted her daughter, the men nodded and silently departed through the front door and out into the morning haze.

CHAPTER 3

As a light rain began, Weston entered the building as a person desperately trying to awaken from a nightmare. As he rounded the corner his lab coat snagged on a nail head sticking out from the handrail at the top of the stairs pulling him backwards. Losing his footing momentarily, Weston's tall, slender frame awkwardly slipped down two steps sending his coffee cup against his chest. "God damn it!" he hissed as coffee splashed onto him.

"Good morning, Doctor Anderson," said a young graduate student who flashed a quick smile as she flipped a strand of blonde hair.

"Yeah, good morning," Weston mumbled barely looking up.

"Jaycee. My name is Jaycee," she offered energetically. "I've been a part of the lab staff for six months…six months today," she added as she straightened her pristine lab coat.

Weston looked up. "Sure. Great," he replied distractedly as he looked around. "You alone?"

"Well, yes…" she said surprised. Then she looked around and whispered, "I'm busy right now, but later…"

"Stay away from my lab," he snapped. Then shaking his head, Weston looked at the newest coffee stain on his coat and tossed his cup into the trash leaving the bewildered woman staring. Weston's step picked up as he walked down the narrow, dismal hallway. Careful not to trip over the lose tiles in the floor, his thoughts focused on the data he had copied onto a flash drive the previous night. Suddenly Weston stumbled into a man leaning against the wall near his doorway.

"Dr. Weston Anderson?" asked the man politely.

"God damn it! Why can't anyone leave me alone?" Weston's eyes darted around the hallway completely bypassing the stranger initially. Then he paused for a moment and looked at the stranger, assessing him with one quick glance. *Pants down to his knees, ignorant goatee. Graduate student* he concluded and then fumbling for his keys, Weston briskly stepped around the man. "Yeah. Yeah. Look I have a very busy d…" Weston stopped. He froze as the door swung open.

The soft squeal of a dying rat could be faintly heard above the flapping of the curtains in the wind. Despite the breeze the horrific odor of seared fur and sulphuric acid burned Weston's nose.

Weston rushed to the animals that lay scattered among the splintered tables, broken vials, and overturned garbage. Lose papers fluttered in the breeze from a nearby open window. Picking up one tiny, brown rat whose body quivered with the last of its life, Weston stroked it for a moment and then placing his thumb and forefinger on each side of its head, he crushed it. For a moment the small furry body continued to twitch, but the squeal was silenced. Weston looked around at the other animals. He stood frozen for a moment, then a paper brushed past him propelled by the breeze like a ghost with a message and Weston snapped into a new reality.

He raced over to the desk and got down on his hands and knees. Running his hands frantically underneath the bottom drawer for several seconds, he stopped just as suddenly as he began.

"The key," he said like a man whose life was being drained from him. "The key is gone." For a moment Weston's large frame cowered beside the desk. His forehead resting against it, his arms curled inward and his legs folded beneath him.

The man from the hallway raced out. Weston looked up startled. Grabbing the desk with both hands, Weston jumped to his feet instinctively ready for pursuit, but then stopped as he heard vomiting.

"It doesn't matter anyway," he whispered into nothingness. "It's gone."

Moments later a pale version of the stranger staggered into the room. Wiping vomit from his mouth onto his sleeve, he paused and then rushed out of the room again.

Weston looked around at the devastation of his lab. Then he spotted a sparkle on the other side of the room where the sun danced on yet another defeat. Weston walked slowly and deliberately towards it. He tossed aside fragments of chairs and tables sending them splintering further against the walls. "Oh, god," he gasped as he picked up the splintered remains of a pink and silver frame that had rested securely in his locked bottom drawer for the past six months. Mangled and smashed, the empty picture frame held a message that was clear. Completely numbed, he continued to play with the sparkles of glass

10

cursing himself for the picture in the first place.

"Dr. Anderson," said the stranger timidly from behind him, "should...should I call the police?"

In despair, Weston dropped it and walked a few feet to the only remaining upright desk in the room. Sitting down on it, Weston ran his hands through his hair and struggled to think clearly. The stranger approached. "Should I call the police?" he repeated.

Weston's despair turned to rage as he turned violently towards the stranger. Grabbing the man by the collar, Weston threw the stranger against the wall. "Who are you?" He demanded.

"Caleb...Caleb Philips," gasped the stranger.

"Who sent you Caleb Philips?" screamed Weston as he lifted Caleb slightly off the floor. Caleb's pale, boyish face quickly turned red and bulging. Struggling, Caleb fought for breath.

"Dr. Anderson!" screamed Jaycee, who had now entered the room.

Weston dropped Caleb to the ground like the rat he had just silenced. "What does it matter anyway? It's over. It's over," he repeated horrified. Shoving Caleb aside, Weston turned away. He could hear Jaycee behind him as she comforted Caleb, but the pair now seemed in a different world from Weston as he walked silently to his now empty file cabinet that lay on its side near the windows at the back of the room. As he ran his hand along the side of the cabinet, he noticed a red streak following it.

"Dr. Weston, you've cut yourself," said Jaycee walking up behind him.

Weston held up his hand and looked at it as if he had no idea it was attached to him. "Yes, I...I..."

Then he looked back at the shards of glass he had just been holding. "What have I done?" he whispered.

"What's going on, Dr. Weston?" asked Jaycee confused. Finally, she nervously cleared her throat. "Do I call campus police first or the city police?" Jaycee asked frantically as she reached out to grab Weston's injured hand.

Weston jerked back. "No...no...I've...already called. You need to leave now. You don't want to get hurt and there's chemicals...just go. Now. And please don't mention this to anyone." He looked at her puzzled face then added, "We want to catch the culprit, not tip him off."

Jaycee silently nodded. Confused, she paused as she passed Caleb and opened her mouth to speak, but no words came. After a few seconds, she silently continued on her way.

Straightening his sport coat, Caleb swallowed hard and then approached Weston again. "I had nothing to do with this."

Weston didn't respond. Instead he stared at the filing cabinet seemingly mesmerized by the drops of blood now dotting its side.

"Animal rights activists?" asked Caleb. As soon as the words came out of his mouth he knew how stupid they sounded.

"Yes, Einstein, they want me to stop hurting their little furry friends so they poisoned them by burning their cuddly bodies from the inside out," replied Weston sarcastically.

"I'm a graduate student. We spoke...on the phone." Caleb cleared his throat.

"Fine. Now get the hell out of my lab and forget you ever saw this."

"And the police?"

Weston turned sharply with fire in his eyes. "The police can stay the hell out too," he hissed.

Caleb approached several dead lab animals lying on the floor nearby. He bent over and started to touch one.

"Stop!" Weston shouted as he raced over to Caleb. "Trust me! You don't want to touch anything in here. Not without gloves."

Caleb backed away quickly. "An experiment gone bad?"

"Not one of mine," answered Weston. He bent down close to the animal. "Burned from the inside out. Acid most likely." He tapped a water bottle nearby. "Probably in their water."

"But that doesn't make any sense," replied Caleb. "Why kill

animals like that? If someone wanted…say…your notes, for example, isn't that a lot of trouble?"

"Well, Mr., what did you say your name was?"

"Caleb…Caleb Philips."

"Mr. Philips, they did indeed get my notes. But in a lab notes are only the paper version of the experiments." Weston swallowed hard. "If you really want to hurt a scientist, you take his notes and his evidence. You just burn it all."

"Evidence?" asked Caleb.

Weston walked over to the sink and began to rinse his wound. He looked at Caleb as the blood swirled in the sink. "Mr. Philips, I don't remember why you're here…"

"Flu…we were going to discuss your work with the flu vaccine and progress on obstructing mutations…" Caleb's words trailed off into nothingness.

Weston interrupted, clearing his throat loudly. He reached over to a rat corpse still twitching on the countertop. Picking it up tenderly, Weston stared at it for a moment as Caleb watched in silence. Then with one abrupt violent motion he slammed it against the wall leaving a grotesque smear. "As I was saying, I don't remember why you are here, nor do I care. Find another scientist, Mr. Philips, or you'll end up like that rat or worse yet….me."

CHAPTER 4

"Hello, Sweetie!" a voice rasped from the shadows of the hallway. Boney arms reached out from all sides.

"Reilly, say hello," Erica said as she pulled back the blanket from Reilly's face. Instead, Reilly turned to bury her face in her mother's neck.

"Hello! Hello! Can I see her? I'd like to hold the baby," soft, ragged voices continued their echoes.

Erica moaned. "I'm just here to see my grandmother and I'm off to work," she tried to explain as she weaved in between all of the wheelchairs and walkers trying to get to her grandmother's room. "Don't ever put Mommy in a place like this," she whispered to her daughter and then kissed her cheek. As she shifted Reilly's weight, Erica's purse slid down her arm and hit a man who sat motionless in his chair. "Oh, God! I'm so sorry!" she said as she tried to turn and see the man while balancing Reilly. The man didn't move or speak. Erica grabbed a tighter hold of Reilly and began to sprint towards room 117.

The room number was obscured by a group of men whispering and huddled around a clipboard. As Erica approached, the whispering stopped. Two men in suits walked away quickly with their heads down, while the man in the white coat made eye contact with Reilly. He smiled slightly as his eyes remained fixed on hers. Instinctively, Erica turned to move her baby away from him. Her lips parted briefly as she began to speak, but he abruptly turned leaving her standing.

"Reilly, honey, great-gramma is in here," whispered Erica as she entered her grandmother's room.

"Why is she here?" snapped an insistent voice from behind her.

Erica turned to see a nurse's aide pushing a cart. She shoved past Erica and then took her seat next to Pearl.

"Someone called me," replied Erica. "They said Grandma was well enough and Reilly could come today. Who were those men at the doorway?" she asked.

The aide completely ignored Erica and instead focused on a manila folder that she picked up from her cart. "Oh, yes, fine...fine," mumbled the aide.

"Who were those men outside?" repeated Erica insistently.

Without another word to Erica the woman turned towards Erica's grandmother. "Pearl, I'm gonna roll up your sleeve now," she said loudly releasing breath that reeked of cigarettes as she rolled up Pearl's sleeve. "Flu shot," she wheezed.

"Well, I'll only be a minute," replied Erica as she leaned over and kissed her grandmother's cheek. "Hi, Grammy."

"I don't want another shot," said Pearl softly as she looked up at Erica.

"It's going to be okay, Grammy," Erica said as she sat on the bed. Reilly reached out for the handle of Pearl's wheelchair. "We'll take gramma for a walk next time, Reilly," said Erica as she pulled Reilly's hand away.

"Your little one there...I wouldn't have brought her," the aide whispered as she motioned towards Reilly, but her eyes darted to the doorway.

Erica followed the aide's stare, but saw no one. "I got a phone call yesterday."

"Hmmm," said the aide looking up quickly. "She's lookin a bit green. If she's sick she ought not to be here round these folks." Then she wiped Pearl's arm with a swab.

Pearl pulled away. "No! I says I don't want another shot!"

Erica felt Reilly's head. "She just had a flu shot," she responded sharply. "And I'm sure she's not sick. Probably just the flu shot. We'll only be here a few minutes," sighed Erica. Then she turned towards her grandmother. "I was just thinking about Momma this morning," Erica said loudly looking into her grandmother's face. "Ann. I was thinking about Ann this morning."

Erica stared into Pearl's eyes. Disappointment swept through her as she looked into Pearl's vacant stare. Erica managed a smile.

"Who, dear?" Whose Ann?" asked Pearl.

"No one, Grandma. I just thought I'd stop by to see you, Grandma," she said sadly. For a moment Erica fingered a bouncy, black curl that bobbed alongside of Reilly's face and then glanced at her watch. "I should get going."

"How old?" asked the aide nodding towards Reilly.

"Eight months."

"Wow! She's a tiny one. My grandson is just about that and he's just a monster." "Hold still now, dear," said the aide as she wrapped her large hand around Pearl's thin forearm and pushed a needle into the skin.

Pearl screamed startling Reilly and causing her to fuss. Erica began to comfort her baby.

"I said...I said I don't want a shot..." sobbed Pearl, "why don't you listen? I don't want a shot again!"

"Again? Why, Pearl, you ain't had no other flu shot."

"Yes, I have." Pearl cried. "I have and I won't take another one."

"Grammy, this will make you all better," Erica said in a comforting tone. "Oh, and look. Reilly and I made this for you."

Reaching into her pocket, Erica pulled out a red construction paper heart. "See it says, 'We love you, Reilly & Erica'." Then she extended it to Pearl.

"Why looky there, Pearl. That's nice," said the aide, who reached out to Pearl's hands, pried them open, placing the paper heart into her palm before the boney appendages snapped closed around it.

"Is this my number?" asked Pearl loudly. "Like the last time?"

Erica shook her head. "No, gramma. It's a heart from me and Reilly."

Reilly began to fuss. "We better go," said Erica in a concerned tone.

"These old folks don't need no fussin, that's for sure," added the aide.

16

Erica glared at the woman. Pearl reached out and began to stroke the baby's soft locks as she rocked back and forth in her seat. The red, paper heart she held in her hand slipped to the ground and slid along the smooth floor finally coming to rest at the closet door unnoticed by Erica. "I didn't want this shot…no, no, no…I said I didn't want another one," moaned Pearl as she rubbed her arm. "I don't feel well again."

"Grammy, I think we'll go for now," Erica said tenderly.

Pearl began to hum and Reilly's cries softened to a whimper. Looking at Reilly, Pearl began to cry quietly. "I did my best for my babies. I did everything I could," Pearl murmured.

"I know that, Grammy," Erica said as she reached out to Pearl. "You did the best you could."

"No. No. No. I didn't have flu shots…no one had flu shots…no…no…no."

Tears dribbled down Pearl's face running along the wrinkles. Erica looked around for a tissue. As she did a bright yellow sticker in Pearl's medical chart that was lying on the aide's cart, caught Erica's eye.

"What does that mean?" she asked leaning over to point to the sticker

Startled, the aide closed the folder quickly. Erica reached out for the folder, but the aide pulled it away. She moved towards the door, stopping momentarily to wipe away the sweat off of her fleshy, flush red cheeks.

"I'm just here to give a flu shot. That's all. Just a flu shot," she said wheezing. "I have to leave now," announced the aide loudly startling everyone and sending Reilly back into loud sobs.

"What clinical trial group is my grandmother in?" asked Erica pointing to the folder in the aide's hand. "Who put her in this group?" she insisted as she stood up.

"Charts are confidential," the aide snapped. Abruptly, the large woman clumsily grasped her folder and supplies close to her body and waddled out the door wheezing as her grotesque weight closed in on her lungs.

Erica sat stunned.

Pearl simply looked down at her own hands, shaking, wrinkled, brown. "My baby Wallace died in these hands," she sobbed.

Erica sighed. "Grandma, it's okay. Really it is," said Erica as she shook her head and looked at her watch.

"Wallace had a rash and a fever," cried Pearl as she rocked back and forth in her chair.

Erica stood up. "Grandma, I have to go now..."

She gave Pearl a quick kiss and walked away holding Reilly tightly. Just outside the door Erica stopped and leaned against the wall. Her cell phone began to ring and she answered it quickly. "Hello? Hello? Weston? You're not making any sense. I have to take Reilly to daycare...I'm with my grandmother right now. What? They called and said Reilly could come today. I don't care what you said. She's my grandmother and I wanted her to see the baby. Fine! I'll stop by there right after I drop her off."

Reilly continued to fuss.

Erica fumbled through her purse for a pacifier. Just then the phone rang again. Trying to juggle Reilly, her purse, and her phone, Erica finally dropped her purse. "Hello?" Erica said into the cell phone. "Oh, uh... I'm going to be late. In fact, list me as not coming in until after lunch." She hung up the phone.

"Don't look in the folder."

Startled, Erica looked up to see Pearl. "Ann looked in the folder. Ann had to die," Pearl added softly and then shuffled back into her room.

CHAPTER 5

"Like you?" repeated Caleb.

Weston focused on wrapping a bandage around his hand and remained silent for a moment. "Mr. Phillips, I have nothing for you today. Even if I did make an appointment to speak with you, which I currently cannot recall, I need you to leave *NOW*." A cool anger tempered Weston's words.

"I can help," said Caleb stepping forward. "I can help you clean up. I can help you get answers. I have connections….a senator or two…or maybe someone else."

Weston walked towards the windows and grabbed a stool that was lying on the floor. Sitting it upright, he pulled it close to the window then he took another step to look outside. Thrusting his good hand into his pocket, Weston stood for a moment gazing out. Then, as he pulled his hand from his pocket, a piece of paper slid to the floor in silence. Caleb's eyes followed the paper, and then they darted to Weston's face to register his awareness. Weston stared like zombie, unmoving, unknowing. Then he whispered, "Erica's coming."

"Who's Erica?" asked Caleb. Cautiously he moved towards the paper until he was close enough to place his foot over it.

Weston looked strangely shocked at the question. "A…a fri…someone I know in our parent company's PR department," he whispered looking out the window.

"I'm sorry…a friend in PR is that what you said?" responded Caleb as he let his jacket hit the floor. Then he bent over and picked it up, glancing only briefly at the pencil marking: 3351 Charlotte. He shoved it into his pocket and looked back up at Weston.

"Something like that. She works for Astrium International. That's the parent company to Zelticor. She'll help," Weston stated somberly.

"How do you know she wasn't part of whoever did this?" asked Caleb.

"She's not." Weston paused for a moment and then continued with a distracted tone as if speaking to himself. "She does media relations or something like that. A few years back she was a great biology student...my student...but now she writes press releases and other corporate materials. That's not a real job for a biologist." After several minutes of silence, the sound of Caleb's sneaker on shards of glass as he shifted his weight brought Weston back to the moment. He stared at Caleb as if seeing him for the first time. "You're not going to school to become a publications specialist for Astrium International, are you?"

Caleb stood silently. Weston stared somberly like a man ready to smoke his final cigarette as he faced the gallows. Caleb cleared his throat nervously. "I'm here to learn about pandemics and right now..."

"Right now it's fashionable to talk about influenza and all the panic. Right?"

"Um," Caleb struggled to respond. "I guess. Um I guess you get lots of people wanting to talk to an expert like yourself now."

"Oh, yeah. The media is ringing my phone off the hook and every graduate student within the United States and a few outside of it wants to work with me."

"I guess so," said Caleb as he attempted to lean against the desk, but misjudged the distance and lost his footing. "Oh god!" shouted Caleb as he hit the floor.

Weston did not react. In fact, his eyes returned to the window, as the reality of the world around him froze again.

"I'm not hurt," said Caleb jumping to his feet and wiping debris off his shirt and the jacket he held. Noticing his elbow was wet he held it up to Weston. "What is this stuff?"

"Take your shirt off." Weston said dryly.

"No, seriously, what is this?"

Weston turned his head slightly to look at Caleb. "Could be any number of things including acid or virus. I'd take my shirt off if I was you."

"Damn!" shouted Caleb. He raced into the hall and removed his shirt.

"Modest?" mumbled Weston.

Caleb returned carrying the backpack he had previously dropped in the hall. He reached for an overturned waste basket. Careful to grab only the edges of the basket, he pulled it upright and then tossed his shirt into it. "Shouldn't this lab be locked up? I mean, you know, shouldn't we get out of here?"

"Little late for that now that you've rubbed your elbows into it, isn't it?" asked Weston with a smirk.

"You're crazy!" said Caleb and he turned abruptly towards the door just as his cell phone began to ring. Looking at Weston he shook his head and then briskly walked out. "Yes," he whispered into his cell. "No, I'm leaving. Look this guy is freaking nuts….and I walked into…into…I don't know what the hell is going on. The lab. It's been vandalized or robbed."

Weston watched Caleb exit the lab. Pausing for a moment, Weston grabbed a piece of paper from the floor and pulled out his pen. "Outside" he wrote on it with large letters and then drew an arrow. After pausing to tape it onto the door, Weston quietly pulled the door shut, locked it, and then walked away as his own cell phone began to ring. For a moment he stared at the device and then he flipped it open as he headed down the hallway in the opposite direction from Caleb.

"Yeah, I got your message. Did you get mine?" said Weston with a sneer. "I know you found the envelope, but that wasn't my only copy, and trust me, that's just a small taste." He paused for a moment and looked around. He saw no one in the dismal hallway, but then he noticed the tip of Caleb's shoe sticking out from a side hall near his lab. Resisting his first impulse to go after Caleb, Weston turned the opposite direction and headed for the exit on the far end of the building.

"I'm still here," he assured his caller after several seconds. "But apparently so is your friend. I ought to kick the shit out of…what? Yes, I said YOUR friend…I don't care what you say. I still hold all the cards." Weston hit the disconnect button as he reached the rear exit to the building. Once outside he leaned against the wall, looked around and pulled out a cigarette. For a moment he simply stood with the cigarette between his lips letting the breeze sweep across him.

Then he pulled out his cell again and dialed. "My lab. It was trashed," he said into the phone as he walked around the corner of the building out of sight of the exit door. "Animals dead, papers everywhere. Beeman, I was collecting evidence. Why? Wake up! Can you honestly sleep at night after what we've done? It's about human life. Damn it, Beeman, people are.... Look I'm sorry I didn't tell you...I didn't want anyone else involved. ...The election is in five days.... I just need to get the truth....yes, I said the truth...look when I'm dead I need my kid to know it was for something."

He paused and took a long drag on his cigarette and walked over to a discarded newspaper sitting on a nearby bench. The headline "U.S. Struggles to Meet Global Demand" caught his eye as the voice in his cell phone droned meaninglessly in his ear. "It's in play now," Weston said over the voice. "Just turn on the six o'clock news and let the death count begin."

CHAPTER 6

Caleb stood and watched the door at the far end of the hallway. Weston never returned, not even for his coat. Then a voice came from the cell phone he was holding in his hand.

"Huh? Yeah, I'm still here. I was just…hell, I'm leaving. This guy's a freak… Look, Senator, you asked me to meet this guy and find out what he's up to. Well, someone has beaten you to it. His lab's trashed and I'm probably dyin or something from this shit on my arm….okay…okay…okay. I'll talk to the guy one more time and maybe snap a few pics of the lab, but that's the end of my roll in all of this." Closing his phone he stuffed it into his backpack and then pulled out the mini-tape recorder from his shirt pocket.

"Damn!" sighed Caleb. Then he rubbed his ribs where the tape recorder had been shoved into him when Weston slammed him into the wall. Pressing the eject button he fingered the tiny tape for a moment.

Just then he saw a petite woman in a suit march up to the lab door. For a moment she attempted to peer into it, then noticing the paper taped to it, she pulled it down from the door. Adjusting her glasses, she pushed back a strand of brown hair behind her ear and turned and walked towards the same door Weston had just used.

Puzzled, Caleb watched the woman step briskly toward the end of the hallway where Weston had just stormed off to with his cell. Putting the tape recorder back into his backpack, Caleb zipped his coat and pursued the woman. As he neared the door, he edged along the wall in an attempt to watch unseen, but he couldn't find a good way to look out the small, square window in the door without being seen.

He stopped a moment and crouched on the floor and pressed his ear against the door hoping to be able to hear something even if he couldn't see. Just then Erica pushed open the door as she called out, "Weston? Where are you?" Just then she toppled over Caleb as he knelt in her path.

"Oh, God! Are you okay?" asked Caleb frantically as he grabbed her arm.

Erica sprawled across the floor and her purse slid beyond her reach sending make up and pacifiers sprawling. Dazed and slightly embarrassed, she looked up just in time to see Weston swing the door open. "Erica!" he shouted and then slammed the door into Caleb pushing them both back onto the floor. Then she saw Weston's body falling onto her.

Weston struggled to regain his footing quickly. Erica laid there dazed for a moment.

"Oh," moaned Caleb. "Is everyone okay?"

"God no!" groaned Weston. "What the hell is going on here?"

Then both men spotted Erica. "Erica!" shouted Weston. "Erica! Are you okay? Come on, sit up."

"I think she had the wind knocked out of her," said Caleb as he struggled to help her to her feet. Erica gasped and as breath filled her lungs the color returned to her face. "Are you okay, Erica?" asked Caleb.

Erica nodded then she looked at Caleb. "Do I know you?"

"I'm..."

"He's a graduate student who was supposed to have left about half an hour ago," interrupted Weston. "Want to tell me what you're still doing here? No, on second thought I don't care. Get out. Get out of this building. Get out of my life. Get out."

"Calm down, Wes," said Erica as she began to gather her items.

Weston leaned over to assist her and began quickly pushing everything on the floor into her red, leather bag including Caleb's tape that has been knocked out of his backpack. "Don't patronize me, Erica. This guy needs to get out of here."

"And don't treat me like a child. This is so typical of you," she huffed.

"Typical of me? What does this idiot have to do with anything between us?" he shot back.

"Why are you yelling at me?" she shouted. "This guy's trying to help."

"Trust me, honey, he's not here to help anyone but himself. He's behind my lab break in…"

"No, I'm not," interrupted Caleb.

"If you have proof call the police, Wes," said Erica ignoring Caleb.

"Good idea," replied Weston sarcastically. "I wish I'd thought of that. You're a genius."

Erica straightened her Ann Taylor blouse as she stood to her feet. "Why did you call me anyway?"

As the two argued Caleb quickly checked the pockets of his backpack… everything was in place….everything except his tape. His eyes scanned the area, and then rested on Erica's red bag that was clutched under her arm.

"I don't know," said Weston. "I was upset and obviously didn't make a sound judgment."

"I need to talk to you about Reilly…"

Weston looked at her somberly. "Erica look around you….my lab's been trashed!"

"And your daughter needs some of your expertise, even if you can't parent…it's flu season you know."

"Get her a flu shot," snapped Weston. "Right here, right now I've got other issues going on!"

"All that education and yet you're still so stupid," shot back Erica and she began to march away.

Weston rubbed his forehead. He watched Erica storm away as he stood silently.

"Wait a minute!" shouted Caleb, startling Weston.

"Leave her alone," Weston growled.

Weston took several steps forward and grabbed Caleb's arm. "This doesn't involve her."

Caleb pulled away. "Then who does this involve?" he snapped, "You said she works for your parent company, right? If someone is after your work on virus production, maybe they should be alerted?"

"Look I don't know who you really are, but if you hurt her or get in my way, you're a dead man." Then Weston ran his hand through his black and gray hair and walked back outside alone.

Caleb ran after Erica and reached the door at the same time as her. "Wait," he said breathlessly.

"What do you want?" snapped Erica.

"Look, I'm sorry we had to meet this way, but I'm really just a grad student who wanted to work with Mr. Anderson on the flu stuff. Things just got...well my timing is lousy I guess."

Rain began to pelt down from the dark sky as they stood on the front stoop of the building. "Don't you mean Doctor?"

Caleb looked puzzled.

"Dr. Anderson?" she said coolly. Then Erica pulled out an umbrella and began to walk towards her car.

Caleb pulled his jacket up over his head and he splashed after her. "Hey can I get some help?"

"You're not wearing a shirt?" asked Erica astonished.

"What can I say? I heard Georgia is warm all year around."

"Well, it's not," replied Erica. She looked at her watch. "I've missed two meetings and I've only got an hour before I have to pick up Reilly from daycare. God damn it!"

"Then you're not busy. Want to go get some coffee and maybe we can figure out what's going on here?" he asked.

Erica sighed, and then motioned to her right. "Coffee shop on the corner."

He reached into his backpack quickly and patted his gun. "Great," he said. "I'll see you there."

CHAPTER 7

"We use to come here a lot," said Erica as she entered the coffee shop a few steps ahead of Caleb. "Wes and me that is," she added softly.

"Not anymore?"

Erica shot him a harsh look. "What did he tell you about me?"

Caught off guard by her response, Caleb hesitated.

"Forget I asked," Erica mumbled as she shook off the rain. For a moment she stared out the door and up at the dismal gray clouds.

"I didn't take Mr. Uptight for being a Starbucks kind of guy," Caleb joked.

"You think that's an odd match," replied Erica, "you should see the crotchety ex-CIA guy who runs the place."

"Ah mystery solved," laughed Caleb.

"Yeah, I guess that's why Weston fits in here."

They approached the counter. "Latte," said Caleb as he reached into his backpack.

"I've got this one," said Erica as she stepped up. "Hot chocolate, no whip."

"Hot chocolate?" Caleb asked. "Not a coffee drinker?"

"Nope. Just not my thing," she said somberly. Then she began to open her purse.

"Oh, hey, let me get this one," Caleb said quickly as he thought of his tape and pushed her purse off the countertop.

"Okay. Thanks. I need to use the restroom anyway. Grab the drinks and find a seat, okay?"

"Um, want me to hold your purse?" he asked quickly.

Erica paused and looked at him puzzled. "My purse? No. No, I'll take it with me." Then she walked away.

"One latte and one hot chocolate no whip," a voice from the other side of the counter announced.

Caleb picked up the drinks and found a place in the corner with two large cushioned chairs. He sat down and propped up his feet on the coffee table. His cell phone began to ring just as Erica re-appeared.

"Is that yours?" she asked.

"Huh?"

"Cell phone. Is that yours ringing?"

"Oh, yeah, but uh, I'm not going to get it right now."

Erica sat down and dropped her purse between her leg and his. "That thing weighs a ton," she said. "Funny after you have kids it seems like you can't leave the house without everything including the kitchen sink."

"Oh, you have a kid?"

"Yes, I do. Reilly Ann." Erica opened her purse. "I'll show you a picture."

Caleb leaned forward and nervously looked into her purse. His hand went towards his gun in its hiding place. Then he spotted the tape. Leaning forward he knocked over his drink. "Oh, God! I'm so sorry!"

Erica stood up quickly. "Oh, it's on my skirt!"

"I'm so sorry," said Caleb as he eyed her purse. "Why don't you go and clean up before that stains. I'll take care of things here." He began frantically wiping with the napkins. Erica paused. "Seriously. You better get that cleaned up," he urged.

Erica headed for the restroom again. As she turned the corner, Caleb reached for the red, leather strap and yanked the purse up. Quickly he began riffling through the miscellaneous hodgepodge that made up its contents. "Pacifier, tissue, Band-Aids, coupons, scotch tape? What the hell? She's got everything in here," he whispered to himself as he continued.

"Yes, I already told you that," Erica said angrily. She grabbed her purse. "Want to tell me what the hell you're doing?" she shouted. The coffee shop suddenly became quiet and all heads turned towards her.

Startled, Caleb dropped the purse and stood up to face Erica's angry glare. "Look," he sighed, "I could lie and cover my ass, but the thing is that I really don't want to be involved in this...this little situation you all have here anymore than I have to be. Sit down and I'll tell you who I am." He sat down, but Erica remained standing. "Please," he whispered.

Reluctantly Erica sat down. "I'm listening, but you had better make this good or so help me..."

"Yeah, yeah, you'll kill me...but you'll have to get in line behind our mad scientist friend." Caleb picked up his cup to take a drink. He shook the empty cup. "Mind if I get a refill first?"

"Yes, yes, I do. I want to know what's going on and I want to know now. Did you have anything to do with what happened in Weston's lab?"

"No."

Erica rolled her eyes and tilted her head sideways.

"Honest to God," Caleb nervously tapped at his cup. "I'm seriously going to need a refill here to go on much farther...otherwise I'm going to say something stupid about how cute you look when you..."

Erica stood to her feet. "Go to hell."

Caleb jumped up.

"I want truth and you're giving me pick up lines?" shouted Erica.

"Okay. Okay, you're right. Not appropriate. Sit here for one minute and I'll tell you everything." He walked up to the counter leaving Erica sitting alone. As she waited, she thumbed through her purse.

When he returned she was sitting quietly sipping her drink. "Okay here's the truth. There's been lots of complaints by grad students about the way Weston..."

"You mean Dr. Anderson."

"Yeah. Dr. Anderson, the way he's been treating students. He pissed off the wrong person. She went to a senator who went to the university president….yadda…yadda…yadda."

"And where do you fit into all of this?"

"I owed someone a favor," he sipped his latte and then swished it around in his mouth for a moment.

"So?"

"So I agreed to come in here and find out what's going on."

Erica reached into her purse and swiftly pulled out the tape. "And where does this come into play?" she asked as she held it up.

"I taped my conversation with him this morning." Caleb stared intently into Erica's eyes.

Without moving, Erica sat and stared at Caleb intently. Then after a minute she took a drink from her cup. "I guess I believe you," she said hesitantly. "So what's your verdict about Weston?"

"I assume today was atypical and there's no way to say."

"So you'll be back?"

"No. I did my favor now I need to get on with my life."

"As a graduate student?" asked Erica cautiously.

"Yeah, as a graduate student," Caleb responded dryly.

Erica took a long drink and looked out the window for a moment. "And where did you say you're a student?" she asked not turning to look at him.

"I didn't," he answered. "Now can I ask you a few questions?"

"Is one of them 'may I please have my tape back'?" Erica asked.

"Ah, yes."

Erica looked over the tape and then tossed it to him. "I have no reason to answer any of your questions or to even stay here another minute."

"You have no reason not to…after all, it may be to your advantage to talk to me and it doesn't exactly look like the two of you are best buddies."

Erica smiled slightly. "That's not completely accurate. You kind of caught us at our worst this morning. Neither of us were having a good day, but go ahead. You can ask. I just may not answer."

"Fair enough," began Caleb. "How long have you known him?"

"Seems like forever, but I guess it's actually only been about five years…yeah…five years ago this week."

"How did you meet?"

"He was my professor."

"Really?"

"Really."

"We were off and on again for awhile. I graduated, got a job at Astrium International so I could be near Weston and not long after got pregnant."

Caleb looked around the dimly lit room eyeing every individual. Moving closely to Erica, he lowered his tone. "Listen I really need to ask you something. How ethical do you think Weston is?"

"Ethical?" asked Erica loudly.

"Shhh. Look I just want a quick off the cuff answer."

"Why are we whispering? Weston isn't around here, I guarantee you that right now he's out looking for whoever messed with his lab."

"Let's just be safe, okay?"

Erica sighed. "When it comes to the scientific community," she cleared her throat for effect and then whispered, "you won't find anyone more concerned about ethics than Wes."

The sound of Mozart's Minute Number 5 began to play from Erica's purse. "Phone. Excuse me a minute." She pressed the green button on her phone and turned away from Caleb. "Hello? Really? Okay, I'll be right there."

Erica's heart raced. She violently shoved the phone into her bag and turned to Caleb.

"Anything wrong?" asked Caleb.

"My baby….the daycare says she has a high fever."

CHAPTER 8

Erica exited the coffee shop without another word. Despite only needing to travel a few miles, she felt mocked by each stop light and every slow driver.

Instinctively she hit the speed dial on her cell and listened. "Mikala Green's office," said a voice through the phone.

"Miki, oh God, I'm so glad to hear your voice!"

"Erica? Erica, girl where you been? Marcus called looking for you earlier. He said you missed every meeting you had scheduled today and that ain't like you!"

"Miki, I've done something really stupid," she moaned.

"Uh huh, I hear that. You went over to see Weston *again* didn't you? You always turn off your cell when you're there."

"Yes, I did, but that's not what I'm calling about."

"Erica Elaine!"

"Listen, I got Reilly a flu shot, someone from Weston's lab gave it to her and now..."

"You let someone from that crazy man's lab give your kid a shot?" shouted Miki.

"They said Weston sent them. He's given me flu shots before. But ..."

"But this wasn't Weston, right?

"Right," Erica said with concern.

"Erica...."

"What? You're breaking up, Miki," said Erica irritated. Then she looked at the display on her phone. "Hold it. Wait. I've got another call. Give me a minute."

"Hello?" Erica said into the phone after switching lines.

"Mrs. Schmidt? This is Dr. Hall's office. We have an open appointment if you'd like to come in," said the voice.

"Yes, I would."

"So what seems to be the problem?" replied the voice.

"She had a flu shot earlier today and now she has a fever according to the daycare center," stated Erica.

"Ms. Schmidt, did you give her some Tylenol?" asked the voice.

"No, but if you have an open appointment, I'd like to just bring her in," she replied.

"Can you come now?

"Yes. Thank you." Then she hit the flash button and returned to Miki.

"Everything okay?" asked Miki.

"The doctor's gonna see Reilly right now," said Erica.

"Bad day?" asked Miki.

"Bad day," replied Erica. "I saw Weston this morning."

"Yeah, so you said."

"Someone trashed his lab," Erica blurted out.

"Really?" asked Miki surprised.

"Just before she died...specifically the morning before...my mom called and told me to put the wedding plans on hold. She said...she said there was something about Weston. Did you know that his grandfather was a scientist?" asked Erica hesitantly.

"No," replied Miki. So?"

Very slowly Erica continued. "He was accused of being a part of a bioterrorism plot AGAINST the U.S."

"Girl, what are you saying?"

"Why would someone trash Weston's lab?" Erica demanded.

"Hmmm, let me see," said Miki sarcastically. "He sleeps with his students. Abandons the mother of his child and he's an all around asshole."

"He doesn't sleep with his students," shot back Erica angrily.

"Wake up, Erica," insisted Miki. "He slept with you while you were his student. You really think you were the first and only?"

Erica bit her lip to hold back her tears.

"Erica? Erica? Girl, I'm sorry," blurted out Miki. "I'm sorry."

"Yeah, sure thing," replied Erica as she stopped the car. For a moment she rested her head on the steering wheel. "Goodbye," she said angrily and pushed the disconnect button. Then her cell phone rang again. Briefly she wiped the tears from her eyes and then looked at the phone number before answering.

"Hello?" Erica asked puzzled by the unknown number.

"Hello, is this Erica Schmidt?"

"Yes."

"I…I'm…this is going to sound strange, but I'm visiting my mother-in-law at the Cherry Hill Nursing Home and your grandmother was just taken to the infirmary. In fact, from what I could tell she was being put into isolation."

"What?"

"Maybe it's standard or just part of this flu epidemic thing, but my mother-in-law was very upset and wanted me to call you."

"Grandma was feeling just fine earlier today when I saw her. Not even a cold."

"I know this sounds strange," repeated the woman.

"Why haven't they called me?" insisted Erica.

"I don't know. You know how the elderly can be…they see

conspiracy everywhere."

"I'm not following," said Erica.

"My mother-in-law seems to think there's something going on at the home and that everyone is trying to cover it up so they won't get sued."

"Oh," Erica replied hesitantly. "Well, thank you. I'll call the home when I get a minute. Thanks."

Erica hit the "end call" button and then pushed her phone back into her purse. Taking a deep breath she left her car and walked briskly into the daycare.

"Hello, Ms. Schmidt. Reilly's in the nurse's office," said a young woman seated at the front desk.

Erica rushed past her and down the hallway into the red door marked "NURSE." She saw Reilly lying on the couch sucking her thumb.

"Oh, sweetie," Erica said soothingly. "What's the matter, baby?"

Just then a large woman in a white smock appeared. "She has a slight fever, so we thought you had better pick her up. We're taking every precaution we can against this flu epidemic this year. Course you know that working for a pharmaceutical company that creating flu vaccines."

Erica scooped up her daughter. "Thank you," she whispered and then carried Reilly out.

"Your arms are pretty full, Ms. Schmidt!" observed the woman behind the desk. "Let me help you," she offered as she came around the counter and grabbed Reilly's diaper bag. As they reached the car, the young woman held Reilly as Erica unlocked the vehicle and put the bag and her purse into the front seat.

"Thank you," said Erica as she reached out for Reilly.

"Feel better soon, honey," said the woman stroking Reilly's head.

As she started the car, Erica looked back at Reilly who was now sleeping in her car seat. "We'll get you into bed and get you feeling better," she whispered. Just then her cell phone rang again.

Looking at the display she saw the same number that had just called her. "Hello?"

"Hello, I'm so sorry to bother you again. I'm the woman who just called you about your grandmother," said the voice.

"Yes, what can I do for you?"

"The nursing home made me leave just now. They gave me a handout about the flu and said that they were 'locking down' the place. Does that sound right to you?"

"That really depends on what's happening there," said Erica puzzled. "Let me check and I'll get back to you...what did you say your name was?"

"Baker. Shirley Baker.'

"Okay, Ms. Baker, I'll get back to you. Can I reach you at the number on my caller ID?" Erica's question was met with silence. She pressed the phone against her ear. "Hello? Hello?"

Taking one more look back at her sleeping child, Erica sighed and began to dial her cell phone. "Hello, Cherry Hill Nursing Home," said a frazzled voice.

"Uh, yes, this is Erica Schmidt. I'm calling about my grandmother."

"Who?"

"Erica Schmidt. My grandmother is Pearl Schmidt. She's been there for four years," she said impatiently.

Erica strained to hear a voice, but all that she received was silence. Then she heard the brief shuffle of papers before the same voice, only now soft and faltering, returned on the line. "Ma'am, are you sure you're calling the right care facility?"

"Is this the Cherry Hill Nursing Home?" Erica asked.

"Yes, but we have no Pearl Schmidt here."

CHAPTER 9

Caleb sat at the coffee shop sipping his drink and thinking as he mindlessly fingered the tape. *There was nothing significant on the tape...just some crazy middle-aged scientist ranting about...about....well God only knows what Weston's whole episode this morning was about...*

"Friend leave?"

Caleb was startled by the question. "What?" He sat up quickly and looked up to see a heavy-set bag of wrinkles standing in front of him.

"Your friend, she leave?" the raspy voice repeated.

"Uh, yeah, I guess. What's it to you?"

Suddenly a hand was thrust into his face. "Carson Jaspers."

Caleb looked at the large hand for a moment. Then shaking it briefly he replied, "Nice to meet you, Carson, but you know right now I'd just like to be alone. Not really in the market for a new friend if you know what I mean."

Carson tossed the white rag he was holding onto the coffee table next to Caleb's drink. Then he dropped onto the overstuffed chair next to Caleb with a thump. "Seems to me a man can use all the friends he can get...especially one with lots of secrets like you."

"And what makes you think that I have lots of secrets, Mr. Jaspers?"

"Carson, if you please," huffed the large man. "Well, I saw you fishing around that young lady's purse. I also know I've seen you in here before and yet you told that pretty little thing that you'd never been here."

Irritated, Caleb stood up abruptly. "What can I say, Carson, love can make a guy do strange things."

"You ain't in love with her," wheezed Carson. "Damn, I wish I could smoke in here...God damn no smoking ordinances."

"Well, I guess you've got me figured out then…oh, and I think you've had more than your share of cigarettes already."

Caleb made his way towards the door weaving around the displays of gourmet coffee and shiny metallic mugs. "All right fine," he heard Carson shrilly shout. "Just thought you might be fishin for some info on Dr. Frankenstein."

Caleb stopped. The few people seated in the coffee shop stopped momentarily as well. Then, as they resumed their conversations, Caleb slowly turned and approached Carson who sat huffing breathlessly from exerting himself in an effort to shout. Standing over Carson, Caleb said sharply, "You know something?"

"Maybe. Maybe not. I thought you didn't need a friend."

"I don't," replied Caleb coolly.

Carson tapped on the table in front of him and whispered, "How about paid informants?"

Looking around for a moment, Caleb pulled out his wallet and sat down. "Possibly," he said. "But first I'd like to know what I'm paying for."

"A little old fashioned conspiracy," said Carson as he wiped sweat from his forehead. "I operate this place. Been doing stuff like this off and on for years since I left the CIA. Anderson's lab is within spitting distance and I hear things. Especially from them youngsters…grad students interning there come in here all showing off. Think cause they're in Starbucks they can blabber their heads off. They just don't get the meaning of confidentiality…or maybe here it don't matter," Carson chuckled showing a tobacco stained teeth. Then he tapped on the table again.

"Sorry, but the daily grind of a graduate student doesn't impress me much," replied Caleb sarcastically. "What I want to know about Dr. Anderson they most likely aren't even privy to knowing."

"Look I been watching you since you first came in here and I think we both want the same thing," rasped Carson.

"World peace and good coffee for all?" asked Caleb pointing to a sign behind the counter.

"Yeah, asshole, that it's. You know, I thought you was interested in finding out why some of the flu vaccines ain't working, but looks like you're just in it for the paycheck. I hope your little tape there helps lots." Carson struggled to get out of the chair, rocking back and forth until he had gained momentum enough to rise. "Damn hippie chairs," he hissed and began to walk towards the counter.

"Wait," said Caleb. "Do you know something….I mean really know something?" he asked.

"You'd be surprised what I know, kid," said Carson looking over his shoulder.

Caleb pulled out $50.00. "How much of what you know will this buy?'

Carson reached out for the money, "Not much, but maybe enough for you…"

Just as Caron's fingers touched the bill, Caleb jerked it away. "First, tell me why? Why do you want to sell this info?"

Carson stood silent for a moment looking like a chubby pouting child about to cry. "Got my bills to pay."

Sighing, Caleb shrugged and then sat down on a stool at the counter and laid the money on it. Carson waddled up and took the money then he motioned to a door marked "employees only." Caleb looked around then followed Carson.

The little storage closet barely accommodated Carson who seemed to be knocking over coffee tins, mugs and boxes as he wobbled his way to the back of the closet. As Caleb entered he thanked God for his own slim build and pressed himself against a stack of boxes to avoid making physical contact with Carson. Although he normally enjoyed the smell of coffee, the aroma was so strong that Caleb felt nauseous. Watching Carson wipe streams of sweat off of his forehead didn't make the situation any better. Caleb turned and surveyed the boxes. His wife, Sandra, had been an avid coffee drinker and might have found this whole situation humorous if the context hadn't been so dang…

Caleb's thoughts were interrupted with the sound of a click. He turned to see the barrel of a gun pointed directly at his face.

CHAPTER 10

"I don't understand," responded Erica, "My grandmother has been in your nursing home for four years!" Her voice was met with only the dial tone. *What the hell was that about?*

Reilly began to fuss. Erica put her phone into her purse and turned to look at Reilly in the backseat of the car. "I swear they have so much turnover at that nursing home, no one ever knows what's happening," sighed Erica. I'll check on Grandma when we get you home and into bed," she whispered to her daughter. After she put the car into gear she hit the radio button.

"…and in the top of the news today, officials are warning communities to step up emergency response training in order to have all states ready for what some are saying will be a pandemic equal to or greater than any the world has seen so far…Here's Mike Niswander with the report from Washington DC…"

Erica shook her head and turned down the radio. Then she reached for her cell phone. As she began to dial she swerved slightly. *Damn!* Glancing down quickly she hit *4. "Hello, Marcus?" she said quickly.

"Hey! Where the hell have you been all day?" an irritated voice shouted through the phone.

"Okay, okay. You have every right to be mad. Now what'd I miss?"

For a moment there was silence.

"Marcus! Hello?" said Erica.

"Vaccines aren't working. There's something wrong," the voice said slowly.

"Wrong?"

"The Secretary of Defense…his people are…"

"Who?"

"Erica, there's something strange going on…something that we don't have clearance for," replied Marcus.

"Clearance?" asked Erica as she balanced the phone between her cheek and her shoulder as she attempted to turn into the parking lot of the pediatrician's office.

"We're talking terrorism here, Erica," Marcus answered sharply. "Homeland Security is all over this and…and there's talk of an investigation of pharmaceutical companies…Weston's company. If you'd been here for a few meetings you might be up to speed more on all of this."

"Sorry, Mother!" Erica replied sarcastically as she pulled into a parking space and let the engine idle.

"Erica, how sure are you that Weston isn't a terrorist?"

"What the hell is wrong with you, Marcus?"

"I resent that," shot back Marcus. "What the hell is wrong with you? Didn't you say he had Muslim friends and once toyed with joining Islam?"

"Oh please! I don't have time for this," replied Erica. "Ever since 9-11 it's all become one big run from the Boogie man!"

"Maybe a little healthy fear would be good for us all. Besides, people are asking questions, Erica. Questions about Weston…questions about you."

"Just in time for Election Day," Erica sighed.

"Look, this isn't about your little love affair. There's a bigger picture," said Marcus. "You've said it a thousand times yourself that people should be taking the flu seriously. Each year 36,000 people die from the flu and another 20,000 are hospitalized with complications from the flu and yet…"

"…and yet something seems different this year." Erica completed Marcus' statement with growing concern clouding her mind.

"Yes," he said coolly. "Working in this field certainly bioterrorism has crossed your mind, hasn't it?"

For a moment there was silence. "Erica, it's just been a very…very bad day," Marcus' deflated voice seemed to drift off farther with each word.

Erica stumbled around the words in her head before blurting out, "Weston's lab got trashed today."

Again there was silence. Then Marcus said in a matter of fact tone, "You see? Do you see what I'm saying, Erica? Stay away from him."

"I'm not with him anymore, Marcus. There's nothing between us."

"I know that. *He* knows that. Do *you* know that?" Marcus said sarcastically.

Erica hit the disconnect button and threw the phone into the passenger's seat. She leaned back and took a deep breath, fighting the urge to cry. Just then there was a tap at her window. Startled she looked up quickly and then began to roll down the window.

"Ms. Schmidt? We're from the United States government. We need to talk to you."

CHAPTER 11

Weston's keys snagged on his bandage as he attempted to unlock his front door. *God damn it! My head hurts. My hand is killing me. I just want to...* then the door swung open. Weston stood silently in the hallway peering into his dimly lit apartment awash in Déjà Vu. Lit by a sole lamp that lay on its side, the typically organized room was a sea of papers, clothing, and over turned furniture.

For a moment he just stood and stared. "I guess it wouldn't make sense if you didn't tear this place apart too!" he screamed as he entered. The door across the hall opened a crack. He whirled around. "Am I being too loud, Mrs. Tipton? How about the assholes that trashed my apartment? Were they loud enough for you to call the cops?"

The neighbor's door slammed shut instantly.

He turned back to his apartment. "It's not yours," he screamed. "Not this time! Can you hear me?" Walking into his bedroom, he saw his mattress had been sliced open. Even his box springs were exposed and pulled apart.

Then he returned to the living room and glanced around before going into the kitchen. Milk had been poured all over the floor along with all of the other items from the refrigerator. "Yeah, I hid it in the refrigerator. You fools don't even know what you're looking for, do you?" he shouted as if the perpetrators were still present.

Weston went over to the kitchen table and with one large sweeping motion of his arm cleared it. Pulling out the cell phone he had just purchased, he dialed a very familiar number. "Hello? Yes, it's me," said Weston. "Don't say any names. I'm using a new cell phone....untraceable...for the moment. Let's just get down to business. The shipment of vaccine being sent to Russia...saline solution and I'll give you just three guesses where RCG35-98 is headed. It'd be rather poetic if it was sent on 9-11. Payback's a bitch."

Weston began to search his pockets for a cigarette. "How do I know?" he asked. "I authorized it," he said slowly with anger. He paused for a moment and caught his breath. "Hey, I need you to check on two things for me. A guy named Caleb Phillips... no, I don't know how to spell it, but he's been messing around. Take him out if you need to….I'm certainly not attached to him. Oh, and…and…I need a personal favor. You look out for my kid." He listened nervously as he tapped the table. "Yes, you can. The kid stays out of it or…or you go down with it all."

Then he heard a rustling sound behind him. "My visitors may still be here," he whispered into the phone. Then he heard another noise. Disconnecting his call he grabbed a hammer from nearby on the floor and looked around him. He saw nothing but the door to his apartment was standing wide open, so he walked over and slammed it shut. He placed the cell phone on the counter and began to hammer it into small pieces. With each smash, Weston's blood pumped faster and faster through his veins. He could see their faces. Their empty words screamed through his mind. *"We don't know how this happened. It's the scientific community that let you down, not the government because honestly, all this was done without authorization….but you can fix it…you can fix it…you can fix it."* The words hurt his head even now and with each slam of his hammer the pain throbbed within him.

Even as the pieces of the phone went flying he continued and began to make dents into the counter top. The little pieces lay scattered in the rubble of his life. Thin, black lines like a bizarre spider web rippled out across the orange Formica counter top where his hammer had fallen. He then threw the hammer across the floor. It lodged in the opposite wall sending plaster down on his home phone which lay on the floor. He began to rub his sore eyes, but hearing a chunk of plaster fall from the wall he turned with a start. There flashing beneath the rubble was his caller-ID unit. Someone had called him. Remembering his argument with Erica earlier, he frantically began to dig through the pile of clothes nearby.

Where's my answering machine? Where the hell is my answering machine?

Moving into the bedroom, he frantically scanned the room. However, unlike all of his other possessions, it was not in a disheveled mess. In his earlier visit to the room, he had completely missed it. He missed it because it sat peacefully on his bed. There was no light flashing on it. *If there were any messages left on it, they've been heard.* Weston hit the button: "Two new messages left today." As Erica's voice began on the machine Weston began to sob.

"Wes, I'm going to see my grandmother today…meet me? You

know where…the Cherry Hill Nursing Home. I'm bringing Reilly…."

Then Weston heard something from the living room. He silently moved to the head of the bed and reached under it for the night stick his father had given him when he first moved to Atlanta. His heart raced as his hand felt only carpet. *Where was the stick? Where the hell was….*

Then he was struck from behind. Weston stumbled over the bed and then grabbed a fork lying on the floor nearby. With all of his force he lunged at the black figure. Unstable from the blow to his head, Weston was only able to hit the figure's arm before falling to the floor himself. For a moment he lay on the floor breathless from the fall. Blood ran down the prongs of the fork and Weston smiled.

"I got you!" he rasped.

The figure turned and raised the black night stick high into the air preparing for another blow to Weston, who narrowly escaped by rolling away. The figure then landed on top of him and began to punch him. Weston got in two solid blows and then half removed the ski mask covering the face of his attacker.

"You?" he gasped. Then Weston fell back onto the shards of glass on the floor and everything went black.

CHAPTER 12

"The government?" asked Erica confused.

"Yes, ma'am. We're from Homeland Security and we need to talk to you about the two men who visited your home earlier today," replied the blonde haired man. His sharp tone alarmed Erica. "Agents Culver and Barclay," he added pointing to the African American man next to him when he said Culver.

"I don't understand," she responded.

"What did those men want?" barked Culver.

Erica froze in her seat. Nervously she fumbled with her keys. "Can I see some identification?" she asked.

The two men quickly flipped open what appeared to be badges or IDs of some sort and then thrust them back into their black overcoats.

"You need to speak with my attorney," she replied and then swung open her car door.

Barclay stepped up and pushed the car door closed again before Erica could step out. "Is there a reason I would need to speak with your attorney?" he asked suspiciously. "Ms. Schmidt, do you have something to hide?"

"What is this about?" Erica insisted in frustration trying to push her door open again.

Barclay leaned into the car window keeping Erica from opening her door.

"This is about what we say this is about," Culver barked.

Erica reached for her cell phone. Barclay reached into the car and slapped it out of her hands. "Who are you calling, Ms. Schmidt? Who do you honestly think you can call?"

"I don't understand," shouted Erica. "Who are you and what do you want?"

"We want to know about Weston Anderson and about his two

associates who paid you a private visit this morning. You see, we get real pissed off when someone threatens our country, Ms. Schmidt. We get pissed off when innocent people get killed by monsters like Dr. Anderson."

"I don't know what you're talking about," insisted Erica. "Please I don't know anything."

"Did two men from Dr. Anderson's office visit you this morning?" barked Culver.

"I don't know…yes…yes okay," she stammered. "Just leave me and my baby alone!" Erica fought back tears as she looked back at her daughter.

"What did they want Ms. Schmidt?

"They wanted…they wanted to know," Erica hesitated and then looked at the keys dangling in the ignition. She took a deep breath and wiped away the tears. With as much calm as she could gather she looked right into Barclay's eyes. "They were investigating Weston's lab being trashed and they wanted to know if I had a key. I didn't. Never have. They left angry."

Barclay turned his head and looked back at Culver for a moment. Erica stared at the steering wheel. As Barclay pulled out of the car a bit, Erica turned the key, threw the car into reverse and with all of her strength hit the accelerator. Barclay fell onto the pavement.

Culver ran after her yelling, "We're watching you, Ms. Schmidt. We're watching you all the time…"

His voice faded as Erica continued to speed down the road all the while wiping away tears. "It's okay, baby!" she cried. "Honey, it's going to be okay. It's going to be okay." Her voice shook as she repeated the words. Struggling to breathe as fear swept over her, Erica headed for her home.

With her hands still shaking violently, she turned off the car after she had pulled into her driveway. She rested her head against the steering wheel and sobbed for a moment. Just then her cell phone rang. "Micki!" she sobbed as she looked at the name that was lit up on it. She covered her mouth with her hands. *I'll talk to her later* she thought as she shoved the phone into her purse. Then she got out of the car and quickly grabbed Reilly. *We just have to get into the house....we just have to get into the house.*

Immediately she locked the door after she entering and took Reilly into the nursery. She felt the baby's head. It didn't feel warm at all. "Finally something good today," sighed Erica. After settling Reilly into bed, Erica fell back onto her couch and for a brief moment just tried to breath. A knock at the door startled her.

Leaving the chain lock in place she opened the door just a crack. "Yes?"

"Erica, the tenants' meeting started about ten minutes ago. Aren't you coming?"

Erica closed the door and removed the chain. Upon opening the door she saw her porch filled with her neighbors.

"Oh! I completely forgot!"

"Yeah, you were supposed to talk to us about this flu pandemic or whatever it is and what we can do...you promised!" sniveled a small elderly woman who jostled her way to the door.

"Folks, I've had a really bad day and my daughter is...not feeling well. I can't come."

There was a loud moan from the collective group.

"Look there's nothing to tell. Wash your hands a lot. Take vitamins and don't go out if you're sick. You can't get the bird flu. Only birds can."

"But my husband has it," insisted the elderly woman.

"No, Mrs. Clements, he doesn't. I'm sure he just has the normal, non-exciting flu," replied Erica as soothingly as she could muster.

"No," replied a tearful voice from the back of the group. Just then a middle aged woman with wild red hair pushed to the front and embraced Mrs. Clements for a moment. "The doctors just called us a few minutes ago."

Mrs. Clements clung to her daughter. "This is my daughter, Julie."

Erica nodded.

Julie cleared her throat and spoke slowly. "They said Dad has a new strain never before seen. They don't even know what to call it and asked us for a list of people with whom he had had contact....they even asked us for a list of any foreign contacts."

CHAPTER 13

Erica let the group into her home. "What do you mean they don't know what strain it is?" She asked.

"That's what they said," sobbed Mrs. Clements.

"Momma, it's going to be okay. Really it is," comforted her daughter.

"Julie, I've got to know. What *exactly* did the doctors say," Erica said to the younger woman.

"I...I...it wasn't a doctor really," stuttered Julie.

"What are you talking about?" asked Erica impatiently.

"The nursing home director...she said the facilities were being locked down because some weird flu had developed there....that my father was...was..."

"Was what?" shouted Erica.

"They don't know...they claim they honestly don't know!"

Julie hesitated a moment and looked at her mother. "People are dying at the nursing home from this thing."

Erica wanted to say this wasn't possible, but the truth was more relevant. "New strains develop all the time, but I can assure you that the CDC is monitoring this closely. Even my own company is keeping a close watch since we manufacture flu vaccines. Maybe they don't have a name, but I'm sure they're watching it."

"How do you know?" creaked an elderly man standing by the door.

"Look, you want to know about flu viruses? Well, I'll tell you, but pay attention. It's not exactly an easy issue to address," said Erica with a patronizing tone.

"We'll try to focus," snapped back the man as more people crowded into Erica's living room.

"Pandemics occur about every 50 years or so and there have been roughly three major influenza pandemics in the twentieth century…and, of course, none yet in the twenty-first century," sighed Erica completely fatigued. "There were pandemics in the years 1918, 1957, and 1968. People died. Lots of people died," she added with emphasis. "Pandemics typically infect about 20%-40% of the world's population."

"Forty percent of the world's population dies? Oh, come on!" replied a man in his thirties seated on the couch.

"I said infect not kill although there is tremendous potential. For example, the Spanish flu of 1918 killed about 40 million people in less than a year," replied Erica.

"So is that what we're looking at here?" asked Julie.

"The Center for Disease Control and the World Health Organization are preparing for the worst in order to keep it from getting there, so you have nothing to worry about."

"Okay, Professor, enough of the history lesson. Tell us about why they wouldn't know about a new strain," stammered the elderly man.

"It could just be a form of the H5N1 from last year," sighed Erica. "The flu virus mutates all the time. That's why each year we need a new flu vaccine. Sometimes the drug companies guess right and sometimes the mutations go in a different direction and vaccines are only moderately helpful. We just have to take precautions and when things are spreading stay off the streets."

"My father wasn't out on the streets!" sobbed Julie. "He was in a nursing home eating soup all day and watching 'I Love Lucy' reruns."

"Is my husband going to die?" asked a frail, soft voice.

"I couldn't possibly tell you that. I'm sure they're doing everything they can," assured Erica.

"If this was someone you loved, would you be reassured by the thought that they're doing everything they can when each moment your father, or mother, or child just gets worse!" Julie shouted.

Erica looked towards the stairway that she had climbed just 30 minutes earlier carrying her own child. The ticking of the clock that rested on her piano seemed to thunder in her ears as all eyes focused on her. She looked at Reilly's picture on the piano...the tiny smiling face. Then Weston's words in the lab shot through her head, "Well, get her a flu shot!"

He knew, right? He knew Beeman injected Reilly...right?

CHAPTER 14

"Hey, man, what's going on?" asked Caleb as he swallowed hard. He slowly moved his fingers towards his own gun that he had tucked into his waist band.

"Put your hands up where I can see 'em!" hissed Carson.

There was a knock at the door. "Mr. Carson? Mr. Carson?" shouted a voice through the door. "We're out of Columbian Supreme blend. Can I come in and…"

"Just a minute, Stacy," shouted Carson.

"Uh, Mr. Carson? I'm Heather."

Carson rolled his eyes. "See that can way up there?"

Caleb nodded.

"You're gonna get it and hand it to the nice girl and you're not going to try anything funny because you don't want shots fired and you or that nice girl gettin hurt. Do you?"

Caleb forced a smile "This is quite a little coffee shop here. Starbucks do any kind of psychological testing on you people?" he asked sarcastically.

"Hand her the damn coffee," he hissed.

Caleb smiled and then reached for the door. Before he could pull it open, however, he felt the gun barrel jab into his back. "Don't be funny, pretty boy," Carson whispered.

"Anytime, fat, old ugly dude," retorted Caleb.

"Just open the door and do as I said," Carson hissed.

Caleb pulled the door open slowly to see a smiling young woman in a red shirt and blue jeans. "Who are…." She began her question, but the moment the coffee can was thrust towards her Carson reached out from behind Caleb and slammed the door shut barely giving Caleb time to pull his arm back.

"Hope this means I get a free cup of coffee for being such a good helper," Caleb retorted. His hand returned to his waist within inches of his own gun that he had put into his waistband. Then he turned to face Carson's gun again.

"Look, you called me in here," said Caleb. "I didn't bring you in here. Put your goddamn gun down and we'll talk."

"I've got the gun for my own protection. I ain't gonna kill you... if you behave," said Carson raising the gun to Caleb's face again.

"What do you want?"

"Are you wired?"

"Wired?"

"Yeah, are you taping us like you did Wes?"

"How do you know that?" Caleb asked.

"Just answer me," rasped Carson.

"No, I'm not taping," Caleb opened his jacket and then patted down his pants pockets.

"Who do you work for?"

"I'm a graduate student just looking for some answers," replied Caleb.

Carson pressed the gun firmly against Caleb's temple. "I'm only gonna ask you once more. Who do you work for?"

"Antigone labs," answered Caleb. "Look, I really am just a graduate student. I'm doing research for Antigone and heard rumors that Anderson was doing something illegal...covert government shit. I thought it'd make me a name if I was the one who uncovered it all."

Carson lowered his gun. For a moment he stared at Caleb and rubbed his chin with his empty hand. "Could you really uncover shit and get the word out?"

"Yes."

"You've got the contacts....an outlet?"

"Yes, why what do you have?"

"There's stuff going on....with this whole flu thing. I've heard people talk in here...the flu is going to be the next A-bomb."

Caleb pulled himself up on a nearby box and sat on it. He looked Carson in the eyes. "I don't understand."

"You ever hear of the Iran Contra crap back in the 80s?"

"Sure."

Carson looked around suspiciously.

"Hey, crazy old guy! Hello?" said Caleb impatiently.

"I outta kill you right now," growled Carson.

Caleb put his hand directly onto his hidden gun. "What about the Iran Contra crap?"

"Viruses. They kill people. Your new friend Dr. Anderson has created a nifty little one and the government's gotten very very interested," replied Carson slowly.

"Biological warfare? Is that what you're talking about?"

Carson nodded silently.

"The U.S.?"

"People in the U.S. But that ain't the half of it," Carson said as he spit onto the floor. "It was meant to go foreign, but someone let the cat outta the bag here."

"In the U.S?"

Carson nodded.

"You have proof?"

Carson leaned into Caleb. "My son. He died. They said he was sick and then he got worse."

"And that means?"

"They were doing experiments. They create viruses and shit. Then they find victims. My son," Carson paused and wiped his eyes before proceeding. "He just couldn't get better, but that's because they didn't want him to. They needed to see…to use him…"

"As a guinea pig?" offered Caleb.

"Yes, and people don't know. They just don't know."

"I'm sorry about your son, but I've got to have more proof than that," said Caleb as he jumped down from the box and reached for the doorknob.

Carson turned away and began wiped his eyes with the edge of his apron. "Get the hell out of my storeroom. Get out and don't come back," he yelled. Then Carson turned towards a small scrap of paper taped to the wall that Caleb had not noticed until that moment. In the dim light, Caleb could barely make out the red crayon images of two stick figures with big happy faces. Carson reached for it and gently removed it from the wall. His eyes remained fixated on it. Pausing for a moment Caleb looked back at the large man holding the frail crayon drawing. Like a piece of modern art commenting on the solitary plight of human suffering, Carson's stout silhouette convulsing with silent sobs among the stacks of coffee boxes. Caleb shook his head and then slowly opened the door and slipped into the dark hallway leaving Carson alone.

After reaching his car, Caleb pulled out his cell phone. "I need some background on a guy named Carson, former CIA he claims….general stuff including his family. You know, kids, wife…that stuff. Oh, and I'm going with the Antigone Labs cover, so give me enough to sound convincing on that…."

CHAPTER 15

Weston lay silently in the rubble that was his home. Beneath his fingers he felt fragments of glass. Blood seeped from his bottom lip and ran down his cheek onto the floor. He opened his eyes and looked up at the ceiling trying to focus. Then he heard footsteps.

"Oh, God!" he moaned as he attempted to turn his head toward the sound.

"Hey, buddy," said Caleb as he bent over Weston. "You sure are having one hell of a day. I didn't call the police, because I know you're not into that…are you?" he asked sarcastically. Caleb walked around the room and kicked at some of the overturned furniture. "I ought to kick your ass for the way you roughed me up earlier today, but I'm not that kind of guy."

Weston tried to focus. "You?" he wheezed through his dry swollen lips.

"Believe it or not, I'm here to help you. There's lots of people who want to know what you're doing…hell, I'd like to know what you're doing…you're in over your head. You need to get out before…"

Weston fell back losing consciousness again. Several hours later he awoke, everything hurt, but especially his head. *God, what the hell happened?* Nothing came to mind…nothing except that graduate student. *He was here….he did this! Why?*

Then, like a sledge hammer striking his skull, his phone rang. Slowly he managed to pull himself upright and look. He couldn't make out the number on the screen…it was all too blurry. Nothing came into focus, not even the buttons…they seemed strange to him. *This phone is lighter than my landline…did I smash the wrong phone?* The ringing continued. Weston finally hit the button to answer. "Hello?" he choked out.

"Ah, Dr. Anderson, you're awake," said the voice.

He made an effort to swallow, but only managed to gag himself. "Who is this?" he whispered.

"You don't need to know. What you do need to know is that

you've been the rouge scientist long enough. When you were hired, you said you'd play ball. Now that we really need you, what have you done?"

"I don't know what you mean."

"Oh, I think you do and if it wasn't for the fact that you're more valuable alive than dead, you wouldn't be chatting with me right now...you know that don't you? We have the key to your little safety deposit box. You do know that any evidence you might have regarding RCG35-98 implicates you just as much or more than anyone else, don't you?"

Weston said nothing.

"Of course you do. So why would you be keeping all this evidence? Tape recording, notes, photos from your camera phone. I really thought you were much smarter. Let me guess...the election is coming up and you thought that if you showed the American people that elements of the current administration were working on the most effective weapon ever created, something monumental would happen? Reagan's people went against the U.S. government completely in the Iran Contra deal and where did they end up? Oh, yeah. Heroes. That's what the American people want....heroes. And guess what, Dr. Anderson? You don't qualify for hero status." Then the phone was silent.

Weston got up and stumbled his way to the bathroom. Splashing water on his face, he grabbed a towel off the floor and wiped it across his bruised and swollen eyes. Then he stoically walked through his home stopping only to glance once more at the little picture frame. He grabbed his keys and under the watchful eye of his neighbor, he pulled the door shut and locked it. "Can't be too careful," he said looking directly into her peep hole.

Swelling kept him from seeing well enough to drive, so he walked to the bar on the corner. He knew the place well enough that vision wouldn't be an issue and before long he found himself on his usual bar stool. "Keep 'em coming all night long," he said to the bartender.

"Wes, we close in half an hour. Go home," came the reply.

"No home to go to, Stan," he snapped.

"What about that sweet little gal you brought in here a few times?"

"Never knew her name," he mumbled.

"Aw hell. Sure you did. What was it...Erin...or something..."

Weston threw his glass against the wall. "I said, I didn't know her damn name."

"Wes, you're gonna pay for that glass. Now simmer down," said the large man behind the counter. "I'll bring you your drinks, but ain't no one gonna get wild and woolly in here."

Just then a thin man with a mustache moved into the seat near Weston. "So what's buggin ya mister? Women trouble?"

"Todd here's a cop, Wes. Wasn't your dad a cop?" asked Stan.

"Yeah. And my good old grandpap was a scientist...just like me," he finished drinking one beer and then reached for the next. Then he leaned in towards his two companions. "Only...only he experimented on people..."

"Scientists do that all the time, don't they?" slobbered Todd.

"Not without the person's knowledge."

Todd began to laugh. "You ever do that?"

Weston stood up and slammed money down on the bar, and then with a sinister tone whispered, "How do you know I'm not doing it right now?" Then he threw another beer glass against the wall and tossed another bill at Stan. "This should cover it for me and let old Todd here take a try." Then he walked out the door stopping just two feet from a green sedan idling at the curb.

The door to the sedan swung open. Weston looked in and then entered without a word. The car pulled out.

CHAPTER 16

Erica's neighbors began to file out as she continued to stare at the stairway leading to her baby's room.

Mrs. Clements stopped in front of Erica and sobbed. "Please...please how do I find out what's going on with my husband? Your grandmother is at the same nursing home. Aren't you concerned?"

Erica numbly turned to look at the woman. Tears rimmed the woman's large, dark eyes as she took Erica's hands in hers. "Please, I just need some answers."

Noticing the Mrs. Clements' trembling hands, Erica quietly offered what comfort she could. "That place is just a disorganized mess in administration and communication, but before my mother put grandma in there she checked and it's one of the best in the state. In fact, my grandmother got sick a few weeks back and they seemed to take very good care of her. It's taken her awhile to get through it, but she has. So call the administrators and keep calling. Go ahead and call doctors. Or go in there yourself and get him out. The flu is a scary thing when it comes to people over 70..."

"...and children under 5," Julie added as she nodded towards Reilly's picture.

Then slowly and silently the last of her neighbors exited her apartment in the dark night. After they left, Erica walked over the couch and mindlessly reached out for a knit doily made by her grandmother and for a brief moment rolled it between her finger tips feeling its pattern. Then she reached for her phone on the coffee table.

"Take charge and get her out of there," she whispered. But before she could even hit a button on the phone it rang. She stirred. For a moment she sat and stared at the caller ID. Then she slowly picked it up. "Hello," she said on the verge of tears.

"Erica? Oh, girl, don't tell me you're throwing yourself another pity party!" scolded Miki.

"Maybe."

"Maybe," Miki repeated. "Dis always happens after you've

talked to Weston. He called you dis evening about his apartment getting trashed didn't he?"

"You mean his lab?"asked Erica.

"Yeah, you know…his lab. Anyway, I'm coming over. Having friends is good medicine."

"Miki, I'm exhausted. Absolutely and completely drained. I just need to go to bed and end this day."

"Dats fine, but I'm coming over anyway. I promised your mom before she died that I'd look after you."

"You're a good friend," said Erica. "I probably could use some company."

After setting down her phone, Erica aimlessly hit the television remote control watching an endless drizzle of nonsense flowing past her on the screen. *People eating worms, rolling in Jell-O and…well whatever…* Just then there was a knock at the door.

"Come in," Erica called out. As the knocking continued, she cleared her throat. "Come in." The knocking continued. "Use your key, Miki!" she shouted as she stood up. Reaching the door she opened it without a thought. The two large men in black suits who had accosted her in the pediatrician's parking lot.

"What do you want?" she asked trying to control her trembling voice.

"Ma'am my name is Barclay. We need to finish our talk. May we come in?"

Erica stood frozen. "No. Now what do you want?"

"We want to talk more about Dr. Anderson."

"I told you everything I know," she said as she began to push the door closed.

"Do you know that we have reason to believe he's been doing experimentation on humans…specifically the residents of two local nursing homes?"

Erica's mouth went dry. "I've known Weston for many years. He…he would never…he's a fanatic about ethics."

"Have you spoken to your grandmother recently?" asked the blonde haired man.

Erica's heart raced. *Her grandmother's nursing home?* Then she spotted Reilly's picture on the piano again and next to the piano the chair she sat in as she held her baby for Beeman.

Barclay cleared his throat. "Ma'am, you can work with us or against us. Either way we're going to get to the bottom of this. The real question is do you want to be a hero or do you want to share a cell with Dr. Anderson?"

"If you're with the U.S. government Weston is working with you. I can assure you of that," responded Erica. She began to push the door closed, but met with resistance as one of the men pushed into the door.

"Have it your way," he hissed.

Just then she heard a voice from behind the men. "Erica, what's going on?"

"Marcus?" she called out on the verge of tears.

A slender African American man pushed his way between the two agents. "Everything okay?"

"Marcus," cried Erica reaching out to him.

Marcus looked at both men and quickly added. "Gentlemen, does this need to become a police matter?"

Marcus slipped into Erica's condo. He slammed the door shut behind him. Shaking off the cold rain, Marcus took off his coat. "So who were those goons?"

"FBI."

"Oh, God. Erica, what's going on? "

"I don't know what's going on," responded Erica in frustration. She took Marcus' coat and hung it up. "This morning Weston's lab was trashed. He called me…that's what I was trying to tell you."

"About that," said Marcus delicately, "I'm sorry I…"

"It's okay. I'm sure I deserved it. I keep trying to move on, but part of me keeps hoping…" she let her words trail off.

Marcus leaned forward and for a moment he seemed unable to speak. Then finally he took a deep breath. "Erica, I know you're all stressed out and I really shouldn't lay anything more on you, but we're getting reports. There's an investigation starting and it involves Weston's lab."

"I know," she said in a shaking voice.

"No, you don't know. There were two clinics whose vaccines were nothing but saline solution. They aren't vaccines at all, but yet Weston's company is selling them as vaccines."

"What are you talking about?" responded Erica in horror. "Weston wouldn't do that."

"I'm not saying it's him," said Marcus as he sat down on the couch. For several minutes he looked distracted as he stared out into the night through Erica's front window. "Look, Weston could be in some huge trouble if his name is even remotely tied to this."

"He's not. Weston is a lot of things, but I'm sure he's not this."

"Are you? Are you 100% sure, Erica?"

Erica stared intently in Marcus'eyes. "Yes."

For a several seconds they stared at one another. Then Marcus looked down at the stack of white wedding invitations that sat covered in dust beneath the end table.

Finally he looked up again. "I've accepted a new position," he said in such a somber tone that Erica was startled.

"Well, that's great," she responded cautiously. "Does that have anything to do with what we've been talking about?"

Marcus ignored her question. "Do you think Weston is loyal to our country?" he asked.

"What's going on, Marcus? I'm really lost here."

Marcus leaned forward. "Would you consider yourself loyal to our country?" he asked with grave intensity.

Reilly began to cry. "I have to go," Erica blurted out startled. She jumped to her feet, but suddenly she felt a sharp pain in the back of her upper arm. She whirled around in surprise to look at Marcus, but then the room began to whirl around her. In her mind she was screaming. "Marcus? Marcus?" Her voice echoed through her body and everything went black.

Several hours later, the darkness lifted. She looked around. No one. Her eyes darted to the clock. "Six? It's six in the morning?" she asked aloud as she walked from room to room dazed. Papers were scattered around the floor of her office and all of the drawers were open in her bedroom and the kitchen. *Did I do that? Wasn't Marcus here?*

She heard Reilly again. As Erica headed for the nursery she heard the phone ring. As she passed her bedroom she reached in and grabbed the phone before walking across the hall to Reilly's room.

"Hello?" asked Erica as she balanced the phone on her shoulder and picked up Reilly. The baby felt warm and her cheeks were red.

"Hey, woman, it's me."

Erica could focus on nothing more than her baby's face. "Huh? Oh, Miki?"

"Who else? Sorry I didn't make it over last night. I called and Marcus said you were headed to bed so I figured you needed the rest."

Reilly began to cry.

"Hey, is that the baby?"

"Yeah, she's doesn't seem to be feeling well today." Erica put her palm on Reilly's forehead. It was burning hot and the baby's face was a solid red.

"Have you taken her to the doctor?"

"No. The appointment got cancelled," she said thinking back to her encounter with the two agents in the medical center parking lot.

"If she's worse, girl, you better take her somewhere," Miki said with urgency. "Last night Marcus said there was some scary shit out there and I just didn't like the way it sounded. In fact, he gave me the creeps altogether last night."

Erica's mind raced. "Will you check on my grandmother?" Erica blurted. "I can't do that with Reilly sick."

"Sure," replied Miki.

Erica clicked the "disconnect" button and let the phone drop from her hand. Quickly she began filling a diaper bag and within minutes she raced back down with Reilly tightly bundled.

She buckled Reilly into her seat and threw some diapers into the car. Then after she had herself situated, she tore out of her driveway at full speed. Then her cell phone began to ring. Reilly was now crying loudly. "Honey, it's okay. I promise you, it's going to be okay." As she pressed harder on the accelerator, Erica stared directly ahead. The phone continued to ring and Reilly continued to wail.

Erica looked back at her daughter. "Honey, we're going to the doctor. You'll feel so much better." Then she glanced down at her cell phone. Weston's home number appeared on the screen. "God, I wish you were here right now," she whispered. Impulsively she grabbed her phone, flipped it open and blurted, "Please don't tell me you're calling because you need me because right now I need you."

For a moment there was silence. "Uh, um, this is Caleb…Caleb Phillips."

Surprised, Erica looked down at the phone. She looked up just in time to see a car from the left lane come over onto her forcing her to swerve off the road. Slamming on her brakes she took a quick glance back at her daughter whose screams were now full terror. Out of control, Erica's Honda spun off the shoulder and into the guard rail. Erica saw a blur of green as her car struck the vehicle that had cut her off. Her hands seemed useless as chaos danced before her eyes. Then she heard a loud pop and everything went black as the air bag momentarily swallowed her in a blistering heat.

Reilly's cries pierced Erica's darkness. *I have to help her. How do I help her?* Erica was screaming in her head, but the words never met the reality.

Then Reilly's voice became distant. *Reilly where are you? Where are you? Why aren't you crying anymore?*

Seconds turned into horrifying minutes until finally a hand touched Erica and moved her slowly back. "Are you okay? Ma'am? Can you tell me your name?" asked a man in a red jacket. "I'm Joe. I'm a paramedic. We're going to get you to the hospital. Can you talk to me?"

"My baby...my baby...why isn't she crying?" Erica tried to turn to the back seat, but Joe held her shoulders.

"Ma'am have you been drinking?" asked Joe.

"No," Erica replied in a stupor.

Joe placed a brace around her neck. Her head ached. Reaching up to touch her forehead she felt a warm liquid. It streamed down into her left eye.

He turned to his partner. "Tommy, do you see a kid around here?" Then he turned back to Erica and pulled her hand away from her head. "Ma'am how old is this child? Was the child buckled?"

"She's a baby," Erica said struggling with each breath. "She's my baby...buckled in the car seat in back."

Joe glanced vaguely into the back backseat as he began to apply bandages to Erica's forehead. "It's going to be okay. We're going to take care of everything," he said calmly.

"There's no baby here. Do I keep looking?" she heard Tommy ask.

"There's no car seat in back," she heard Joe reply above the sirens that screamed louder by the second. "Check that the kid ain't been thrown from the car, but I don't see any evidence whatsoever that there was ever a kid in this car."

CHAPTER 17

"No. No. No!" repeated Pearl as she scurried past one white wall after another. *White everywhere! White everywhere! It was just...where was the end? Where was the end? Why were all the walls so white?* Pearl reached out to touch one. It moved. "It's laundry day!" she sang out like a child. "Sheets hanging for laundry day!"

Playfully she peeked under a sheet. There were beds upon beds of skeletons with thin wispy flesh hanging off of them.

"Help me," they whispered in great echoes around the room. Pearl bit her lip. *Where am I? Where am I?*

Then she saw the silver trays by the bedsides. She walked over to one skeleton and bent over while trying not to get too close. "Where is my husband?" she whispered. "We brought him to the hospital...yesterday. He's got the flu, but he's a young man. He'll do fine. Just tell me where he is."

The skeleton blinked, "Help me," it whispered.

"It's not my fault...I didn't kill my babies," Pearl began to scream. The skeleton seemed startled for a second and then lapsed back into its hopeless plea for help. Pearl walked away screaming, "I didn't kill my babies. I'm just 18...I don't know how to take care of sick babies and now Paulser is gone...He's here in the hospital. I need him!" A nurse came over and reached out to Pearl. "Stay away from me," Pearl screamed then she punched the nurse in the nose. As blood spurted out, Pearl smiled at her own strength. Then she scurried away.

"Pearl!" shouted a nurse from the far end of the hallway. "Come back here!"

Shuffling along, Pearl began to pick up her pace. *Where is this? Where am I? Not this hallway. Where is my brass bed? Paulser bought it for me...for me...for me; it was that year that the crops were good. My bed! Where? Where?*

She wiped at her face. *No one should see a real lady cry, wasn't that what mamma had always declared?* But her fingers wouldn't release from a clenching fist. *Something's wrong...why won't my fingers open?* Each effort to wipe away the mixture of snot and tears turned into a punching match as her fist met her face. And something wet was coming off of her arm, something wet. *What is happening? What is happening?*

Then she turned the corner to see a room she recognized. It had color. No white walls. There were books and a television. She shuffled over to it. Just then a soft warm voice called out, "Mrs. Schmidt? I'm Miki. Your granddaughter sent me to check on you."

"My granddaughter?" she asked puzzled.

"Yes, Erica. Remember Erica?"

Just then a harried nurse appeared from around the corner. "Pearl!" thundered the voice from the petite frame. Then she spotted Miki. "May I help you?" the nurse asked softening immensely.

"Yes, you can tell me why you're screaming at a little old lady like that," snipped Miki.

The nurse struck an indignant pose. "I need to take Mrs. Schmidt back to her room now."

"Please, no!" shrieked Pearl grabbing onto Miki.

"I'm going to visit with Pearl right now. I'll take her back to her room when we're done," Miki replied commandingly.

"I'm sorry, but you can't do that. The facility is in lock down right now," she replied sternly.

"I'm afraid she's right," said a nearby doctor who approached and joined the conversation. Smiling, the man seemed to exude an overabundance of the warmth that the nurse lacked. "Hello, I'm Dr. Randall." He extended his hand and then cupped her hand in both of his.

Miki smiled back flirtatiously. "Well, since she's already out here, there's really no reason I can't visit with her. Is there?"

"You can't do that," interjected the nurse.

"Certainly a few minutes sitting right here won't hurt anything," said Miki staring into the young doctor's eyes and smiling. "Besides, her granddaughter is going to be asking lots of questions...and do you really want someone who works for one of the largest healthcare management companies poking around here? She knows people at the CDC you know."

Dr. Randall looked around. "We're not hiding anything," he replied somberly. Then added in a hushed tone, "A few minutes….just sitting right here."

Pearl's bony hand griped Miki's arm. "I have to leave here," Pearl whispered. "I really do." Tears flooded her face.

The doctor remained frozen, fixated on Pearl. "Is there a problem, Mrs. Schmidt? Perhaps this is too much and you need to return to your room?"

"No, no, no, no," replied Pearl as she began to rock back and forth.

"You said a few minutes," reminded Miki glaring at the doctor.

He turned and slowly walked away.

"Hang tight, Granny," Miki whispered to Pearl.

The doctor turned and looked at them from the counter across the room where he was writing. Miki mockingly smiled at him.

"Granny, you just sit tight. Old Miki's gonna take care of everything," she whispered. Then, looking directly at the doctor she said loudly while holding up her cell phone, "I've got to run out to the car and take this call."

She stood up, but Pearl's bones wrapped around her wrist. Pulling at Pearl's fragile fingers Miki feared she might break them, but she needed to leave…immediately. Miki stayed focused on a car that had pulled into the parking lot. She had to get to it. "Let me go," she hissed to Pearl. "Please. I'll come back. I promise."

Finally breaking free she raced out the door and over to the car that had just parked. "I can't believe it!" she shouted. "I just can't believe it!"

"What's the matter lady?" asked a round middle-aged woman in a ragged cloth coat.

"I can't believe they're covering up a sexual assault!" Miki squealed.

"What? What are you talking about?"

"In there," Miki pointed to the nursing home. "There's a good-looking doctor in there and he's sexually assaulted a group of patients, but they ain't doin nothing. He's still on duty. Look here, what's your granny's name?"

"It's my aunt...her name is Millie Kreiger."

"Millie Kreiger! Oh you gotta get in there...her name is the one the nurses keep mentioning."

The woman shoved Miki aside and stormed into the building. Miki could see her smacking Dr. Randall. Two orderlies came out and a larger fight ensued as nurses and other visitors flooded the lobby.

Miki quietly slipped into the lobby and grabbed Pearl's hand. "Are we escaping now?" asked Pearl.

Miki put her forefinger to her lips. "Shhhh. Yes, we are," she whispered. "Quick now!" she ordered attempting to rush Pearl to the car. The elderly woman hobbled along and Miki at times had to practically pick up the frail grandmother to keep her moving. "Good thing I'm a big woman," whispered Miki.

"You are strong," mumbled Pearl as Miki pushed her into the car and buckled the seat belts.

Miki slammed the door shut and raced around to the driver's side and threw herself into the car. As Miki started the car, Pearl looked out the window and said softly, "Goodbye." She raised her tiny knotted hand to the window.

"Look, Granny, we ain't gonna be gone that long," said Miki. "I just promised Erica I'd find out what's going down with you."

"It doesn't matter," Pearl said matter-of-factly. "They'll all be dead soon...even the doctors."

CHAPTER 18

Miki looked over at Pearl. "We gotta hurry though. It won't take long for them to spot us."

Just then she saw two orderlies dashing into the parking lot.

"And away we go!" shouted Miki as she pushed on the accelerator.

The orderlies began to run towards the car.

"Get the hell outta my way!" said Miki as the tires squealed. "Okay, now, Granny. I need to know what you're talking about. What do mean everyone is gonna be dead?"

Just then her cell phone rang. "Damn," she said as she reached for the phone. "It's Erica. You hold on one minute, Granny and then we gonna talk." She flipped open her phone. "Hello? Hello? Erica? What? Hon, I can't understand you. Slow down."

"Tell my granddaughter that her baby is in danger. Tell her! Tell her!" Insisted Pearl as she grabbed for the phone.

"Stop it! Stop it, Granny! Stop!" shouted Miki as she struggled to maintain control of the phone. Just then she looked up. Dropping the phone, Miki grabbed the steering wheel and swerved to stay on the road. Then she made a sharp right and turned into a Bob Evans parking lot and shut off the car. "Goddamn it! Don't you ever do something that like again!" she shouted to Pearl. Miki placed two shaking hands on her steering wheel and took a long deep breath. "Dios Mio! You could have gotten us killed. Do you understand that?" she screamed. "Do you?"

Pearl sat silent. She straightened her back and raised her chin as she looked away from Miki. With an icy voice, Pearl spoke slowly and clearly, hiding her tear rimmed eyes. "That baby is in danger."

"And everybody at your home is gonna die," Miki snapped sarcastically. "Dios Mio! Granny, come on." Then in the reflection of the window, Miki saw Pearl wipe away a tear. "I'm sorry. Look I've never been too good with old people....I mean, I don't have lots of patience with...with anyone. We're going to see Erica. She's at da hospital emergency room...at least I think. I couldn't quite understand her."

Pearl unbuckled her seat belt and began to open the car door.

"Whoa! Hey, Granny, where you going?"

"I don't want to go to the hospital," she said flatly.

"What?"

"I don't want to go to the hospital," she repeated.

"Look, I ain't taken you. I'm going to see Erica. Remember? Your granddaughter? You said her baby was dyin or something..."

"Dying? Her baby is dying?"

Miki threw up her hands. "You! You said that she was dying!! Now shut dat door and get back into da car! We're going to help Erica. She's in trouble."

"I'll ride with you, but I am not going into the hospital," Pearl slowly said with a calm, smooth voice.

"Fine. Fine, crazy lady. Fine." Miki started the car and pulled out.

They both sat silently lost in their own mazes of confusion and fears for the entire twenty minute trip. Although not sure what she might encounter, Miki was relieved when she saw the hospital. "We're here," she sighed.

Pearl turned to her with tears running the lines across her cheeks and whispered, "I was never the favorite."

"What?" asked Miki.

"My father died when I was young...in the hospital waiting room my mother hugged my sister, Fanny, and told us all that she was Daddy's favorite," Pearl said so softly it was almost inaudible. "Why wasn't I ever the favorite?"

"I don't know," replied Miki. Turning her attention back to the keys in the ignition she blankly repeated her words. "I just don't know."

Miki put her hand on Pearl's and looked at her in the eyes. "Your eyes have so much pain," Miki said as she softly brushed Pearl's check with the back of her hand. "I understand," she sighed. "I really do understand, but we have to go now," Miki whispered. "Erica needs us....she needs us both."

Pearl nodded vaguely. Then her bony fingers griped the door handle and she swallowed hard. "Paulser died here..."

"Who?" asked Miki as she helped Pearl out of the car.

"My husband....my husband and my two sons." Pearl stood and stared at the building. Then slowly she moved towards the building with her head down.

Miki stared at Pearl for a moment. Then she took a deep breath and reached for Pearl's arm. "Let's go."

By the time they entered the building, Pearl's body convulsed with soft sobs. Miki could barely keep the elderly woman upright. "Do you want to stay in the lobby?" she asked.

Pearl gripped Miki tightly for a moment and then nodded and released the younger woman's arm. Then she meticulously positioned herself in front of a yellow, vinyl chair and eased into it. Her back straight and her chin high, Pearl focused on the bright colored vending machines on the far wall. They were bright and new and watching people approach the machines and walk away with their treasures made Pearl feel better. In fact, Pearl didn't hear another word that Miki said. She didn't see Miki leave. She also didn't see the van from her home pull up in the parking lot.

CHAPTER 19

"Excuse me," said Miki as she approached the receptionist's desk. "I'm looking for my friend."

"What is her name?"

"Erica Schmidt."

The woman behind the desk hit a few keys on the keyboard in front of her. "I'm sorry but I don't see anyone by that name. When was she admitted?"

"I don't know if she was...I think she came in by ambulance."

"She's probably still in the emergency room then." The woman raised her arm to point, but Miki was already racing down the hallway. As she approached the large, white doors that read EMERGENCY she heard Erica's screams.

"Erica! Erica!" yelled Miki. She burst through the door and frantically looked around. Then she spotted several nurses wrestling with her friend. Erica was kicking and screaming wildly as she thrashed around on the examining table. One of the nurses held a syringe. Erica looked horrified. "Leave her alone!" Miki screamed as she raced forward. In her effort to be heard her voice reached a level of shrillness that she had never before heard from herself.

Suddenly all was quiet and still. For five seconds all eyes focused on Miki and no one moved. Then, as if a button had been pushed, everything resumed, but on a much quieter level. Erica collapsed in her friend's arms. "Oh God!" she sobbed.

"Erica, baby, what's wrong?" asked Miki as she embraced her friend.

"I can't find Reilly," she wheezed.

"What?"

A middle aged, bald man walked up. Smoothing out his white coat and taking a moment to straighten his hospital badge, the doctor cleared his throat and said, "Do you know this woman?"

"Yes, of course I do," replied Miki.

"Is she...under any care at this time?"

"Care? What the hell are you talking about?" shot back Miki.

"She claims to have a child. She hasn't been willing to let anyone treat her until she sees this child, only we can't seem to locate one. The paramedics said she was alone in her vehicle...she didn't even have a car seat in the back."

"Doctor, give me a minute with my girl here," stated Miki as she looked around the room. "Please. I know her."

The doctor nodded and everyone left.

"Lay down," whispered Miki. "Just lay down and let them treat you."

"But Reilly!" pleaded Erica.

"We been through a lot together in the four years I've know you, right? Remember when things exploded with you and Weston? And when your mom died who was there for you?"

Erica laid down.

"You trust me?" asked Miki.

Erica nodded silently.

"Then you let dhem treat you and I'll take care of the rest of dis mess for you...I got your back." Then Miki stood up and left the room.

As she looked for the doctor, Miki rounded the corner and ran into Caleb. "Get out of my way, idiot!" she said.

"I'm sorry," apologized Caleb.

Miki continued around the corner.

"Wow! Who was that crazy Amazon?" he asked a nearby nurse. Before she could answer he spotted Erica. Walking quickly over to her he reached out and took her hand. "Hey," he whispered.

"Huh?" Erica looked up dazed. Then recognition slowly crept

across her face. "Why are you here?" she asked amazed.

"I'm uh...I'm visiting a friend here in the hospital.

"What?"

"I heard someone calling out your name and thought I'd see if it was that beautiful lady I met yesterday. So what's going on?" Caleb asked as he rubbed her hand.

Just then a nurse approached. "Are you calm now?" She asked sharply as she looked at Erica.

Erica glared at the nurse, but nodded silently.

"Good, then I'm gonna give you a little shot and you can get some rest."

Erica began to sit up, but Caleb gently pushed her down. "You need to take care of yourself."

The nurse proceeded to inject Erica. Caleb sat down next to her and stroked her hand. "It's going to be okay," he said.

The words blurred into a stream of colors in Erica's head. She tried to focus. The nurse had several plastic bags...like at the nursing home. Red...yellow...all full of syringes.

"No," Erica whispered as she spotted a large yellow label on the papers the nurse was holding, a label that looked just like the one on Grandma's chart. "No," she mumbled. "No..."

Meanwhile Miki continued to rush down the hall. She pulled out her cell phone and hit a button. "Hello?" a voice replied.

"Hello? Where's da kid?" she demanded. "Where's da kid? We've got the virus. Da kid she ain't got nuthin to do with this," Miki said. "You can't deport me. I kept up my end. I got you the stuff and...ask Mr. Beeman. He's your guy for dat. I said just git me the kid she belongs to her momma. Right now!"

"Where are you?" asked the voice calmly.

"I ain't gonna tell you dat now am I?" she shot back.

"Are you with Erica?"

Miki was silent.

"Answer me, you damn wetback!"

"You got nerve. I hold da cards now and I ain't from Mexico, idiot!

"You hold nothing. Do you hear me? You hold nothing. The stakes just got higher. RCG35-98 has been verified in three local counties. Weston thinks he's called our bluff, but the funny thing is....we weren't bluffing. And what he's done now is treason. Killing Americans on American soil."

"Now what's dat got to do with me?" shouted Miki into her phone as people passing by stared at her. Then she turned and pulled back into a doorway and whispered, "I got you dat virus and I destroyed his evidence against you. Done. I'm done now and you don't go hurtin that baby or Erica. I'll tell dem all! What I know makes what Weston had on you look like nutin."

"Don't do anything stupid. Weston infected Erica's grandmother as part of a trial now it's spread through the nursing home and anyone who's had contact. If you've been with Erica, you've been exposed. She's got to be quarantined and now so do you."

"You're lyin. You lyin bag of crap," hissed Miki. "Dis is all so you can control it. Control everything, but you ain't controlling nuthin and you ain't controlin me!"

"Fine. Die. I don't care. What I do care about is we've got our own home grown epidemic of a virus only Dr. Anderson potentially can stop. You want out of this nightmare? Well, too late. And Erica? Well, she just picked the wrong guy. You want her kid safe? Then shut your mouth and don't draw attention to this kid because if you think the wrong people have her now just wait until the potential buyers for the virus find out what's happening."

"What you gonna do about dis virus?" Miki whispered.

"The best we can. Your new contact is a guy named Marcus. Don't call me again." Then the phone went dead.

"Marcus?" asked Miki incredulously. Then she saw the doctor. Disconnecting her call, she grabbed the man's arm. "Doctor? You're da one working on my friend?"

"Yes, thank you for your assistance. She's resting comfortably now."

"Is she sick?"

"Sick? Looks like a minor concussion, that's all. What do you mean sick?"

"Flu?"

"No, no she doesn't have the flu," responded the doctor. "We are concerned because she keeps claiming to have a child."

"She doesn't have a child," blurted Miki.

"What?"

"She doesn't have a child," she repeated. Then she looked out into the waiting room. Pearl was nowhere in sight.

CHAPTER 20

Pearl looked up and saw a child in the hallway leading out of the hospital lobby. He was alone. Standing up slowly she shuffled after him weaving through the chaos of the room as the orderlies from her home entered. Glancing around for a moment, they approached the receptionist and then headed for the elevator.

As the kaleidoscope of colors and sound whirled around her, Pearl slowly stepped through a door in time. The chaos around her dissipated and she was walking down that quiet hallway…the one that lead to the horrific pain that crushed her daily, but never had the compassion to simply kill her.

She stopped. There was no sound. *Why was there no sound?* Her babies had cried for days on end and now there was nothing. *Why?* Paulser would help her. He would make things better. His room was on the left. Flu patients lined the hallway, so many coughing, moaning, and so many crying.

"Ooooomm," hummed a woman on a gurney in between lung spewing coughs. A man covered in his own phlegm gurgled as she walked by his emaciated body.

Two small children huddled against a body that earlier in the day was raging hot, but now grew cold. In this hallway of bodies no one even noticed…no one except the newly orphaned children who now sniffled and wheezed from the virus infecting their lungs.

Pearl tried to avoid the eyes on the faces of those still alive…those who waited for help, those who were far beyond help. She wondered if death really was a man in a black robe and if so, had she brushed against him in these narrow halls. But for as much as she hated this hallway of death, Pearl had to come. Like the hundreds of others who now crowded in and around the hospital, in the makeshift tents outside, in the hallways, she had to be here. She needed help.

Her legs wobbled slightly as she weaved through her delusion of the scene that horrible day. The babies had cried all night. Her husband had moaned. She had sat vigilant believing that she herself could ward off death if only she stayed awake near the cradle of six-month-old Wallace and the ragged bed of three-year-old Irving. She sent her seven-year-old daughter, Franny, to care for the others in the house.

All the coughing, the vomiting, the tremors…all raged in the tiny bodies near her. For a few seconds here and there her delusions also took her to the Arkansas land that once surrounded her. That beautiful farmland became so ugly to her. She didn't want to be alone out there. As midnight had passed, the land turned into a black box surrounding her. She tried to look through her husband's books, but the lines and dots just danced around as they always had for her. Until she married Paulser, she had never been in one home long enough to enroll in school. Her life had simply been one town after another riding on a broken wagon, sometimes simply walking, as her father begged for work. There had been no books, no reading.

She had been a beautiful child and her father used her often to get food. All she did was pout and say she was hungry, and anyone in hearing distance would quickly buy the family a meal. But then she turned 13 and wasn't quite the cherubic figure anymore. She remembered one day when Papa had sat her on the steps of a small church and told her to sit still and wait for an angel. Despite the howling winds, the bitter ice, Pearl had sat very still all night. Then an angel did come…a woman who took Pearl into the building and warmed her.

Though still living on scraps, Pearl stayed at that church for one year, until the day a traveling teacher came and married her. One year later Franny was born and they moved into a tiny cabin on a farm left to her husband by his uncle.

Life had been good until that horrible winter just a few years later. The flu struck while she was pregnant and she lost the baby in the middle of the night. Paulser had been traveling…selling crops in nearby towns. Franny was only six, but she held Pearl's hand until dawn. When the morning sun came, Franny looked like an angel as she stood over Pearl holding little Ann's hand.

But Franny couldn't help Pearl that terrible night weeks later. As Franny held her little sister's hand, Pearl fought the fever that her and Paulser, and ultimately claimed her unborn child.

"Momma, we got to go to the hospital," Franny begged.

"No, they can't do nothing there we can't do here," snapped Pearl.

"But, Momma, Daddy...he's...Momma, please," cried Franny.

Then the babies stopped crying. At first Pearl thought that was a good thing. She wiped her brow and said a silent Hallelujah. Her joy was only momentary.

"Momma, why is Wally's lips blue?" screamed Franny. Poor Ann curled up in the corner and covered her eyes.

Pearl looked down. She grabbed the child and held him up. The sweat on his body ran down her arms as she shook him. "Wake up, Wallace!" Then she looked at Irving. He was still breathing, but it was shallow and his eyes were closed. His body didn't move.

"Run get Papa!" screamed Pearl.

"I can't wake Papa up!" screamed Franny. "I tried to tell you that! I can't get Papa up!"

Pearl wrapped her arms around herself and began to rock back and forth. Franny screamed louder and louder. Then the door swung open. A man entered. "I could hear screaming from the path out there....you folks need help?"

Pearl remembered nothing else. The hour ride, the doctors who met her at the door...she remembered nothing. The doctors took her babies. "I didn't kill Wally!" she sobbed as they covered his body with a sheet. Irving disappeared in the arms of a nurse, a dumpy woman with a scowl who returned moments later to say that Irving was dead as well.

Now she had to find Paulser. He had to take her home. They would go home and she would fall asleep in his arms tonight. Things would be so happy...but the hallway never seemed to end. The pale lumps of flesh, the eyes begging for help, the smell of sweat and vomit.

"Paulser!" she screamed. "Help me!"

Then the nurse appeared. That dumpy lousy bitch who took Irving's last few minutes on this earth. Those last precious minutes! His momma should have been the last face Irving saw! Now that horrible face that stole Irving was telling her to go home. Call family. Paulser is dead. Pearl doesn't belong there anymore...too many sick...bodies need to be moved to make way for those with hope.

Who has hope? Pearl wondered. *Ann always had hope.*

Through the confusing mist she saw Ann, her youngest daughter. She was holding a black and white picture in her bloodied hand. *Ultra sound...Erica's baby...*the words drifted through Pearl's head. The doctor, the man who was with Erica so many times before, he took the picture covered with bloody finger prints and put it in his pocket leaving Ann's body at the bottom of the stairs.

CHAPTER 21

As Erica drifted to sleep, Caleb looked around. Taking a moment to look at his notebook, he stood up slowly and looked around again. A figure rounded the corner; he instinctively thrust his hand into the pocket where he kept his gun.

"Erica!" shouted Miki as she raced into the room. Then she stopped abruptly. Confused she cocked her head as she looked at Caleb. "Excuse me? Who are you?"

"I'm Caleb. I met Erica at Weston's lab."

Miki bypassed Caleb and sat on the edge of Erica's bed. "Did they…"

"Yeah, they uh, gave her something to help her sleep. Quite a nasty blow to her head, I guess."

"Are you a part of…are you…do you know Marcus?" Miki asked stumbling.

"No," Caleb replied.

"It wasn't supposed to have happened dis way…" Miki said, fighting tears. She looked down by Erica. "dose terrible men did dis to get you here," she whispered.

"What?" asked Caleb. "What do you mean?"

Miki swallowed hard. "I just mean something like dis shouldn't happen. dat's all. But it's going to be okay now," she said softly. Then she looked up at Caleb. "Erica's granny. I left her in da lobby. Now she's gone."

"I can help you look," Caleb said.

"You know Weston?" asked Miki.

"Yes."

"Do you know where he is right now? I can't reach him at home or on his cell phone…and his lab it has been sealed off by police or somebody," said Miki.

"It has? By who?" shot back Caleb.

"I just said SOMEBODY. How da hell am I supposed to know? I don't know and I don't care. I need to find Weston and I need to find him now," said Miki. She turned towards the window and began to chew on her thumb nail.

"Look, lady. Do you want my help or not?"

"I don't even know you, so don't be trying dat shit on me. For all I know you're one of dem."

"Why is everyone I've met in the past two days crazy?" said Caleb as he headed towards the door.

"Reilly is missing," blurted Miki.

Caleb froze. Then after a few seconds he turned slowly. "What?"

"Are you deaf?" snapped Miki. "I said dat Erica's baby is missing. Granny kept snipping about everyone dying and Reilly is gone...I didn't take dem seriously, but now Reilly is gone. I need to find her," Miki pleaded. Then she wiped a tear from her eyes. "I thought I was helping...I thought I would say in dis country. Erica is my friend."

"Look, crazy lady, start searching the hospital for Granny....I've got some calls to make."

Miki hesitantly left the room. Caleb rushed past her and dodged down the opposite hallway as he dialed his cell phone. Then he paused and yelled into his cell, "Who the hell is Marcus?"

Miki disappeared down the hallway without looking back.

Caleb shook his head. Then, spotting a janitor's closet, he slipped into it and returned to his call. "Do you know anything about this kid getting snatched?" he hissed into the phone. "Don't play dumb. Personally I don't give a damn what happens to that idiot Weston. Kill him. But a kid's a different story....and an old lady. ...hey, listen, bastard. I'm done. I think you've lied to me and now I'm done....Don't give me that shit! I don't know much, but what I know I think it's time the authorities knew and it won't be long before that friend of Erica's....she's going to the authorities herself. I ain't going down with this shit."

Caleb stormed out of the closet, knocking over a nurse as he swung open the door. "Project RCG35-98?" he blurted.

The nurse stood up dazed.

"I said Project RCG35-98!"

For a moment she raised her arm and point to the hallway to the left. Caleb tore away in the direction she pointed. Reaching a door with black paint over its window, Caleb raised his fist to pound on it. Before his knuckles could make contact, however, it swung open. Pearl tumbled out the door and onto the floor.

"Oh, dear God!" she wailed.

"Here, let me help you. Are you okay?" he asked.

"Please get me out of this terrible place," she sobbed. Then she pointed to the door from where she had tumbled. "There...in there...have you seen? In there...people are dying. They're everywhere...dying. I didn't get to hold my baby. He died."

"He died in there?" asked Caleb frantically.

Pearl stood and looked at him for a moment. Then she looked around her and at her wrinkled hands. "I need my granddaughter, Erica" she said slowly and clearly. "Her doctor friend killed my daughter."

"What?" Caleb blurted shaken.

Pearl nodded.

"Was his name Weston?" asked Caleb softly.

"I live in the Cherryhill Nursing Home. I don't want to go back."

"I'm asking you a question. Did Weston kill someone?" Caleb asked urgently.

Pearl cocked her head to the side and began to rub her hands together. "I live at the Cherryhill Nursing Home. I don't want to go back," she whispered.

Caleb put his hands up to his face as if to block the world for a moment. Then he took a deep breath. "How about we take you to Erica's home?"

"I'd like that," she replied. "Where is Erica?"

"She's sleeping right now."

"Weston's part of the plan," whispered Pearl.

"Excuse me?"

"He said the virus didn't belong there. I heard them talking about him at the Cherryhill Nursing Home. Maybe they can save my baby. One was still alive when I got here," she said.

"Yeah, maybe," said Caleb distracted. Then he began to guide her down the hallway.

"Is it very far?" she asked.

"Not too much farther and I guarantee you that no one is going to bother us."

Pearl looked at the gun handle protruding from Caleb's pocket. "Because you have a gun?" she asked.

Quickly he pulled his coat over the gun and put his forefinger against his lips. "Shhhhh!" he whispered. "Our little secret."

"That sign says 'employees only'," pointed out Pearl as they entered a narrow hallway. "Do you work here?"

"Sure," he said patronizingly as he continued to guide her down the hall.

They emerged into the rainy day and then heard a loud shout. "Granny!" Pearl looked up to see Miki.

"That's the lady who brought me here," she whispered to Caleb. Pearl turned to Miki and pointed at Caleb. "He's taking me to Erica's house," she said happily.

"You know where Erica lives?" asked Miki as she stepped between Caleb and Pearl.

"Yes, I do." He said dryly.

"How come Erica never mentioned you? I'm her friend. She tells me everything....EVERYTHING! How come she didn't say boo about you?"

"As long as we're asking questions, maybe you could tell me something," Caleb shot back staring intently into Miki's eyes. "Why did you trash Weston's house and what did you find that you're still hiding?"

CHAPTER 22

Erica slowly opened her eyes. White blurs skated around her in a room with no shape or depth.

"How are we feeling?" asked a form hovering nearby. "Would you like some TV? I'll put it on while you wait for the doctor."

Erica blinked several times and then tried to swallow. Her tongue refused to work. She closed her eyes again. Her left arm throbbed. For a moment sleep found her again and she smiled as she saw Weston approaching with flowers. Then in her dream she saw blood everywhere. It was all over Weston and her. Weston was yelling at her. "Where's the baby?" he screamed. "Where's the baby?"

Erica woke abruptly with every muscle in her body jerking in a painful state of tension. She opened her mouth, but air didn't seem to enter.

Air. I need air. Can't breathe. I'm dyin. Someone...someone...If I lay her I'll die. I've got to...I've got to...what the hell is this...out of bed....

Delirious, she thrashed around pulling the IV out of her arm and sending herself tumbling out of the bed. As she hit the floor she caught a breath. There in a pile on the floor her gasping became breathing and then she remembered.

Reilly? Where is Reilly? How long have I...

"Good God! Nurse! Help me!" shouted a man's voice from above her. Then Erica felt hands reaching down. There were lots of hands pushing, pulling. She closed her eyes.

"Ms. Schmidt? Ms. Schmidt?" the voice said again.

Erica opened her eyes. "Hmmm?"

"Do you know where you are? Can you tell me what day it is?"

Erica looked around the room. Yes, she felt moderately certain she knew where she was, but her mouth remained closed.

"You had an accident yesterday," replied the doctor through a white mask that covered his face.

"Yesterday?" she croaked out through a dry mouth. "No, I had an accident this morning."

The man shined a small light in her eyes and then grabbed her wrist as he looked at his watch. "No, you've been sleeping," he said firmly. "How do you feel?"

"I need to get out. I have a baby. I need to go home right now! Why are you wearing a mask?"

"You're looking better, but I want to give you a complete exam before we let you go," he said looking at a clipboard.

"Doctor?" said a voice from behind him. "You're needed in room 311."

"I'll be back in a few minutes and then we'll talk about you going home," he said to Erica. As he left the room he paused by the door. "She's still talking about a baby. Where's the results of the CAT-scan just to make sure we've caught everything."

The doctor exited as the nurse returned to Erica's bedside and asked, "Would you like something for the pain?"

Erica stared mutely at the nurse who also was wearing a thick, white mask. "Why are you wearing a mask? I had an accident. That's not contagious."

"I'll get something for your pain." She left.

Then phone began ringing…. At first Erica looked around confused. She rubbed her arm and then noticed the yellow plastic band around her wrist. Then slowly she turned to the phone beside her bed and picked it up. "Hello?"

"You're in danger."

"Weston! Oh, God, Weston!"

"Shut up, Erica. I'm not even supposed to have access to this room. Listen. You're in danger. You're right in the center of a biological warfare development site. You were exposed to a virus at your grandmother's nursing home. An experimental virus called RCG

35-98 and your car accident was not an accident at all! They want you there."

"Am I sick?

"I...I..I honestly don't know, Erica. You've been exposed. It's my fault."

"Your fault?" Erica asked in surprise.

"I can't explain now. Just know that I didn't plan it this way. It was all an accident. Just one horrible accident. I should have locked down the nursing home right away, but I didn't want panic.

"What are you talking about, Weston?" asked Erica with urgency.

"Let's get you out of there. I know this virus. I can help, but not there. Not now. They've turned it all around. An accident that they're going to use to their advantage. Just get out of there."

"But what about Reilly?"

"Right now, get yourself out. Trust no one. Just get out." Then the phone went dead.

Erica hung up slowly and looked around. She had no windows. She was surrounded by four white walls.

Just then the nurse returned and began setting up the IV.

"Where am I? Why don't I have any windows?" asked Erica.

"Um, well, we're underground. A lower level of the hospital," replied the nurse.

"But I wasn't when I first came here...and I thought that patient rooms were all above floor three."

The nurse looked up surprised. "The doctor can explain." Then she pulled out a syringe from a red package.

"What's that?" asked Erica.

"Your pain killer."

"I'm fine now. I decided I don't need it," Erica said quickly.

"Oh, I think you'd better. You want to get feeling good again, don't you?" insisted the nurse.

"What type of pain killer is it?" asked Erica.

"What?" replied the nurse surprised.

"Type...I want to know what you're giving me *exactly*!" insisted Erica.

"The doctor can explain," replied the nurse as she gripped Erica's arm.

"Stop saying that!"

"I'm going to get the doctor," snipped the nurse.

"Fine. Go get the doctor," Erica replied in panic as she pulled away. "I'm going to the bathroom and I'll be in there for quite a while."

The nurse rolled her eyes. "I'll be back in a few minutes and then we're going to do the IV." She left as Erica scanned the room for her clothes. Then the television caught her eye. There was a picture of Miki.

Erica froze as the words "PARKING LOT ATTACK" scrolled across the screen. Hitting the sound button, the voice of a stranger delivered the news. "According to security tapes at the condominium, the two women were attacked from behind. The younger woman was left in a pool of her own blood, but the whereabouts and identity of the older woman who was with her is still unknown."

CHAPTER 23

Erica sat stunned. *Miki dead? Miki, the foreign exchange student she met in graduate school whose goal was to meet Brad Pitt and to eventually have lots of babies with someone who looked like Brad Pitt, was dead? And who was the elderly woman with her?*

Erica slumped onto the bed and put her hand in her hands. *Could this be related to Weston's lab being trashed? What have I done getting Miki involved?*

For a moment she sat shaking with tears running down her face. Then she remembered Weston's words. "Right now, get yourself out. Trust no one. Just get out." Slowly she stood up. Then wiping her face with the back of her hand, she raced to the door and looked down the empty corridor. Staring intently down the florescent tunnel she listened to a slow, steady hum of a floor waxer and an occasional groan. Nothing moved in the hallway. A florescent light flickered almost in time with the soft ghostly groaning that had become steady.

Closing the door, Erica scanned her room again and spotted her clothes sticking out of a small, white cabinet drawer near the door. Erica pulled them out and began to dress quickly. As the cabinet door swung closed, she noticed a small tag on the door:

POTENTIAL EXPOSURE VICTIM

What? Erica studied it for a moment and then she thought she heard movement outside her door.

The sounds of movement were now accompanied by a groaning that grew louder every few minutes. "Help. Please?" the voice begged.

Once she was fully dressed, Erica slipped out of her room and down the hall towards the groaning. The smell of sweat and vomit became intense as she moved towards the final door in the corridor. The flickering fluorescent brought a horror movie quality and Erica hesitated to open the door.

This is ridiculous. I'm in a hospital. There is nothing weird here.

She swallowed hard and then swung open the door as she flung her body backwards against the wall. Nothing happened. Her heart was a stealth bomber in her throat as she pushed her body against the wall and waited. Still nothing...nothing but that horrific stench. Then she looked into the darkness. She could make out one empty patient bed and nightstand near the door. The rest of the room was swallowed by the darkness, but she heard nothing.

This is crazy, she thought to herself. *There's nothing going on here.* She moved into the darkness and sat on the edge of the bed nearest to the door to think for a moment. *I need to get out of this horrible smell. And I need to get help finding Reilly...and Grandma. Poor Miki. What happened?* Her thoughts tumbled one after another.

Then out of nowhere an arm. A boney, sweaty, shaking hand clamped around her wrist like a metal handcuff. Startled, Erica jumped, but was pulled onto the bed with sudden force. As her head hit the mattress, what appeared to be a skull with eyes thrust up from the other side of the bed.

Erica screamed. The skull talked. "Help me, please. Help me!"

"Oh, God! Oh, God! What the hell!" Erica tried to free herself, but stood in horror at this figure that appeared to have stepped directly out of a picture of holocaust survivors.

"My name is James...I'm sick...take me to a hospital..." he gasped.

"But you...you are..."

Suddenly the handcuff released. The boney hand and the skull slipped down to the other side of the bed onto the floor.

Then Erica heard footsteps. "I'm sorry. So sorry. I'll get you help," she whispered.

"Go to the room marked 3-B. It's a back stairway to the parking lot," whispered another voice from deep in the darkness.

"Who are you?" asked Erica trying desperately to see. She reached for a lamp, but hesitated as she listened for the footsteps.

"Go! Go now!" said the voice with growing urgency.

Erica peered out into the hallway and watched as the nurse

headed towards her room. *When she sees I'm gone they'll start looking for me.* As soon as the nurse disappeared into Erica's room, she raced out the door. First she turned to her left. *Damn! Everything is marked "C."*

Frantically she turned just in time to see the nurse emerge from the room yelling into a cell phone. "Has someone come for Erica Schmidt?…Hey! Stop! You need to go back to your room!" she shouted as she spotted Erica. "I've got her. Send containment!" snapped the nurse into her cell phone.

When she spotted the door "3-B" behind the nurse, Erica took a deep breath and raced at her causing the woman to dodge to the side. Grabbing the door handle, Erica thrust it open. *A patient room? Oh God!* She raced to the back of the room, and then, after pulling down the white gauze room divider, Erica saw a green door. *Please don't let it be locked! Please don't let it be locked! Please don't let it be locked!* Then she turned the handle and pulled it open with so much force she almost fell to the floor. Stumbling through the door, she pulled it closed behind her and then she pushed in the button on the door handle. A split second after the door slammed closed, the handle jiggled.

"Open this door!" shouted the nurse. "You've got nowhere to go! You're sick. Let us help you!"

Erica turned and raced up the stairs bypassing the first floor. *They'll expect that. I'll go to three. Was Wes right?*

Reaching the third floor she tried the handle. Locked! She headed up another floor. Breathlessly she reached for that handle. The door opened! She burst out into a hallway into the middle of a flurry of people. She shuffled into the crowd and then into a visitor lounge. Seeing a red, leather coat flung over a chair in the corner, Erica slowly walked over to it and sat down. She looked around to see if anyone was watching and then pulled on the leather coat and a white, yarn hat lying nearby. Then she returned to the crowd and walked towards the elevator.

With the coat collar pulled up around her face, Erica exited the elevator and quickly walked through the lobby. Spotting a cab out at the curb, she rushed outside towards it, opened the door and as she flung herself into she said, "313 Brookwood Way."

"Huh? Oh, you the lady who called? Cause I'm here to pick up someone…"

"Yeah, that's me," said Erica excitedly. "Could we speed it up a bit?" she shouted as she glanced back and saw that the nurse who had been pursuing her had reached the lobby.

They pulled away and Erica sat back and took the first deep breath she had taken in what felt like years. *Weston, what have you gotten me into?*

"That's something, ain't it?" asked the cab driver as he turned up the radio.

"What?"

"A U.S. scientist gone rogue. Really something, ain't it?"

"Ummm," she said still not hearing the words as she closed her eyes to rest.

"We're here," called out the cab driver. "Hey, lady! You awake?"

Erica shook herself and looked around. She was indeed home…but now she needed to find Reilly.

"That will be $47.95."

"Huh?"

"I said that'll be $47.95."

Erica realized for the first time that she didn't have a purse. Reaching into her jean pockets she pulled out a $5.00 bill. As she fumbled around her pockets, she tried to stall the driver. "So…uh…what was that about a scientist killing people?"

"What? Oh, that thing on the radio half an hour ago? Some guy working for the university. Killed a pretty Jamaican lady and some old lady."

Erica paused and looked up. "What was the name of the guy? Do you know?"

"I don't know. Hey, lady, you got the money or not?"

"Was it Anderson?"

"Yeah, I think it was. Yeah, Anderson."

Just then Caleb walked up and opened the cab door. "Need some help?"

"Yeah, she needs $47.95. You got it, buddy?"

Caleb reached into his khaki cargo pants and pulled out three $20.00 bills. Here. Keep the change," he said as he helped Erica out of the cab.

As the it pulled away Erica stared at Caleb. "What are you doing here?"

"You're welcome. I'm here to talk to you."

"Look, I don't know who you are, but I sure don't want to talk to you now. Ever since you've been around there's been trouble everywhere."

"You noticed that too, huh?" he replied as he began walking towards her building. "Your condo, right? You live here? Let's go inside." He motioned to the doorway.

"What are you doing here?" she repeated firmly.

"Look we really need to talk…inside your place," he snapped. "Dr. Anderson has gotten you into a whole hell of a lot of trouble… Miki is dead, who knows where your grandmother is…"

Remembering Weston's words of warning, she stood frozen. *Trust no one.*

Caleb walked a few steps and then turned when he saw Erica was not following. "What has this guy got on you? He's a murderer. Do you know what he's been doing in his lab? Do you really know?" Caleb began to walk away. Then he paused and looked over his shoulder. "Your baby's life may depend on this conversation."

CHAPTER 24

"Hey, bartender!" shouted Weston loudly.

The large man behind the counter looked up dutifully. "Yeah."

"What do you call 100 scientists at the bottom of the ocean?"

"I dunno, Mac."

"A good start!" hooted Weston as beer laced spit flew from his mouth.

"Don't you mean lawyers?" asked a guy nearby nursing a gin and tonic.

"Did I say lawyers, you shit head?" slobbered Weston.

The man picked up his drink and moved away.

"You got a problem with scientists?" asked the bartender.

"Man, if you only knew…if you only knew what goes on in labs," said Weston as he wiped sweat from his forehead.

A waitress approached the bar. "Two gin and tonics," she called out.

"Hey, Ginger!" shouted Weston.

"You don't need to shout, cowboy. I can hear just fine," she said brushing back the frizzy, red curls that draped her face.

Weston looked up into her face and smiled. "Did I ever tell you that you look like someone I know?"

"Yes, Weston, you tell me that every time you come in here. So where you been recently?"

Weston took a long drink of the beer sitting in front of him. He stared at the dark circles under her eyes that hid in the shifting shadows of the bar, but yet could not dim the light in her eyes that miraculously remained even after five years under a bartender's thumb. Then he smiled. "I went to visit some friends…well, not friends, but scientists.

The world's about to face the biggest plague we've ever seen before and guess what?"

"What?" she asked as she hurriedly placed drinks on her tray and turned to leave.

"I may have started it...all because I didn't go to the doctor with my pregnant girlfriend when she got her ultra sound!" For a moment he stared emotionless at the mirror behind the bartender. Then as tears rimmed his eyes he began to laugh maniacally. Then put his head in his hands as he somberly added, "Yeah, everyone's gonna die." He took another long drink.

The waitress turned and put down her tray. Then she sat down the stool next to Weston. "Weston, go home. You need to get some sleep. Is there anyone I can call for you?"

Weston held up his new cell phone. "It's new," he whispered. "It's my death watch phone." Then he slumped over the bar dropping the phone onto it.

Ginger picked up the phone and hit "redial." The phone began to ring at Erica's condo just as she and Caleb entered.

"Hello?" said Erica.

Ginger took the gum out of her mouth and wrapped it around the bare ring finger on her left hand. "Uh, hello. Um...this is kind of awkward, but do you know a guy named Weston?"

"Yes," said Erica confused.

"He's here at the bar and needs someone to take him home...right now," she whispered as she noticed the bartender eying her.

"Is he hurt?" asked Erica.

"No, drunk. Look the bar is at the corner of Mohican and Third." Then she hit the call end button and slipped the phone back into Weston's pocket.

Weston looked up as Ginger picked up her tray and walked away. "I can't do anything...now they have my notes and so they can duplicate this...this evil virus. That is if there's anyone left to kill with it later."

"Hey, Ginger, get them drinks out," snapped the bartender.

"I like it better when Stan tends the bar," complained Weston.

"So do I, Sweetie. So do I," whispered Ginger. "Look, I'm on break in just a minute. You go sit in that booth and I'll join you for a few."

Weston slowly stood up and wandered over to the booth in a drunken haze. Ginger dropped off her drinks to four people sitting at a round table in the center of the bar. Then as she headed for Weston, she tossed her tray on the bar. "For God's sake, Wes, move over if you want someone to sit with you," she said as she slid into the booth and elbowed him. "Now tell me what this is all about. I haven't seen you this drunk since that graduate student showed you the two pink lines."

"I got a job a few years ago for a pharmaceutical company," he said with sudden clarity.

"Yeah?" asked Ginger as she pulled out a nail file.

"I wanted to find a way to limit or at least more successfully predict mutations of flu viruses."

Ginger blew a bubble with her gum as she looked at Weston. "So that's good, ain't it?"

"I...I created," he paused as if he were having trouble breathing. "Somehow I created a new virus."

"Okay," said Ginger slowly. When Weston didn't respond she added, "The virus that's gonna kill us all?"

Weston ran his hand through his sweaty hair and then reached for his beer. He took a long slow drink and then put it down. "They wanted to use my virus as a weapon...send a warning," he said adding quote marks with his hands.

"Who?" asked Ginger alarmed. She sat up straight and reached out to hold Weston's hands. "Who wanted to use it?"

"That doesn't matter anymore because...because..."

"Because what, Weston?" Ginger asked urgently.

"I missed the ultra sound appointment," he said again on the brink of tears. "God, you must be what 21?"

"Twenty-two, but who the hell is counting?" she joked.

"Your sister still at the university?"

"Yeah, thanks again."

Weston shook his head and waved a hand in the air. "Glad to be able to help someone...just once in my life do the right thing."

"Why do you talk like that? You helped my sister get into college when God knows my worthless family wasn't going to help...you're so smart they hire you to create cures for things like cancer. Why do you talk like this?"

"I didn't cure cancer, but the guy who did is either dead or sleeps with the devil."

Ginger moved the beer out of Weston's reach. "You've had enough."

With a violent lunge, Weston grabbed the beer twisting Ginger's arm in the process. "Enough? Enough? Hell yes! I've had enough," he screamed. "Now nothing left to do but die...correction...watch other people die!

"Damn it, Weston!" Ginger said jumping up and rubbing her wrist. "That hurt."

Weston got to his feet and grabbed her shoulders. "Have you ever heard of the Tuskegee Syphilis Study?"

Ginger stared wide eyed at Weston and shook her head. Her body frozen, she stared at the wild look in his eyes and held her breath.

"People had syphilis and were told that they were getting treatment, but they weren't. They were being watched and charted by scientists...U.S. scientists...who wanted to see how the disease developed. Penicillin could have successfully treated it, but were they given it? HELL NO! They just sat and died."

"I don't understand," said Ginger as she tried to move out of Weston's grip.

"There are a lot of ways to control people...keeping them sick is a great one...oh, and a nasty life threatening virus also makes for a damn good weapon. You can block missiles, but what the Sam freaking hell are you going to do when a virus infiltrates your country and you have no vaccine?"

CHAPTER 25

Erica hung up the phone and turned to Caleb. "Weston needs my help," she said bluntly.

"Oh, my god!" said Caleb as he shook his head in disbelief. "Erica, this man is not a good man. He's done shit that you have no idea."

In a burst of tears and frustration, Erica turned on Caleb. "Why don't you tell me who you are? Huh? Since you've been here, Weston's work has been destroyed, Miki is dead, and my grandmother and my baby are gone." Erica paused as she choked back tears. "And at the hospital...in the emergency room...I couldn't even get them to take the report. Apparently my daughter doesn't exist! So what the hell is your role here? You show up out of the blue—coincidentally on the day that Weston's lab gets torn apart and then you proceed to just keep showing up! You are not a God damn graduate student...you want something. That's why you're here. So why don't you tell me what you want and let's get this over with because you telling me Weston is no good really doesn't hold any credibility? Weston is going to help me find Reilly."

Caleb silently stood with his mouth slightly open for several seconds. Shoving his hands into his pockets, he took a deep breath. "Weston has problems. Big problems. Either he's delusional and a danger to himself and others, or he's secretly involved with biological warfare...and not for our government."

Erica put her hand over her mouth to hold back the tears. "I need to find my baby. I just need to find my baby."

"I believe Reilly is being used to manipulate Weston."

"Used?"

"Possibly for an experiment or maybe just to get back at Weston...or maybe both."

Erica turned away as the tears streamed down her face. "Please leave. Leave me alone."

"Look I can work with you to help or I can just follow from the shadows, but the person who is paying me isn't going to let this just go away. Things are already in motion. Apparently, Weston's little experiments have gotten out of hand. There's an epidemic beginning and Weston and his little group of friends have lost control."

Erica walked to the couch and picked up one of Reilly's blankets. Holding it she walked to the window.

"What if he killed your friend?" asked Caleb. "What if he took your grandmother as well as your daughter? How are you explaining all of these things in your mind?"

"I don't know…I don't know what happened to Miki or my grandmother, but if he took Reilly she's safe."

"Why?"

"Because she's his daughter."

"Yes, and he's such a doting father," shot back Caleb.

"He cares."

"Oh, come on! You're an educated woman. You certainly can't tell me that you thought this was a good idea. Or wait. Let me guess. You're one of these *he'll come around eventually* women?"

"I fell in love with him and, yes, I want to Reilly to have a father."

"But he doesn't want to be a father."

"He never said that."

"Oh, good God!" shouted Caleb. "Do you hear yourself? It's really no wonder that women have never achieved equality…you're all set to take shit from anyone who says they love you."

The phone began to ring again. At first no one moved. Then Erica glanced that the caller ID unit and saw a familiar number, but then turned away.

"I've got to go, and you better leave because I'm calling the police, the FBI and anyone else I can about you!" Erica screamed.

"Like I said…I can come with you and be a part of this thing to help you or I can simply follow you and watch it all go down. Quite frankly, I think you need me," Caleb said calmly as he sat on the arm of the couch. "If I'm right about Weston, I can be of help. If I'm wrong he can beat the shit out of me again like he did yesterday morning."

Erica hesitated for a moment.

"I know people and I know more of what's going on here than you do. Do you want your baby back?"

With her hand pressed against her lips and tears streaming down her cheeks, Erica nodded. Caleb slowly stood up and walked over to the door. "You gonna get that?" he asked nodding towards the phone.

Erica ignored the question and motioned towards the door. Caleb shrugged and walked out, followed closely by Erica who slammed the door to her condo just as her answering machine began to take the message... "Erica? Hello, Erica? It's Marcus. Look that guy...the grad student hanging out with Weston. He's a hired gun, Erica. He killed his wife."

CHAPTER 26

The bartender, tired of hearing Weston's rants, reached for the television remote control. Turning up the volume massively, he then began to flip channels looking for a ball game.

Annoyed, Weston stood up, dusted off his clothes with his hands and then stumbled towards the bathroom. As he disappeared from sight, his face appeared on the 72 inch television screen for the whole bar to see.

"Weston Anderson is wanted in connection with the murder of Michala Gonzalez and the disappearance and possible murder of Pearl Schmidt," roared the voice from the television. "There is a reward for any information leading to his arrest."

The bartender stared at the screen with his mouth open. Ginger dropped the rag she was using to clean tables. Everyone stopped talking. Then the bartender looked at the men's room door…the only thing that separated him from a reward.

Coming eye to eye with the cook who had emerged from the back room, the bartender nodded towards the men's room. Then he picked up the phone and turned his back as Ginger dodged out the front door. The cook disappeared into the kitchen and returned with a plate and a burlap potato sack. He waited silently by the men's room door.

As Weston exited the men's room the plate crashed over his head. He stumbled as the burlap sack was thrust over his head and everything went black. He struggled to breathe through the burlap that covered his face, drawing in more dust and fibers than air. Then as a fist repeatedly slammed into his stomach, vomit spayed across the inside of the bag.

Weston fell to his knees. In a blur of burlap and vomit, he fell to the ground.

The bartender approached Weston's motionless body. "To the storage room," he grumbled to the cook. "I don't care if the reward is only a quarter; it damn sure feels good getting this guy to shut up." He began coughing. "Damn!" he wheezed. Then the bartender leaned up against the wall as Weston curled up at his feet. "I don't feel so good." Sweat rolled down his forehead.

"You should go home," replied the cook as he kicked Weston in the side.

"Yeah, right, Charlie. I go home and you collect a reward. I don't think so," the bartender shot back as he wiped his forehead with his apron. Another patron could be heard in the background coughing. "Damn flu season," added the bartender as he watched the patron run past holding his mouth and stomach.

"Go home," Charlie repeated. "Come on, man, I'll split the reward. You hacking up a lung around here ain't gonna help no one."

Weston began to move. "Take him in back and tie him up," instructed the bartender. "Keep em there till the cops come. I'm goin into the office and get some sleep…but I swear if you don't holler when the cops come I'll bust your head in." Slowly he walked away.

"Officials continue to warn about a possible flu pandemic," blared the television in front of the cook as the sounds of vomiting rang out from the men's room behind him.

"Life is good, ain't it buddy? I need some cash and here you come just in time for a reward…life is good," he said to Weston. Then, stepping on Weston's back, the cook headed for the storage room to grab rope.

In front of the bar, Ginger paced nervously. Pulling the frazzled fake fur that lined her sweater collar closely around her thin figure, she walked quickly to the corner and back. Her sharp, pink heels clicking on the sidewalk, she wobbled back with brisk steps. Then she peeked into the front window. Inside she saw Weston with the bag over his head and vomit running down his neck from inside the bag. His large frame curled in fetal position. He was a fallen giant among a crowd of little people, none of whom bothered to even look up from their beers.

Come on. Come on. Come on. Come on. She kept repeating the words in her head. Then she saw the cook leave Weston when he headed to the back room for rope.

Looking up into the stream of oncoming traffic in the hazy twilight, Ginger bit her lip and dodged back into the bar. She raced over to Weston. "Wes, get up. Come on. Right now, please," she whispered frantically into his ear. She couldn't pull him alone, but she knew she had to act fast.

She raced behind the bar and grabbed a pair of scissors. Then she came back and put one of the blades up against Weston's neck. "Now don't move," she whispered. With all of her force she clamped the scissors closed right on the rope that surrounded his neck closing the bag.

Weston gasped for breath. He began to vomit on Ginger's sweater. She struggled to sit him upright. "Wes! Come on, Wes!"

After a moment the violent retching stopped. Weston wiped his face with his sleeve. "Oh, God! I feel like shit."

"Can you stand up?" asked Ginger.

"I uh…I don't know," he replied in a disoriented haze.

Ginger could hear the cook in the back and then she heard the door to the bar open. A young couple walked in giving Ginger momentary hope that help had arrived, but then they headed to the far back corner of the bar and lit up cigarettes. "Where are your friends?" asked Ginger frantically looking around.

"What happened? What's going on?" asked Weston.

Ginger looked at Weston intensely. "Lay down up against the bar and outta sight," she commanded. Then she got up and ran to the back room. "Charlie, he just left and he's headed out window in men's room!" she shouted.

Charlie raced into the men's room and then back out. "Window's open, but ain't no way I'm getting through it," he said patting his large belly.

"Back door!" screamed Ginger and he took off through the back of the bar.

As soon as she heard the back door opening, she headed back into the bar where she spotted a petite well-dressed woman looking around. The woman had a faced shaped like hers and the same bouncing curls lining her face. *I do look like someone he knows,* she thought to herself. A younger man burst into the bar a moment later.

"How do you know he's even here? This could be a trap," said the younger man.

Ginger raced over to the woman. "Are you looking for Wes? Weston Anderson?"

"Yes," replied Erica. "Are you the one who called me?"

"He's over there," she said pointing to the floor. "And you've got to hurry. The bartender knows there's a reward."

"Why aren't you trying to collect a reward? This guy is wanted for murder and you're helping him get away?" asked Caleb breathless.

"I thought I was calling his friends," she snapped back sarcastically.

"We are...or at least I am," replied Erica glaring at Caleb. "You must be a friend also?"

"Yeah, he helped my kid sister get into college...I owe him one," she whispered as she looked over her shoulder at the storage room door. "We have to move fast."

"Erica!" said Weston as he raised his head from the floor.

Erica looked at the bloody mess on the floor. "Wes?" For a moment she stood horrified. Then Ginger shoved her forward. "Come on! We've got to go."

Quickly, Erica grabbed a man's coat and a hat from a nearby rack. The young couple in the booth was tangled within each other's arms and no doubt wouldn't miss it.

"Put these on him," she instructed urgently as she thrust the items towards Caleb.

"They won't fit," said Caleb.

"We're not doing a fashion show here, it just needs to cover him," replied Erica as she draped the coat over him. Then she pulled the hat over his head.

"Oh, yeah. This'll work," sniped Caleb.

"Look you have to leave and leave now," snapped Ginger.

"Grab that side of him," Erica whispered urgently to Caleb.

Caleb began to shoulder Weston's weight. "Ever heard of Slimfast?" he asked Weston. Then as Weston turned towards him, Caleb gagged. "Good God you stink!"

"Out...out...out!" hissed Ginger.

Then the bar was full of light...flashing blue light. All three froze. Weston groaned.

"Sit down. Here in this booth. I'll distract the police," said Ginger. Then she disappeared out the door.

Caleb and Erica did their best to hunch over Weston. "This isn't going to work," whispered Caleb.

"Shut up!" snapped Erica.

Silently they waited. Nothing happened for several minutes.

"What's going on out there?" asked Caleb.

Then Ginger re-appeared. "Cops everywhere, but I've told 'em I saw Wes headed towards the back alley, so they're all running like crazy that way. You go out the front!" Ginger snapped with urgency. "Go now!"

Struggling and panicked they half dragged Weston as he staggered between them. They could see police officers at the back of the parking lot talking to a group of men in dark overcoats. They were engaged in a heated debate, but none of the words were audible to Erica as they headed to her car.

"Hold it there!" a voice yelled from the group of officers.

Weston tried to turn and look, but Caleb grabbed his arm. "Get in the God damn car right now!" screamed Caleb as he pushed Weston into the car.

Erica threw the keys at Caleb. "You drive!" Then she hopped into the car and locked the door bracing for a wild ride.

Instead of landing in Caleb's hand, the keys clanked to the ground. "Great!" he hissed as he bent over to look for them.

"I said, hold it!" screamed a voice even angrier than before.

Caleb could hear the footsteps running towards him, beating almost as fast as his heart. *I could just let it all go down right now,* he thought. *Right now solve my problem by letting the police arrest him and then sort it all out the right way. But sorting it out means sorting out Sandra's death...*

CHAPTER 27

Caleb quickly stood up holding the keys. He looked at the police office running towards him and then inside at Erica. Her eyes stared straight into his…she knew…she knew he was weighing options, options that could impact whether her baby lived or died. Then he looked back at the officer. He was running more slowly and no one was joining him. Something was wrong.

Caleb jumped into the car and started it up. Taking one last look at the officer and the handful of others that were finally turning their attention on him, Caleb squealed out of the parking lot. Going at top speed he raced down the road.

"Something's wrong," he shouted.

"Other than us harboring an alleged murderer as we break all speed limit laws, what could be wrong?" shouted back Erica.

"They're not chasing us," he observed.

Erica turned and saw nothing but the twilight traffic milling down the road. Then in the distance she spotted a small flashing light. "Yes, they are…in a manner of speaking," she said puzzled.

"They want us to go someplace," murmured Weston.

"Shut up and sleep, Wes," snapped Erica.

"Actually, I think he's right," said Caleb slowly. With a quick jerk of the wheel, he pulled into a parking lot. Then he threw off his seatbelt and turned back to Weston with a vengeance. "Where?" he shouted angrily.

Weston appeared startled. "Huh?"

"I said where, old man!"

"I'm only 52 asshole, which doesn't qualify me as old," hissed Weston as he grabbed Caleb by the collar and pulled him halfway into the backseat.

"Stop it!" shouted Erica. "Stop it right now!"

112

Both men got silent. Weston glared at Caleb and then slowly released him. Caleb slid back into his seat.

"Where, Weston? Where do they think we're going?" Erica said impatiently.

"To get the evidence."

"Evidence? What evidence?" The shock on Erica's face burned into Weston's brain.

"It's not what you think," he said slowly.

"Really? Because what I think is that you're into something big. Something terrible. What I think is that every minute we spend here is a minute my baby is in someone else's hands."

Weston put his hands over his battered face. Every bone in his body ached and he desperately wanted another drink…just one to get him through this. "Yes," he said somberly. "Yes."

"Yes?" Erica screamed.

Weston swallowed hard and sat silent for a moment. He rubbed his face and looked out the window. Then he took a deep breath. "I tried not to get you involved. I tried to keep you and Reilly out of this, but your mother…

"My mother? My mother? She's been with me through everything with Reilly, even when things got complicated at the end of the pregnancy and there was an additional ultra sound done. Where were you?"

"You're never going to let me forget that ultra sound are you? It was nine months ago and yet as recent as a month ago she was waving it in my face saying I wasn't a fit father. If you recall I was at Reilly's birth!"

"And then you called off our wedding less than a day after my mother died!"

"Whoa! The two of you need to stop this. Right now! This is not about your God damn love affair. It's about…" just then Caleb spotted Weston's cell phone. His eyes grew wide.

"What?" asked Erica.

Caleb put a finger to his lips, and then pointed to the cell phone. Pulling a scrap piece of paper from his pocket he began to scribble as he talked. "We need to go to your place, Erica," he said slowly and clearly. Then he held up the paper for Erica and Weston that read, "Follow my lead." They both nodded silently.

"That's a good idea. We'll be safe there and I can tell you all what's going on," said Weston.

Caleb frantically waved for silence. Then he wrote, "Give me your cell phones."

They all silently handed Caleb their cell phones. Then he turned up the music in the car. Then he drove towards the Starbucks near Weston's lab. Turning the volume up even more, Caleb parked the car and motioned for everyone to exit. They all carefully exited the car. The cell phones remained. Caleb grabbed his backpack as Erica grabbed for his purse. She looked at him puzzled, but he avoided her stare.

Caleb nodded towards the Starbucks. "This guy is former CIA and lives on the edge...he'll help us," Caleb whispered.

Weston hesitated, but then as he watched Erica dash towards the building he followed shaking his head.

Upon entering the coffee shop, Caleb marched up to Carson. "I need your office, man," he said softly into Carson's ear. "Something bad's going down." Carson nodded silently and motioned to the rear exit of the building. They all followed and then stood on the back steps of the building. Carson emerged carrying a long metal wand with a black box attached via a thin cord.

"What are we doing out here?" asked Weston rubbing his neck.

"Bug sweep, Professor," growled Carson.

"Is this for real?" asked Erica.

Carson ignored her and waved the wand over her. "Your shoes, Sweetie Pie."

"Excuse me?" she snapped back looking at him incredulously.

"Take 'em off," he said pointing to her shoes.

"Oh, please!" she said as she rolled her eyes. For a moment she hesitated.

She began to take off her left shoe and Carson snatched it away toppling her over. She grabbed onto Caleb who helped steady her. Then Carson ripped the sole out of it…nothing. Then he tore off the heel…nothing.

Carson looked puzzled. Then he motioned for her other shoe. He repeated his actions…nothing.

"You sure you know how to use that thing?" moaned Weston as he looked around nervously.

Ignoring Weston, Carson waved it over him and then turned to Caleb.

"Hold it! Hold it! Hold it!" Caleb objected. "Now I know your thing ain't working cause this is the guy they're after," he said pointing at Weston.

Caleb stepped towards Carson and the machine began to beep loudly and he flung his backpack to the ground. "Carson, let us into your office!"

Carson cocked his head an eyed Caleb. Then he grabbed for the backpack. "Hey, that's mine!" Caleb shouted.

Carson shoved him away and then reached in and rummaged around. After throwing out a sweatshirt and a few notepads, Carson pulled out a transmitter. "This yours too?" he growled.

"No, man, I don't know where that came from," he insisted.

"I think you do," said Weston stepping forward.

Then they heard the police sirens in the distance. "Get into my office and sort this out," growled Carson.

"Whoa!" said Weston stepping back. "Why the hell should we trust either of you?"

"You're the one wanted for murder," shot back Caleb.

"I may be the one wanted for it, but I suspect that you're the one who did it!" shouted Weston.

"Stop it!" screamed Erica. "My baby is missing and that's all I care about right now. And my grandmother…I don't know if she's dead or alive. I need you both…I need to put the puzzle pieces together and the two of you seem to be holding quite a few of them. I need help," pleaded Erica.

Erica stepped towards the building and then there was a soft clicking sound. Everyone froze. Caleb bent over and touched the edge of Erica's pants. Something silver was sticking out from her hem and hitting the sidewalk. Caleb pulled at it and then held up a tiny silver transmitter. Everyone stood silent.

"At the hospital," Erica whispered in disbelief. "Someone bugged me?"

Weston put his arm around Erica. "Let's go in and think this through," he said. As the sirens grew louder they dashed into the Starbucks and down the hallway to the room marked "office." Caleb pulled the door closed quickly behind them.

"We need to go to the cabin," Weston said as he grabbed Erica's shoulders and looked her squarely in the eyes.

"Why would we do that? And what the hell is the cabin?" asked Caleb.

"When I said 'we' I wasn't actually including you," Weston stated flatly.

"You want your kid back?" he asked.

Then Weston slammed Caleb's chest with his fist and pinned him to the wall. As Caleb gasped for air, Weston growled, "You want to tell me what that means or should I just God damn beat it out of you?"

"Do you know where Reilly is?" pleaded Erica. "Or my grandmother?"

Caleb struggled for air. Weston eased up slightly. "No, I swear," gasped Caleb. "But I might know who's doing this." Weston released his hold.

"You better start talking and I mean now!" he hissed.

"Look I was hired by Senator Harris…he was worried that there were some people…powerful people who wanted to get into some good old fashioned bio warfare…"

"Using a virus?" asked Erica astonished.

"Yeah, I guess. Anyway, they wanted me to pose as a grad student and see if you were getting pressured or if you'd sold out…"

Weston landed a right hook on the side of Caleb's face. Caleb staggered sideways and fell against a stack of boxes. Struggling to his feet he rubbed his jaw.

"What the hell was that for?"

"For just being you," replied Weston. "And what do you mean 'they'?"

"Harris and his business partner…Lewis…"

"You mean Reverend Lewis?" asked Erica.

"Trust me he's reverend in name only," answer Caleb as he continued to rub his jaw.

"What are you talking about?" interjected Weston.

"This guy's leading a pocket of supporters who are really growing in power. They've got this whole 'old time religion' and wrath of God stuff going on, but it's all a cover for a political agenda…HIS political agenda," answered Erica. "He's supporting lots of politicians in this week's elections with his own eyes on the presidency." Erica and Weston both stopped and looked intently at Caleb waiting for a response.

"I'm not with them. I don't know," Caleb said finally.

"Funny, you just said you were," shot back Weston.

"All I know is that they said they just wanted me to check up on you," said Caleb. "I owed them a favor."

"Why would they want Reilly or my grandmother?" asked Erica.

"A favor?" asked Weston.

"I think Weston can answer that one," replied Caleb ignoring Weston's question and staring at Erica.

Erica turned and looked at Weston with great intensity.

Weston refused to meet her stare and instead turned to Caleb. "You're not going with us," he stated flatly.

"You need a car," said Caleb. "Mine is parked at Erica's place."

"No," shot back Weston. He turned to Erica. "I'm going to the restroom. I'll be right back and then we leave, Erica." He opened the door and looked around and then walked out.

Caleb turned and grabbed Erica's shoulders. Looking into her eyes he said, "Erica, you obviously don't know this guy as well as you think you do. You can't be serious about going with him alone. Come on. Think about it. Do you want Reilly back or not? Look I only want to go with you because I feel responsible. I didn't get into this to hurt anyone and now there's a baby and an old woman involved. If this is my fault I can't just walk away."

Erica silently stared at him. Then she walked out the door towards Weston. Meeting in the hall they embraced. "I'm going to get Reilly back…safe and sound…I swear," he whispered. "And your grandmother. I swear I didn't kill anyone."

"I know. Look I think we should take this guy…" Weston pulled back and started to open his mouth. Erica put a finger to his lips. "We need to keep an eye on him…he's obviously got more business with us…maybe we can use him to our benefit."

"He's after his own agenda…"

"Look I don't know and I don't care right now what's going on with you or him. Our baby needs us. That's our number one priority."

Weston nodded silently. Together they re-entered the room.

"Have you got your car keys?" asked Erica.

Caleb began to feel his pockets. "Oh, damn! I left them on your coffee table!""I'll call Marcus. He has keys to my place. He can bring the car to us, but are we safe here until he comes?"

Just then Carson entered the room. "Yes, ma'am you're safe here. The government...they killed my boy. He was 11...you know how they did, Professor?" he said nodding to Weston. "I've heard you talking...I've gone to your lectures about politics and medicine. You understand..."

Weston nodded vaguely. "Sure."

"I'm going to get that little baby back for you...or I'll die trying," Carson said.

He handed Erica his cell phone. While keeping a suspicious eye on Carson, she dialed the phone. "Marcus? Oh, thank God! I need your help. There's keys on my coffee table. They go to a...a..." Erica turned to look at Caleb.

"A black Chrysler Seabring," whispered Caleb.

"...a black Seabring parked out front. I need you to bring that to the Starbucks on the corner of Third and Charlotte...What?" Erica pressed her ear against the phone and listened intently for several minutes. "I don't understand...I don't....well, just come right now," she said and then she disconnected the call. She stood silently deep in thought.

"What's wrong?" asked Weston.

"According to Marcus the authorities want to talk to me about....about...about Reilly's murder."

CHAPTER 28

"That's just more bullshit," said Weston.

"Did he say they found a body?" asked Caleb.

Weston turned angrily and shouted, "Shut up!"

Erica slumped to the floor, flung her arms around her knees and rocked back and forth as tears etched her face.

Weston knelt next to her. "She's not dead. They're missing a key piece of what they need to create RCG35-98 and only I have it. And…and they want the evidence I have against them. They wouldn't kill her…she's their ace. They need her alive," he assured Erica. Then he put his arms around her.

Erica shoved him aside. "This is your fault!" she screeched. "This is your fault. You should have told me all this before…before…before you endangered our daughter's life."

"Told you what? Hey, honey, I think the government is going to use my research for political gain, so I'm just going to hide it. Okay?" he said mockingly. "Is that what I should have told you? The truth is that I braced for this… but I never knew for a fact this would happen. Who really wants to think that their government is playing games with their own lives?"

"What are you talking about?" asked Caleb. "You're the one playing the game, Professor. You're the one who released RCG35-98 on OUR own people. I heard on CNN this morning that the pandemic has begun…people are sick and they're dying…meanwhile you're sitting in your lab playing with rats? Oh, and let's not forget that someone from your lab is selling saline solution to earn a few extra bucks by saying it's flu vaccine."

"I don't even know why we brought you with us, but so help me God you are one person I would love to watch die," Weston stated bluntly to Caleb.

"Weston, stop that!" shouted Erica.

"Ask him, Erica. Ask him how he knew the cell phones were

bugged or why he was so protective of his backpack."

"The cell phones weren't bugged, you idiot!" replied Caleb.

"But someone was listening to us, right?" asked Erica.

"Yes. You see, they send a signal…"

"They?" asked Erica.

"Yeah, THEY, Harris' people I assume or maybe one of Weston's friends. They send a signal to shut off the ringer and to set it to automatic answer after two rings. Then they call it and simply listen. It can all be done remotely."

Everyone stared silently for a few moments. "You think I'm lying?" asked Caleb finally

"I want to know about your backpack," Weston sniped.

"You have your secrets and I have my mine, old man," shot back Caleb. A car horn tapped three times. All three stood up and walked towards the door. "Oh, and by the way anything over 35 is old," shot Caleb as he dodged out the door into the dark hallway. Weston trudged behind glaring.

As they reached the exit door, Erica turned to the two men. "Stay here. Marcus is willing to help me, but I don't know how he feels about the two of you." She took a deep breath and then wiped the tears from her face.

Weston leaned over to kiss her forehead, but she moved away without speaking. Then she disappeared as the door closed behind her.

"Marcus! Thank you for coming!" she said as she raced towards him. "Thank you."

They embraced for a moment and then Marcus pulled back. "Listen, Erica, you're in trouble."

"Why do they think I killed Reilly?" she asked.

"Sweetie, you're sick. You need to come back to the hospital. You left heavily medicated saying strange things about Reilly. Let's get you some help and maybe we can figure this whole thing out," said

Marcus in a patronizing tone.

Erica turned cold inside. She stepped back. "How do you know that they want me back or that I left while medicated?"

Marcus looked flustered. "Look, you're sick and... and... and you look exhausted. Let me take you to the hospital. Where's Weston?" he asked as he looked around.

"Weston? Why do you think he's with me?"

Marcus shrugged. "I just assumed."

Meanwhile Caleb and Weston returned to the storage room. Together they peered out the darkened windows. "What's going on out there?" asked Caleb.

"I don't know...she's moving away from him. I don't know what's..." then Weston stopped.

"What's wrong?" asked Caleb.

"Look at his face," whispered Weston with an eerie tone.

Caleb pushed against the window and attempted to look closer. "What about it?"

Weston whirled around and raced to Caron's office. He returned momentarily with Carson's gun and motioned for Caleb to follow him as he ran down the hall to the back door.

Caleb chased after Weston. "Where the hell did you get that?" he asked breathlessly

"On the shelf next to the Caribbean blend," Weston hissed as he raced out the door. "Get away from her!" Weston screamed at Marcus.

Erica and Marcus both turned abruptly with complete surprise. "Weston!" shouted Erica.

"Erica, get away from him," shouted Weston.

"Wes, what's wrong?" asked Marcus in shock. "Come on, man. You know me. I've worked with Erica for two years now."

Weston held the gun steady as he approached Marcus. Waving the barrel of it towards Marcus' left cheek he asked, "What happened?"

"Huh?" stammered Marcus in shock.

"How did you get those scratches across your face?" shouted Weston.

"Fight...I got into a fight with an old girlfriend...her new stud jumped me...it was just a fight."

"I thought you were gay?" asked Erica stepping back slowly.

"You know, I bet Miki put up one hell of fight in the parking lot. Didn't she, Marcus?"

Just then Caleb sailed out the door holding up keys. "Carson's truck," he said breathlessly pointing to a Ford F-10 parked nearby.

Erica stalled for a moment as she looked at Marcus in horror. "Get into the truck," commanded Weston.

She opened her mouth to object, but then looked into Marcus' eyes. Quickly she dashed over to the truck. Caleb jumped in and started it. Walking backwards towards the truck, Weston never moved the end of the gun from its target—Marcus' heart. As he reached the truck, he raised the gun above Marcus' head and fired. "Send that message to your friends....oh, and next time I promise not to miss."

As the truck pulled away, Marcus narrowed his eyes and then shouted, "You'll never see Reilly alive again...the clock is ticking, Wes. You aren't the only one who can play scientist."

Weston turned to Caleb. "Go back!"

The truck whirled around spraying dirt everywhere. "Weston, he knows about Reilly!" sobbed Erica.

The truck came to a stop near Marcus. Weston opened the door with deliberate force and approached Marcus. Then he stared him in the eyes. "Say that again," he hissed.

"Beeman's spilled it," Marcus hissed as he leaned close to Weston. "Your dirty little secret about Erica's mother. *THEY* know. Beeman had to bail himself out, so he gave you to them."

Just as Weston reached out to grab Marcus by the collar, a shot blistered the air. A bullet ripped into Marcus' skull. Blood sprayed onto Weston's face and chest as reality lapsed into slow motion. Marcus fell to the ground.

Everyone turned to see Carson standing at the door lowering a riffle. He somberly looked at them all and then disappeared into the building. No one spoke.

Weston wiped blood spatter from his mouth and after several seconds said, "Let's go. If Reilly is with them, she may be infected with RCG35-98 and for a baby…" his voice trailed off momentarily. "She may only have a matter of days…maybe hours."

CHAPTER 29

Weston marched over to the driver's side. "I'm driving," he announced.

Caleb's lips parted with a ready objection, but one look at the intensity on Weston's blood spattered face told him that now was not the time. Silently Caleb moved to the center of the cab. Erica sat on the other side of him dazed.

For several miles they maneuvered the freeways in complete silence, each person drowning in private nightmares. Then, like the shattering of fine crystal during an elegant dinner party, the silence came crashing to the floor.

"I want out," Caleb announced.

Erica and Weston jerked from their thoughts and looked towards the middle of the cab. "What?" asked Erica.

"I want out. Just stop the car anywhere. I can't help you and I shouldn't be here anyway. I want out." Caleb never took his eyes off of the road ahead of them.

Then, as if complying with Caleb's request, Weston spun the steering wheel towards the exit they had just moved past. "Watch out!" yelled Erica as they ran a red Mazda off of the road.

Weston's eyes fixated on the road ahead as he somberly stated, "Our exit."

"Pull over anywhere, man," said Caleb as he caught his breath and turned to stare at Weston.

"No, junior. You're coming with us now. That's what you wanted wasn't it?" said Weston in the same eerie monotone with which he had announced the exit.

Caleb pulled his backpack onto his lap. Then the sound of a gun cocking rang through the cab. Erica jerked around to see Weston holding a gun to Caleb's head. "I'm ready to pull this trigger...and I can do it long before you can ever get that pistol out of your little purse there. So with that in mind, Junior, give the bag to Erica very slowly." For a moment no one moved. Then Weston began to wave the gun from side to side. "How about I count to three and then shoot?" he asked.

Caleb handed the bag to Erica. By now the truck was weaving among trees along a path that could barely be considered a road.

"Erica, throw the bag out the window," he said in a barely audible voice.

"What?" she asked.

Hitting the button to lower the glass on the passenger side, Weston repeated his statement loudly. "Throw the God damn bag out the window."

Startled she heaved the sack out and watched in the rear view mirror as it thudded to the ground under a pine tree.

Weston continued to hold the gun level at Caleb's head. He pulled the truck to a stop. "They have my life in their hands and I have yours in mine," he announced softly. Rage seethed from his eyes. "Not the same I suppose, but you're all I have to work with, so you'll do. Now you contact your people and you get Reilly back."

Caleb leaned back as he stared into Weston's eyes. "I don't know what you mean, man. My people are just trying to find out what you want. That's it. No one I know has taken your kid."

"You want to play games?" Weston hissed. With angry, deliberate motion he struck the button to turn on the radio. Then he hit buttons until finally coming to stop at a manic voice:

"The death toll for the state of Georgia is currently at 100 known cases this week and authorities say it may be rising. You are advised to stay in your homes and to report to a hospital immediately if you are ill," the voice from the radio announced.

"You're the one who unleashed this new virus!" gasped Caleb.

"Were there 100 deaths this week?" asked Weston. "Maybe. Maybe not."

"I don't get what you're saying," said Caleb.

"Wes, I don't know where you're going with this either," added

Erica.

"There's political capital in fear. Look I came up with RCG35-98 as part of my work. Someone in my lab leaked to the higher ups and they saw a chance for a higher profit margin. There's a market for…for new weapons let's say. "

"My grandmother," gasped Erica. "At the home…there was stuff happening."

"Weston knows that, don't you, buddy?" Caleb said snidely.

Erica looked at Weston puzzled.

"That's not some vague faceless spy ring. It's your own Weston Anderson running that show!" Caleb added.

"Wes?" asked Erica softly.

"Things got out of control," Weston said as he turned and took Erica's hands. "RCG35-98 was accidentally released in your grandmother's nursing home. I was just there to try to regain control. Beeman and I…"

"You infected my grandmother?" Erica slowly pulled away her hands and stared in horror.

"No. A carrier…someone got exposed in my lab and went there," he said in an apologetic tone. "It was not intentional. I swear, Erica! I would never hurt anyone…I would never hurt your grandmother. It happened and then there were these agents with Homeland Security who came in and…and…and," Weston stuttered to silence. He looked at Erica's expression and turned away.

"My grandmother?"

"She's there," said Weston.

"Where?" asked Erica.

"At that nursing home…they don't want to lose her if she's part of their study and I'm guessing that she is." Weston flipped on the safety lock and thrust the gun into his belt. "If we get her, we can prove what they're doing. We'll have leverage….to get Reilly." Then with deliberate motions he started the truck and whipped the wheel around spinning the vehicle. They headed back for the freeway.

"Go left right up here," said Erica. "What are we going to do?"

"We can't just run in and grabbed an old lady," said Caleb.

"WE aren't. YOU are," said Weston.

Erica sneezed and pulled a blanket from the floor up around her.
"You okay?" asked Caleb.

"I'm just a little cold," she replied.

"You don't have a fever do you?" asked Weston.

"No, no. I'm just cold," she sniffed. Then she sneezed again.

"Go get Erica's grandmother out of that place and I won't place
a call to Senator Harris," Weston continued.

"What are you talking about?" asked Caleb.

"I'm talking about your little backpack there...the people
following us picked it up I'm sure. Now you're in as much trouble as we
are because you've gone rogue...or at least they think you have," he said
with a wry smile. "I took the liberty of including a few items..."

CHAPTER 30

Caleb stared at Weston completely dumbfounded.

"What was in the backpack?" asked Erica breaking the tense silence.

Caleb and Weston exchanged glances.

"I'll go and get your grandmother out of there…" said Caleb somberly.

"And you'll get some nursing notes. There's bound to be something at the nurses' station that can help us figure this out," added Weston.

"Turn right at the next light," Erica instructed.

"And then maybe we'll have a little chat about your backpack and about what Senator Harris really has in mind for RCG35-98."

"Man, I have no idea what you're talking bout. Anyway, we can't just go in the front door," Caleb stated as he motioned for Weston to drive past it.

"Why not? They don't know you…do they?" asked Weston as he gave Caleb a quizzical look.

"They might," Caleb responded. "Go around left and drive into the neighborhood that backs up to it."

Weston followed Caleb's directions and then pulled into a driveway. "Looks like no one's home here…we'll sit tight for a few minutes. Then we'll pull around front and meet you and Pearl."

"How the hell am I supposed to make a getaway with an old lady who can't move faster than a turtle?"

"Well, seeing as how you were able to find her at the hospital and get her into a vehicle there, I think you'll once again amaze and astound us all," said Weston.

"What is he talking about?" asked Erica.

"Later," Caleb said. "I'll explain it all later."

"Oh, and, Junior, you may need this," Weston said as he tossed a security name tag towards him.

Erica grabbed it in mid-air. "What is this?"

"It was in his backpack. I found it when we were back there at that coffee shop. Seems our little friend here has lots of connections."

"For a man who created and exposed the whole world to a deadly virus, you're pretty impressive yourself," snarled Caleb as he got out of the truck.

"Are you sure he's coming back?" asked Erica as she watched Caleb walk away.

"Positive," said Weston as he rubbed his eyes. "God I need some sleep."

"We are going to get Reilly back, right?" she asked somberly.

"Yes, we are," he sighed.

For a moment they stared into each other's eyes. Erica reached out her hands and held his. He raised her hands to his lips and kissed them softly.

"Where are we going after this?" she asked. "How do we get Reilly back?"

"Cabin," he replied.

"Why? Reilly isn't there!"

"We'll get her back…but the stakes are bigger," he whispered as he turned his head. "We'll get her back."

They waited through 20 long, painful moments of silence. Finally, Weston took a deep breath. "Let's go."

He pulled the truck out of the driveway and back down the tree lined street. Then he rounded the corner and began to approach the nursing home.

"I don't see them," said Erica.

Silently Weston drove past and then circled back. Still nothing. They repeated this cycle several times. "Wes, we can't do this all day!" said Erica. Her voice was laced with panic.

"Okay, okay, okay," Weston whispered to himself as he thought.

"Wait! There's Grandma!" shouted Erica. "But where's Caleb?" Just then Pearl walked back into the nursing home. "Park! Something's gone wrong."

Weston drove the truck back to the street behind the building and ran back. "Let's go in the side door here," he said motioning to an emergency exit propped open.

Awkwardly Erica tripped into the building. "Shhh!" hissed Weston as he turned to her. "Where is Pearl's room?"

Erica silently pointed. Then she smelled the same vomit and sweat from the hospital. The smell became more overpowering as they walked.

"Just act like you're here to visit," instructed Weston. Then he grabbed flowers from a vase on a nearby window sill and began walking with impeccable posture.

Erica shook her head. "You don't exactly look like a typical visitor...and besides that...where the hell are the visitors? Or anyone for that matter?"

They both stopped and surveyed the hall way. Other than the stench of illness they were greeted with emptiness. Nothing moved and silence permeated the grey dimly lit corridor.

Weston motioned towards the double doors at the end of the hallway. Silently they moved through along the surreal path that seemed to narrow into a tunnel for Erica as she followed Weston. Then they passed an open door. Weston stopped abruptly and Erica, still looking from side to side, bumped into him.

"What?" she asked. Then she followed his gaze. There is the room were bodies...at least four that she spotted instantly. Each body had a wrist band the same color as the label on her grandmother's chart.

Weston moved into the room like a man in a trance. He was drawn to the bodies…grandparents…great-grandparents…someone's family members. He reached out for a limp hand hanging down the side of the bed. "RCG35-98—Group 2" the tag on his arm read. No names were listed.

"Wes!" whispered Erica from the doorway. She was waving a face mask and rubber gloves.

Weston turned back to the cold, wrinkled hand he held.

"Wes, you don't want to get contaminated!" she said straining her voice to be heard by Wes while not moving far above a whisper.

"Long ago," he replied vacantly with an overwhelming sadness. "I was contaminated long ago."

Then Erica looked down. The room was all white, sterile, empty aside from the beds and the bodies piled on them, but yet there sticking out from the closet next to her was something red. She slid her hand into the rubber glove she had offered Weston and she bent over to pick it up. It was a heart…a red construction paper heart with the words "We love you, Reilly & Erica." Erica felt like puking as she stepped into the hallway to look at the room number.

Weston exited the room and looked at Erica. She stood completely frozen and then finally turned to him with tears in her eyes and pointed back to the room. "I've got to go in there. I've got to look," she pleaded.

"Pearl's not in there," Weston said. "I'm positive." Then they heard sounds. "Someone's coming," stated Weston. "Let's go."

They heard the steps from a nearby stairwell growing louder as they frantically raced down the hallway and towards the double doors. Their heartbeats echoed in their ears like gunfire with each breathless lunge the pair made as they rushed through the first set of double doors and then 100 feet further to a second set. They burst out into the south wing of the building and heard voices coming from down the hall. Constantly looking over his shoulders, Weston motioned for Erica to keep up as he raced to the lit doorway. As he entered, Weston bent over to catch his breath. Seconds later Erica arrived. They both stood for a moment catching their breaths before continuing. As they moved into the room, a tiny woman with pure white hair met them with a smile.

"Are you my granddaughter?" she sang.

"No, I'm sorry. I'm not," Erica said sympathetically. "My name is Erica Schmidt. I'm looking for Pearl. Pearl Schmidt," said Erica.

"Are you my grandson?" she asked of Weston.

Weston gently touched her arm. "No, ma'am," then he moved her very carefully aside so they could continue walking. "I'm so sorry," he whispered. They headed towards a table of elderly woman playing cards. "Poker night? Hey, that's great. Has anyone seen Pearl Schmidt?"

"What happened to your face, honey?" asked one woman at the table.

"Oh screw him, what's your bid, Emma?" asked a rotund woman at the far side of the table.

Weston reached into his pockets and then carefully placed a $100 bill on the table as Erica walked to the far side of the room to look down another hallway. "Pearl Schmidt. Where is she?" he asked in a soft, but commanding tone.

"Oh, my!" fluttered the voices surrounding the table...all except the large woman who reached out and grabbed the bill. "In her room," she growled. Then stuffing the money down her shirt, she turned back to Emma. "What's yer bid?"

Weston looked up and spotted Erica on the other side of the room. He motioned to her. The woman who had met them at the door came up again. "Pearl's yellow, I am blue do dah do dah," she sang.

"Okay, thanks," said Erica gently. Then she turned and followed Weston.

"Did you notice the colored sheets of construction paper?" he asked pointing to a blue sheet taped up near them.

"Yeah, I've never seen them here before," she said.

"I'll bet..." Weston began. "That the colors coincide with the wrist bands the patients are wearing. We need to find yellow..."

As Weston nervously looked around, Erica quietly pulled up her sleeve to look at her own yellow band. Her hands began to tremble as she reached out to Weston to show it to him, but then suddenly a woman in a nursing uniform appeared. Erica pulled back her arm and covered the band.

"Excuse me? Excuse me? We aren't allowing visitors today," she snapped at them.

Weston's eyes darted to her badge. "Ms. Williams, I'm Pearl Schmidt's physician and I need to see her right now."

"I'm…I'm new here. Are you a part of the project?" she asked slowly with caution.

"Yes, yes, I am," he replied.

"Then I need to see your security badge," she replied.

"Look I'm Pearl's granddaughter. I want to see her right now!" Erica commanded.

The woman suddenly looked flustered. Her voice changed dramatically and her eyes darted past Erica. "Oh, I didn't realize you were family," she said nervously. "The project is simply an educational study…we received a grant. But if you're family, we certainly can't stop you from seeing your grandmother…unless she's ill."

"Ill?" shot back Erica.

"Is there a problem here at this facility?" asked Weston stepping in front of Erica.

"Just the flu…we're trying to keep it contained," she responded matter-of-factly.

"Any deaths so far this year?" asked Weston.

"Don't I know you," asked the woman puzzled. "And you," she added pointing at Erica.

"We come here often. You probably know us from…"

"Where did you say Pearl is?" Weston interjected.

"Wait here a moment and I'll check," she responded suspiciously as she turned and pulled out her cell phone.

Erica looked around nervously. "We've got to go."

"Do whatever you have to and get out of here. Meet me in the back employee parking lot," stated Weston as he took off down the hall.

Before Erica could speak, Weston was gone. Shaking her head she turned in the opposite direction of the woman who had just been speaking with them and began to run. She came across the room where the women were playing cards. Erica darted in and raced over to the woman who had taken Weston's money since she appeared the most vocal and coherent person in the room.

"I need a quick way out of here," she said breathlessly.

"Don't we all, honey," said the woman without looking up from her cards.

"Please, I need help," Erica said watching the door as she spoke. "Look, we gave you $100. The least you could do is help."

The frail woman to the right of her looked up at the bulletin board in the corner. Erica followed her gaze. Rushing over to the corner, Erica moved aside a large bulletin board. "Ah ha! The emergency exit," she whispered.

"Good job, Gertie," replied the large woman sarcastically still not looking up from her game hand. "Might have been worth another $100."

Erica began to push on the door when the woman who had met them at the door earlier came up. Still singing softly to herself, she titled her head and looked at Erica.

"Oh, honey, don't open that door. It makes lots of noise and you'll get into big trouble," sang the shaky voice.

With all of her might, Erica shoved the door wide open and ran out into the street and then into the neighborhood behind the facility as the alarm blared. As she approached the van, she saw a police car parked nearby with its lights on, so she quickly returned to the nursing home and raced around to the back. There she spotted a rusty white van with the words, "Cherry Hill Nursing Facility—a true home for your loved ones."

Erica rolled her eyes as she read the slogan. As she raced over to the van she constantly looked around. *Why isn't anyone coming out? The emergency alarm is blasting, but no one is leaving?* Her plan for escaping during a chaotic scene appeared to have succeeded, but not due in any measure to chaos because there was none. She breathlessly reached for the van's front door handle, her thoughts focused on the unlocked door to complete her escape.

The door came open the instant she pushed the button. Jumping in frantically, she felt around under the seat for the keys. Nothing. Then she lowered the visor and keys flung down onto her face.

Which key? Which Key? Which key? She fumbled with the keys trying one then another. Finally, she thrust one in and it fit. Then she looked up to see Weston and Pearl standing at the back door. As she put the van into gear, suddenly she began to have a coughing fit. Hacking and wheezing she couldn't stop.

Weston and Pearl frantically motioned to Erica. Weston looked behind him at the door. Jerking it open he pushed the locked button and slammed it shut. Then he grabbed Pearl's arm. "That's only going to buy us a few seconds," he said motioning to the door.

Pearl shuffled along as Weston attempted to gently rush her. The 200 feet to the van seemed like miles. "Come on, Pearl!" he whispered frantically as he looked up at Erica still hacking.

Finally, he lunged ahead of Pearl and helped Erica into the backseat. Throwing the van into gear he met Pearl not far from where he had left her.

Erica flung open the side door and grabbed Pearl. In her panic she gave one strong jerk and flung the elderly woman into a heap in the van floor. Just then Caleb appeared. Grabbing the front passenger door, he opened it and tumbled into the seat. The job completed, Erica closed the side door and began shouting, "Go! Go! Go!"

As the van took off, Erica saw several people emerge from the back of the building. Two men chased the van for a few feet yelling.

"Grandma, I am so sorry," said Erica as she reached out for the elderly woman. "I'm so sorry, but I had to get you in."

Pearl was shaking as she looked up at Erica. "Am I dying too?"

she asked.

"No. What are you talking about?" Erica asked. "You're safe now…here with us."

"Where's Ann? Where's my Ann? I saw that man…he hurt Ann. I saw it."

"Who? What man, Grandma?"

"That man who said he was your friend," she whispered.

CHAPTER 31

"We don't have time for this!" Weston shouted. "Everybody buckle up."

"Wait! Weston, what is she saying?" asked Erica as she grabbed Weston's arm.

"Nothing! She's a crazy old woman who is obviously ill and delusional." Weston focused on the road ahead of him.

"Look at me God damn it!" she pleaded.

"I'm driving," he replied. "Just get in back with your grandmother. Check on her. She's probably been exposed..."

"Exposed?" repeated Erica as she jumped into the van and slammed the door shut. Silently she stared at Weston, but he never flinched. Erica bit her lip as tears rolled down her cheek. Weston, however, focused intently on the road taking deep breaths every few seconds. "Stop crying. Please just stop crying," his voice shook.

"Where's Reilly?"

Weston swallowed hard and ran a hand over his face trying to wipe away any emotion. "If she's with the people who are trying to get me to hand over my final notes so they can manufacture the virus themselves, she's going to be okay," he said. "My notes are hidden... we need to get them and make a deal. They'll bring her to us." His face tightened as Erica leaned into the front seat. Briefly he looked at Erica out of the corner of his eye.

"Great plan, Einstein," mumbled Caleb who sat in the front leaning against the passenger door.

"Why are you saying that?" asked Erica.

"What makes you think they don't already have the virus figured out? If you could create couldn't someone else? Maybe someone in your own lab?" Caleb said somberly.

Weston's fingers visibly tightened around the steering wheel. "Wow! Aren't you smart? Yes, someone else could, but it took me four years and they want to offer it as a weapon possibility now. Oh, and I have evidence of all of this…going all the way to the man who's the Vice President's chief of staff."

Weston's words hung in the air as everyone stared at the road ahead of them. The silence seemed to squeeze Erica's lungs making every breath a labor.

Weston looked at her in the rear view mirror. He could see her body shaking as sweat rolled down her forehead. "Are you sick?" he asked with a note of tenderness that made both Erica and Caleb look at him.

"I just want Reilly," she whispered.

"That wasn't my question," Weston persisted.

Erica turned to look at him as she folded her arms to keep warm. "I'm fine."

"That a cell phone?" he asked as he pointed towards the passenger door.

Reaching into the pocket of the door Caleb pulled out a cell phone. "Yeah, looks like it."

Without a word Weston grabbed the phone from Caleb's hands and dialed. "Peter? I've got something you want. You've got something I want. Let's make a deal."

"Wes, you've made a mistake. You've made a big big mistake," growled the voice from phone. "I know about the vaccine, or should I say the lack of one."

"What are you talking about?" asked Weston confused.

"Beeman told us everything.

"Look I'm talking about RCG35-98. The virus. I know what the company's planning to do with it."

"And I'm talking about saline solution being sold as vaccine and a dead woman at the bottom of the stairs."

Weston dropped the phone. With one quick jerk he swerved to

the side of the road and slammed on the breaks.

Erica was thrown up against the front seat. "Wes? Wes, what's wrong?"

Weston put his head down on the steering wheel.

Caleb and Erica exchanged terrified looks. "Dude, you're completely white. You sick? Hey, you're shaking. Dude, what's wrong?"

Weston sat unmoved for almost a minute. Then he unbuckled his seatbelt and in morbid silence reached for the phone that lay at his feet. Finally he spoke into it again. "I don't know what you're talking about," he said slowly annunciating each word.

"We've taken over your little experiment at the nursing home also," hissed the voice. "You've unleashed bioterrorism in your own country."

"What do you want from me?" Weston snapped back.

"We need someone to take center stage for awhile and you're just dancing your way into the limelight, pal."

Then the phone went dead.

"Who was that?" Erica demanded. "Where's Reilly? Where is she, Weston?" Her hands twitched nervously as she stared at him. Then with an eerie coolness to her voice she asked, "Did you kill Miki?"

"Oh, God! Yeah, that's it, Erica. I killed Miki. Didn't I, Grandma?" he said looking back at Pearl.

"No," Pearl whispered meekly. "No, you didn't."

Erica rolled her eyes. "She thinks the year is 1937, and you want me to take her word?"

"Let me tell you a little about the United States bioterrorism program...it's been going on for years...for decade," hissed Weston. When Miki was being killed by one of *your* little friends, I was in a rather hostile meeting with a group of scientists about RCG35-98 and what they could do to ...to salvage the mess," Weston put his forehead on the steering wheel. "I put my career on the line, but I had to call someone who could help. People are going to die because of my mess. Someone needed to help. I was at a bar getting drunk when they picked me up for the meeting and then I came back to said bar to finish the job. That's where you found me. I screwed up, Erica. I screwed up bad."

For several moments Erica sat and stared into the eyes of the man she once hoped to marry. Erica blew her nose on a tissue and then turned away from him. Then with a stoic tone, she announced, "We have to go to my office. Marcus was on some special task force. I never understood what he was doing, but one afternoon I grabbed one of his files by mistake. There were notes that I think you need to see. Notes that may lead us to Reilly."

"I don't think you have anything that I don't..."

"Shut up, Weston," Erica snapped. "I may possibly have a piece of this deranged puzzle."

Silently Weston made a sharp right turn from the left lane to a chorus of honking.

"I don't feel well," replied Pearl from the back seat.

"Pearl, the man who took Reilly, did he say why?" asked Weston.

"He said she was sick and he was taking her...taking her....to be...to be *observed*," Pearl began to cry and rock back and forth in her seat.

"What? What's wrong?" Erica asked urgently.

"I saw her. I saw her body being carried away, just like Irving that last time. His tiny rag doll body covered in sweat, shaking. His little fingers curled in my hand. Then the nurse and doctor removing him...taking him away limp...eyes closed. No. No. No," she whispered frantically. Then silence.

"Irving?" asked Weston.

"Her baby. He died during a flu epidemic one winter," Erica said tenderly as she patted Pearl's back softly.

"Pearl? Are you okay?" asked Weston compassionately.

"Reilly...she had a red band on her arm...the yellow band people live," said Pearl in a dream-like state. "Or maybe the red band people live...no I think they all die."

"Thank you, Pearl," said Weston quietly avoiding Erica's stare. "We'll remember that." Then he turned back to driving for several minutes before daring to steal a glance at Erica. "It is going to be okay."

Weston turned back to the steering wheel and started up the car. They drove for several minutes listening to Pearl hum. Finally Weston broke the silence. "We're almost there. What's your plan?"

"Stop a block away and let me go alone. I'll meet you back," she replied.

"Hold it!" Caleb blurted. "Let me out too. I have some business."

Weston motioned towards a bright blue sheet of paper in the door pocket where the phone had been. At the top it stated "EMERGENCY INFO."

"Does it say anything about the cell phone?" Weston asked.

Erica studied the case. "Yes...or at least it lists the 'van phone.' So I guess it's to this phone."

"Write it down both of you and call me on it if you get into any trouble," he said.

Erica took a piece of paper out of the glove box and scribbled out the number twice. Tearing the paper she handed one to Caleb. Then she stuck the other into her pants pocket.

Silently he got out of the van.

Weston looked at Erica. "Are you ready?" he asked.

"Yeah," Erica replied as she unbuckled. "But wait," she said as she threw Weston a puzzled look. "I don't understand something...you created a deadly virus mutation and you let it out?"

"No, Erica," Weston said somberly with his voice choking. "Your mother did."

CHAPTER 32

Caleb ran for several blocks, then spotting a cab he ran up to it and got in. "Take me to 3351 Cadillac," said Caleb as he got into the cab. Then he tapped on the back of the sticky, vinyl seat. "And hurry, man."

"Going to see the Senator?" asked the cabbie.

"Yeah. How'd you know?" asked Caleb. "Don't tell me...you're the guru of Atlanta."

"Naw, I just believe in being aware of my government," said the driver as he stroked his grayish black beard. "Important to know your elected officials and stay up with things, don't you think?"

"Oh, yeah," said Caleb as he leaned back and closed his eyes. He began to rub his wedding ring finger as he relaxed for the first time in days. *Everything on me hurts,* he thought to himself.

The cab driver's voice droned in the back ground, but Caleb's eyes didn't open until he felt the car come to a stop. "Hey, buddy. Hey! You awake? We're here," shouted the driver.

Caleb began scrounging through his pockets for money. The cabbie looked around pretending not to notice. "You got an appointment? Cause I hear Harris don't see nobody without one," he said as he turned on the wiper blades to clear the rain smearing down the front window.

"He'll see me," Caleb said as he examined the wads of paper and fuzz that came from his pockets. "Yo, here, man," he said finally as he pulled out a few bills.

Before the man could count the money, Caleb dashed into the small, brick building.

As he entered the brightly lit room, Caleb couldn't help but grimace at the Martha Stewart catalogues on the coffee table. The entire room from the lacey curtains to the frilly couch covers, seemed like one big belch from those books.

"Uh, may I help you?" asked the woman behind the desk.

143

Touching her silver stack of hair cemented perfectly in place by what Caleb could only guess to be a dozen cans of hair spray, she cleared her throat and then tilted her glasses to look over them.

"I need to see the Senator," he announced as he headed towards a door marked "Private."

"Do you have an appointment?" barked the woman as she stood to her feet and rounded her desk.

"No, Martha, I do not," he quipped pushing her aside.

"My name is not Martha and you are not to enter that room without permission," she commanded stepping in front of him.

Caleb's first impulse was to simply shove the woman, but he paused. "Look, my beef isn't with you," he said grabbing her elbow firmly. "I just need to see the Senator."

"And just *who* are you?" she snapped pulling away her arm.

"Tell him I have the 411 on RCG35-98."

"I will tell him no such thing. I will, however, check the appointment book, and before calling security I will once again ask, young man, *who are you?*"

As she stepped towards her appointment book, Caleb lunged past her. He grabbed the door knob as the woman gasped and raced around her desk. "Get away from that door this instant!"

Caleb pulled on the door knob, but it wouldn't budge. He stepped back, preparing to ram it with his shoulder and then saw the brass handle wiggle slightly. Then it turned. A tall, athletic man with graying hair stood motionless in the doorway. He glared at Caleb for a moment and then turned to his secretary. "Give Mr. Phillips, a 15 minute head start and then call the police. I believe they're interested in speaking with him," he said slowly with each word carefully meticulously annunciated.

Caleb returned Harris' glare and stepped up inches away from the elder man's face. "We're going to talk," said Caleb.

As if looking completely through his visitor, Harris continued to speak with his secretary. "Commence the 15 minutes now." Then he turned back into the dark hallway from which he had come, walking confidently.

Caleb followed him. "We need to talk," he repeated firmly.

"Spend your 15 minutes however you like, Caleb," he sneered. Then he veered left and entered an elegant office with a large, mahogany desk. He walked briskly around it and took his seat in the large, leather chair.

Caleb entered the office and pulled the door shut behind him. "What's going on?"

"Excuse me?" asked Harris. He rose slightly leaned on his fists firmly planted on his desk. "Perhaps you could tell me? I paid you to follow Weston Anderson, not to take his kid or kill some woman walking a granny through a parking lot! Our connections are severed, my friend. I can't be associated with you. I told your father you were a monster. If he hadn't been my college roommate I would have let you hang for what you did to your poor wife."

Caleb swung at Harris who intercepted the younger man's fist with his own large hand. He then tightened his grip on the fist, sending Caleb to his knees. "Don't mess with a professional body builder…even if he is now an over the hill senator." Then he released the fist.

Caleb rubbed his hand. "You mean former body builder…you asshole. And I don't know what you mean. I didn't kill anyone and I haven't had any contact with that kid. I've been talking to your retarded punk of a son, Chip, all through this little project…maybe he's got the kid. Maybe, just maybe it's Chip who only has 15 minutes," hissed Caleb as he grabbed the phone from Harris' desk.

"You leave Chip out of this. I told him from the beginning that dealing with you was a waste. You're a waste…your old man is a waste…just a bunch of losers."

Caleb angrily grabbed the door knob and flung open the door. Then he turned and took a long look at Harris who stared down at the papers on his desk pretending to focus intently. Then suddenly Caleb turned back towards the senator. With one viciously jerk, Caleb slammed the door closed and then flung himself into a chair. Putting his feet up on Harris' desk, Caleb folded his arms and looked at the senator.

"It's your 15 minutes," reminded Harris still not looking up.

"You're right. It is," said Caleb. Then he began to hum and look around. He paused momentarily. "I want to be right here so that the police only have to go to one location to grab us both," he said. Then he returned to humming.

Harris shoved Caleb's feet off of his desk. "Get out of here," he hissed.

"After you tell me what's really going on here," insisted Caleb. "You paid me to follow this guy...I only agreed because...because..."

"Because your father begged me to clean up that little mess with Sandra, and you owed me one...I think we all know that part of the story well."

"Because I'm an investigator and you needed someone who knew what he was doing and that you could control. Now tell me what I was really doing or so help me, you'll go down with me. After all, you're in this as deep as me."

"I wash my hands of all of this. I have a career to think about. You get out of my office you little piece of vomit and get this mess cleaned up. If you killed anyone, I'll hang you myself," he shouted. Then regaining his composure, Harris picked up the phone. "You're being watched...you and your little band of hooligans. There are people watching Anderson...people I don't even know."

Just then Caleb heard Mozart's Waltz. He looked around and there in the corner he spotted his backpack, the backpack that Weston had flung by the side of the road. Harris waved the telephone in his hand. "Good. Your cell phone still works. Now take your backpack and get the hell out of here."

Realizing that he wasn't going to get any more information, Caleb picked up his backpack, slung it over his shoulder and walked out of the office down the narrow dimly lit hallway. As he entered the reception area, he waved at the woman behind the desk. "Keep it cool, Martha," he grumbled and then walked out into the cold.

As he pulled his jacket up around his face, the Waltz began to play again. "Give it up, Asshole," he said. But as the tune continued he stopped at the building next door to Harris' office. Leaning against the wall of a two-story accounting building, he pulled the cell phone out. He didn't recognize the number. "Hello?" he asked.

"Is this Caleb?" came the voice.

"Yeah, who wants to know?" he replied.

"This is Carson...the coffee shop, remember?"

"Yeah, Carson. I rarely forget someone who puts a bullet into another man's chest right in front of me," snapped Caleb. "How'd you get this number?"

"The Senator...I called his office...said you just left and gave me this num...who cares? Listen. When they came to get the body..."

"What, Carson? What?" he asked impatiently

"They left something. A pile of baby blankets."

CHAPTER 33

Spotting a bike just inside the doorway of the accounting building, Caleb looked around hastily looked around, then opened the door and grabbed it. Peddling as quickly as he could, Caleb headed for the Starbucks where Carson worked. He could hear every pebble, every tiny piece of asphalt as his tires rolled into the parking lot. Then he saw the pile lying in the middle of the rocks and mud covered with a pink blanket that clung to the shape beneath it. The heavy rain began to soak the blanket. There was no movement underneath it.

Reilly! Caleb's heart beat faster. *Oh, God! Reilly!* Everything inside of him seemed to freeze as he approached the shape. Shaking his head in disgust at Carson's failure to take action himself, Caleb dropped the bike a few feet from the pile and raced over to it.

Just then Carson emerged. "Hey! Over here!" shouted Carson from the doorway.

Caleb looked up startled.

"She's in here!" he yelled.

"Then what the hell is this?" asked Caleb.

"Shit," shouted back Carson.

Caleb picked up the damp blanket. There was a large diaper bag and a few toys. Kicking them angrily, he pulled his coat up over his head to shelter from the rain and dashed to the building.

"Where's the kid?" responded Caleb as he pushed past Carson.

"In my office…"

Caleb rushed past him and into the office where the crying baby lay on the desk shaking. "Don't you have any blankets?" he snapped. Then he quickly pulled off his jacket and threw it over her.

Carson wheezed for breath as he lumbered into the room. "Yeah, kid. I sell coffee and blankets."

Caleb rolled his eyes. "Reilly? Kiddo, can you hear me?"

Reilly's crying now turned to screams.

"We've got to get you to the doctor," said Caleb as he scooped her up into his arms.

"Call a doctor? Are you kidding me? Have you missed the whole past 24 hours or what? You idiot!" huffed Carson. "Do you honestly not see what's going on around you?"

Holding Reilly tightly, Caleb turned with vengeance. "Why don't you just tell me? Huh? Let's just get it all out on the table...what the hell is going on?"

Carson narrowed his eyes and stared at Caleb. "I'm gonna get this kid some juice. You call her mom...her dad...he'll know what to do. She needs medical care."

Caleb sat down and rocked Reilly for a moment. He wiped the rain from her forehead and kissed it softly. "Hang on, baby..." for a moment his mind wandered to rainy night so long ago, a night when he spotted a tiny, blue baby bootie sitting in the middle of his dining room table.

"Either you've really shrunk the laundry or my feet have grown today," he joked as he turned towards his wife.

"No, silly. It's for the baby," whispered his wife.

He whirled around in surprise. "Baby?"

He remembered the smell of jasmine in the air, the flickering candles his wife had lit, the gentle summer breeze fluttering in off of Lake Michigan and the sound of the soft spring rain.

"Hey," barked Carson as he returned carrying the juice. "You make the call?"

Caleb jolted back to the moment. His gaze focused on Reilly's small face. Then he reached into his backpack on the floor near his feet. Trying to carefully balance Reilly, he fumbled through it until he found the phone. He paused.

"What now?" snapped Carson.

"She doesn't have a cell phone," Caleb replied somberly.

"Call the girl's office," shot back Carson.

"What?"

"Call Erica's office. Maybe she's checked in there...maybe the good doctor's headed there to get help."

Reilly began to cry. Caleb offered her juice, but as he tried to pour it into her mouth most of it ran down her chin. Caleb looked up at Carson.

"She's only going to get worse," said Carson. Then he nodded towards the red bracelet on her wrist.

Taking a deep breath, Caleb dialed 411. "Zelticor Corporation, please," he mumbled. He waited a moment and stared at the small child he held. So tiny...so beautiful. "Oh, uh, yes, I'd like to speak with Erica Schmidt." Surprised, he looked up at Carson and said, "They're connecting me." He waited another moment and then sighed. "Answering machine," he said to Carson.

"Leave a message...it's all we got," replied Carson.

"Erica? This is Caleb...look I have Reilly. She's safe, but I need to hear from you right away. Look I don't know what's going on...but I have her and she's safe. We need to get her help. She's sick...very sick. Maybe she's still in danger. Call me at 555-3301." Then he hung up. Still rocking Reilly, he looked up at Carson. "Now! Now I want the truth!" he demanded.

Carson took a deep breath and sat down. "I can only give you *my* truth. You'll have to ask the skirt or the professor for their versions."

Caleb stared at Carson intently without blinking. "Then start with your version."

Taking out a cigarette he started to light it when he looked at Caleb whose stern expression warned him otherwise. He sighed, put down the cigarette and then said slowly, "Do you believe that bioterrorism is real?"

"Yes. I try not to think about it, but I know there are countries engaged in it."

"The U.S. I'm talking about OUR country using bioterrorism to get what it wants."

"Are you just going to give me your delusional CIA bullshit or are you going to tell me why I've been running for the past day now with psycho scientist?"

"I had a son," Carson said choking up. He wiped his eyes for a moment with his apron.

"I'm sorry, man. Really. We all have our own pain, but I need to know…"

"Shut the hell up, you little puke," Carson snapped. "I'm getting to it. My son went into the hospital to get ear tubes put in…he died from pneumonia. Or at least I think that's what the doctors tried to say. He wasn't sick when he went in…he died because of me."

"Because of you?" asked Caleb skeptically.

"I was in the CIA, about to blow the whistle on some of my colleagues, and Toby died. I'd been warned…I'd been warned. I'd been warned. Oh, God."

Caleb stood up and put Reilly up on his shoulder. "Hey, crazy, man. You got some children's Tylenol or anything?" he asked.

"Did you hear what I said? The government was behind it all," snapped Carson.

"Behind what?" asked Caleb softly trying not to wake Reilly who now seemed to be settling down to sleep on his shoulder.

"I don't like your tone," snapped Carson.

"My tone? I asked for the truth…I'll take whatever tone I want," Caleb snapped back.

"There are experiments going on all the time…they use everyday people without their permission. No one is exempt. They slipped my kid into it all just like they did this kid."

"So you think she should die because yours did? I'm taking her to the doctor right now," he snapped. "Even if what you're saying makes any sense whatsoever, that doesn't mean this kid don't need help and sitting here in the back room of a Starbucks is not helping her."

He reached the door just as the phone rang. At the same moment police sirens reached their ears.

CHAPTER 34

Erica whirled around angrily and narrowed her eyes as she glared at Weston. "What?" she snapped. "How dare you blame your failure to keep security in your lab on my dead mother! Real good, Wes! A new low even for you!"

Weston sat staring forward at the steering wheel.

"Say something!" Erica insisted.

"I missed the ultra sound appointment," Weston said softly still not facing Erica.

"I know that! I definitely know that!"

"That morning you and I had the fight about the wedding," Weston took a deep breath, "your mother came into my lab screaming at me. Waving the ultra sound picture. She said I was just like your father and that I wasn't a good father."

Erica looked at him in surprise. "My mother came to your lab?"

Weston nodded and then rubbed his eyes with his hands. "I didn't mean to miss the appointment, but I was knee deep in...I had just realized RCG35-98...what it was...that it was something..."

"The doctor thought there was something wrong with our baby and you made me face that alone," said Erica sadly.

"Yes. Okay, I'm a jerk."

"And my mother?"

"She came racing into the lab screaming." Weston finally turned to look at Erica. "Yes, I know. I was supposed to have the doors locked, but they weren't. She burst in and knocked over several test tubes. Then she raced out almost as quickly as she entered." He stopped to take a deep breath. "The tubes..."

"...contained RCG35-98," whispered Erica.

Weston nodded.

Erica sat in stunned silence biting her bottom lip. Finally, she opened the van door. "We're not done with this discussion," she said somberly.

"No, we're not, Erica," shot Weston. "No we're not."

For a moment she stared at him in surprise and then after a moment Erica cautiously stepped out of the car. She could hear the sounds of the traffic on the nearby I-75. Pausing for a moment, she thought she heard the sound of a child crying somewhere in the distance and immediately she felt sick. Eric choked back vomit in her throat. She turned to look at Weston one more time before leaving.

"Later," he whispered softly. Then he added with urgency, "Go!"

As if seeing him for the very first time, Erica stared at Weston and took in every detail. She saw the flop of salt and pepper hair, the purple bruises along the distinguished wrinkles that lined his deep blue eyes, the soft lips that made her feel so amazing when they smiled.

"Go!" he shouted and the moment was shattered.

"Stay here until I call!"

Weston remained silent and motionless as Erica turned and walked away. The echo of her footsteps in the parking lot filled the silence. Each footstep shouted a declaration of intention for Erica. "I'm ready," she whispered to herself as her office building came into sight.

Once in the parking lot she saw several co-workers approaching their cars. The words "Isn't that her?" echoed. However, before she could turn she spotted her boss emerging from the door.

"Erica!" he shouted extending his arms. But then something caught his eyes and his arms dropped. Looking past Erica, he quickly wiped his hands on his coat and straightened his tie. His eyes focused on something just past her.

She turned just in time to see a flash. "What the hell?" she yelled as she put up her hands to shield her eyes. Then there was another flash and another and another.

"Ladies and gentlemen, there will be a formal press conference in the press room on the third floor," McHann directed.

"A what?" asked Erica.

"A press conference," he repeated as he slid an arm around her back and began to guide her towards the building. "Come on. It's cold out here," he whispered in her ear.

Erica turned to look at him just as another flash burst in her face. "Do you have any statements to make?" shouted a faceless body behind the flash.

"What?" asked Erica.

"Ms. Schmidt, what is your response to the kidnapper?" the voice shouted. "Is this a love triangle?"

"A love…" Erica tried to respond, but the questions and bodies whirled too quickly.

"Is this kidnapping just a hoax to draw attention away from Dr. Anderson's illegal human experimentation?"

"Were you a part of Dr. Anderson's experiments?" yelled a voice from behind her.

Suddenly there was a hurricane of reporters all around her. "Were you a victim? Does Dr. Anderson believe that he is God's messenger of death?" The voices shot at her from all sides.

"What are they talking about?" she asked McHann. He merely smiled. His hands remained firmly fixed on her body. One hand gripped her elbow another clamped around her back…both guiding her through the chaos. She felt his breath on her neck, the strong smell of Listerine and musk stung her nose.

"It's okay. Really it is," he continued to whisper. His nimble, anorexic frame moved quickly through the crowd with her.

"Hold it," she said turning towards him. "What are they talking about? What's going on?"

Her slight hesitation allowed the flood of reporters to engulf them again just as they reached the building. Instantly the door swung open and two armed men walked out. The men began to block the reporters.

Inside of the building, Erica turned and looked back briefly. "Now what's going on?" She asked frantically.

McHann ushered Erica down the hallway. "Come to my office, Erica. We need to have a conversation." The tiny man made no further sounds as he dashed up the stairs towards his office.

They entered his office and then McHann grabbed a nearby can of Slimfast and took a long drink.

Let the show begin, grimaced Erica as took off her coat and threw it onto a chair. Then she paced impatiently.

"Erica, I've worked with you for what…about six months now?" he asked as he attempted to sit on the edge of his desk.

"What is going on?" she insisted.

McHann put a smooth white finger to his lips to motion for silence. "I believe I'm trying to help you," he said with an air of control. "I've never liked your association with Dr. Anderson. He's a dark, ungodly man, but I don't interfere with the lives of my staff…you know with your education there's no reason you couldn't be doing more in this department…but I guess that's another day's issue."

Erica picked up her coat and turned towards the door.

"Wait!" shouted McHann. "There's something you need to hear. He then played a tape:

"Erica? This is Caleb… I have Reilly. … I need to hear from you right away. Look I know what's going on…but I have her. … she's in danger."

Erica stood frozen. "Where did you get that?" she said in horror. "And how long ago?" she flung open the door. "I have to find my baby!"

McHann flew around his desk and jumped between Erica and the door. He thrust the handle from her fingers and slammed it shut. "That's all anyone wants. Your baby was never going to be a part of this…but now she is and she's a wonderful media tool. Her adorable little face…a victim of the flu…perhaps an epidemic created by her very own parents.

Either way the camera loves her."

"What are you talking about?"

"There's a group of…well let's just say Americans concerned about national security. I've been doing a bit of work for them."

Erica shoved McHann backwards.

Suddenly he appeared panicked. "Marcus…Marcus was with them. They're part of our government…a…a hidden part, but a necessary one. You need to get Weston to play ball with us. That's really all this is about. What he's doing is terrorism…after all, he created this new virus AND he unleashed it. Hitler…remember him? That's what Weston really is…people are dying, but yet his cause is more important." McHann's voice had degenerated into a slime that Erica could almost feel on her skin. "You can stop him, Erica."

"Stop him? Good God, he's been walking around a free man…hell most of the time he's been a stinking lousy drunk…and your people can't locate him? That's bullshit."

"We want his notes…we want his allegiance…"

"Allegiance?" shot back Erica. "To what?"

"America. That's it. Pure and simple," hissed McHann. "We're fighting a war…the next big world war. Whose side are you on?"

Just then the door opened. Three men in suits marched into the office. One quickly moved behind the desk, while another stepped within inches of McHann's face. "Mr. McHann, you can go now."

"Go? I don't think so. I'm on your side, fellas."

"We're in charge now, Mr. McHann. The United States government thanks you for your service and we'll let you know if we need further assistance," boomed the man's voice.

Then the man behind the desk looked up from the folders he was flipping through and added, "Howard, take a break. Get some coffee and go to the press room. I'm sure your media skills will be very valuable there."

McHann left without giving Erica another look.

For a moment no one spoke or moved. The man behind the desk simply continued looking through his folders. Then he looked up and nodded slightly. The three other men surrounded Erica. One grabbed her wrist. "Erica Schmidt, for violating Section 12, paragraph 34 of the Homeland Security Act, you are placed under arrest for terrorist acts leading to the death and injury of American citizens."

CHAPTER 35

Caleb listened to the sirens for a moment. "We gotta go," he whispered to Reilly as he picked her up. He looked at her red swollen face. She whimpered softly. "Grab more juice and...and some cookies," he blurted out to Carson. "We've got to get her help."

Carson disappeared for a moment and returned with his arms full. "Around to the left," he shouted as he lead the way to the back door.

"What?" asked Caleb as he rushed out with Reilly.

"My delivery vehicle is around the back on the left side of the building," huffed the stocky man as he waddled out into the afternoon chill.

"Man, you run a Starbucks...what do you deliver?" said Caleb trying to maintain a hold of Reilly and move quickly at the same time. Then he reached the end of the building and saw Carson loading the juice and cookies into a hearse.

"What the hell?" gasped Caleb. "Seriously, man, I ain't getting in there."

"It's a vehicle and it sort of delivers things...well people. Just get in, Mary," he said sarcastically. "Just get in. I guarantee that we'll slip right through the police," he chuckled.

Carson pulled out the keys and Caleb reached out for them. "Whoa, fat man, I'm driving," Caleb said.

"No way, punk. This is my transportation," he shot back.

Caleb jogged around to Carson and pushed Reilly towards him. "You said you had a kid? Well, then I guess you'll know what to do with this one. Besides, I don't trust you driving. I know where we're going. You can stay here. You can go with. But you ain't driving."

The sirens grew louder. Carson rolled his eyes and then took Reilly. "She's wet," he moaned.

"That's a good sign...means she's not completely dehydrated

159

yet…" replied Caleb as he got into the driver's seat.

"Or that no one has changed her in two days," shot back Carson.

"Change her…oh, and give her more juice," replied Caleb.

Carson climbed into the back with Reilly and began to change her as the hearse peeled out of the lot. "Slow down, idiot!" shouted Carson. "You don't see no hearse in the Indy 500. Cop is gonna spot you in a flash."

Caleb slowed the vehicle as they saw the approaching lights of several police cars. As the sirens blared, Reilly cried. "She crying tears?" asked Caleb.

"Why?" asked Carson.

"Cause that shows she's okay. Man, I thought you said you had a kid."

"His momma took care of him…" He looked at Reilly and saw no tears on her cherubic face. Silently he looked out the window and wiped away one of his own.

Caleb focused on going slow. Every impulse in his body wanted to hit the gas and hit it hard. *Stay slow*, he told himself. *Steady, even, slow…*

"I'm going to circle a few blocks around the building and find a good place to park," he announced. "Then I'm going to leave you two in the car while I see what I can find out," Caleb said. "She okay?"

Carson continued to look out the window. "Yeah. That's a good plan. Just hurry."

"I thought you said…"

Carson gripped Reilly and began to rock her. "Just do whatever," he shot back.

Just then Caleb saw the nursing home van parked along a side street under a maple tree. He pulled behind it.

"I'll be right back," he said as he kept his eyes fixated on the van.

"What are you doing?" asked Carson.

As if in a trance, Caleb moved out of the hearse and towards the van. As he did, he heard a voice coming from inside of the car. "The national Amber Alert has been cancelled. I repeat the national Amber Alert has been cancelled. I regretfully report that the child's mother, Erica Schmidt, has confessed to killing the child...what a tragic..."

Caleb banged on the driver's side window startling Weston. "God, you scared me! What are you doing here?" said Weston looking beleaguered.

"What are you doing here? And what did I just hear?" he asked looking into the van.

"Radio. Erica went into that building about an hour ago. I've been waiting here for her...to be honest, I've been waiting for Homeland Security. They must know I'm here and I'm pretty sure that Erica went in to turn me in..."

"And yet you waited?"

"They don't want me," replied Weston shaking his head. He rubbed his forehead with the palms of both hands and then ran them through his hair.

"Then who do they want?" asked Caleb. "Me?"

"No....I mean...I don't think so," Weston sighed. Then he replied somberly. "I think...I think they want her."

Caleb paused for a minute. "Just a minute..." he said and then he ran back to the hearse.

Opening the back seat, Caleb bent over and picked up Reilly.

"What's going on?" asked Carson in surprise.

Caleb said nothing, but instead jogged up to the passenger side of the van and awkwardly knocked. Weston swung open the door and gasped. "Oh, my god! Quick get her in back."

Laying her in the back seat, Weston began to examine his daughter. "She needs an IV to hydrate her and we need to bring down her fever. I've got to get her..."

"...to the hospital. That's exactly what I've been telling Cars..."

"...to my cabin," said Weston urgently.

"What? This kid is sick, really sick, dying and you want to take her out for a little fresh air?" snapped Caleb.

In a flash, Weston turned and grabbed Caleb's shirt collar. Tightening his grip he hissed, "My daughter is NOT dying and I am going to do everything within my power to make sure of it!" Then he threw Caleb against the seat.

"Stop doing that, asshole," said Caleb as he shot back as he got out of the van.

"Stop talking to me, dumb shit," replied Weston. Then Weston got out of the back seat and slammed the door. He moved to the driver's seat.

"Where are you going?" shouted Caleb.

"What's it to you?" asked Weston as he started up the van.

Caleb swung open the passenger side door as the van began to move. "I don't like to be a chump," he said. "Besides, old man, you're gonna need my help to get Erica out of there."

Weston paused for a moment as Caleb climbed in. "You are going to get Erica, right?" Caleb asked.

"I have to get Reilly help. That's what Erica would have wanted and you know it."

"Hey, let me in!" shouted Carson as he slammed his hand onto the side of the van.

"What the hell? Who else did you bring?" snarled Weston.

Caleb hit the unlock button. Weston rolled his eyes and then looked back at Reilly. "Every second counts," he said as he hit the gear stick and the van peeled out with the back door still open.

"Holy shit!" screamed Carson as he struggled to pull it closed. For one brief second he saw the pavement whirl just inches from his foot. With all of his weight he hurled himself into the seat and slammed the door behind him.

Weston looked back at Reilly in the very back row of seats buckled in awkwardly. She didn't stir at all. Weston looked at his watch and back at his silent angel bundled in blankets. Then he turned all of his attention to the road and went screaming through a red light.

"Why do they want Erica?" asked Caleb.

Weston rubbed his forehead. "Does she have a wrist band on?" snapped Weston as he motioned towards Reilly.

"Yeah," growled Carson as he moved a blanket from her tiny arm.

"Red or yellow?" Weston asked.

"Red," Carson huffed.

Then Weston nodded towards Pearl who was sleeping in the middle row of seats near Carson.

"Her...what does she have?" he asked.

Carson and Caleb exchanged glances. Then Carson took a deep breath and reached for Pearl's wrists. "Yellow," Carson replied.

Weston sighed. "They found them," he said hopelessly. "They found Erica and Reilly and now somebody out there is just sitting back and watching them die."

"Hold it! Hold it right there!" shouted Caleb. "What about you? What about all this shit about your notes and evidence?"

"It's a part of it to. Have you ever heard of Zelticor?"

"No," answered Caleb.

"You should learn to read then," interrupted Carson. "That's a drug company just landed a major account with the government to produce vaccines."

"That's who employs my lab. That's who wants RCG35-98. They think I double crossed them because not all of the vaccines work," added Weston.

"What?" asked Caleb shaking his head.

"Are you an '*A is A*' type person, Mr. Philips?" asked Weston.

"As opposed to what?" Caleb responded.

"I take that as a yes," replied Weston. "I used to be one as well. The thing is that A is not always A....sometimes there are things going on. This is one of those times."

"Skip the lecture and get to the point," shot back Caleb.

"The Secretary of Defense is a major stockholder in this company...and so are a few other members of this administration," he explained.

"If the vaccine doesn't work then they don't get any money," interrupted Caleb.

"While I had my hands full with RCG35-98, one of my assistants found a way to make a few extra bucks. He sold vaccines to clinics that were nothing but saline solution. But that's nothing. That's just a dancing monkey compared to what's really going on."

"A dancing monkey? What the hell are you talking about?" asked Caleb.

"You see, kid," wheezed Carson, "if we develop the virus and find the only vaccine for it...that can only mean..."

"...more profits and the U.S. can be savior to the world...especially if U.S. scientists are being told that to share with scientists from other countries is an act of betrayal in the eyes of the Patriot Act," added Weston.

Silence filled the van. Then Caleb's eyes diverted to a sight to the left of Weston...Erica emerging from the south end of the building in handcuffs.

CHAPTER 36

Weston turned to follow Caleb's gaze. "Oh, god!" he gasped.

"Turn on the radio," ordered Carson. "The all-news station."

Weston's eyes remained fixated on Erica as he turned on the radio. "The afternoon continues to be chilly and blustery. We'll dip down tonight and a frost warning is in effect. Now for the headline news," announced a voice. "The FBI has announced that a suspect has been apprehended in the Marcus Smith murder. Erica Schmidt, a colleague of Smith's has apparently confessed. Schmidt and two male companions are wanted by Homeland Security for suspected terrorist acts against the United States. More information to come. The housing market today..."

Weston turned off the radio as they watched Erica being led through the crowd of journalists.

Caleb opened the van door. "Ready?" he asked.

"For what?" responded Weston incredulously.

"To get the hell out of here with Erica."

"How, Einstein?" Weston shot back.

Caleb held up a pack of fire crackers he had pulled from his back pack. "Be ready to grab her," he ordered and then he jumped from the van.

Weston took a deep breath as he watched Caleb run to the east side of the building. "Hold onto the door. Keep it ajar, but don't close it," he ordered Carson.

Carson pulled the door within an inch of latching and then braced himself as the van revved up.

POP! BAM! POP! POP!

Weston peeled out and headed towards the crowd which had begun scrambling in chaos across the parking lot. The agents holding onto Erica drew their guns and turned towards the noise. Caleb raced through the crowd and grabbed Erica just as the van pulled within feet of them. Slugging one agent and ducking another's fist, Caleb jerked Erica's arm throwing her towards the van. Carson swung the door open and Erica hurled herself into the vehicle.

The vehicle swerved through the crowd tossing its occupants from side to side. Carson grabbed for Reilly as Erica fell to the floor. Pearl landed on top of her.

"Oh, dear heavens!" wailed Pearl. "Oh, dear heavens!"

"Grandma! Move!" groaned Erica. Then she heard Reilly. "Reilly!" she screamed. However, the carnival ride was not over yet…as Weston twisted and turned behind the wheel racing over lawns and the sidewalks heading for Caleb.

"Leave the kid," shouted Carson.

"No," snapped Weston. "If we leave him, he's a dead man."

Erica shoved Pearl aside and stumbled towards Reilly who was a limp rag doll across Carson's shoulder.

"Reilly!" Erica screamed again.

"Sit down!" commanded Weston. Gun shots could be heard around them. "Everyone get down!" Weston shouted again as he tore down the street leaving the chaos behind them.

"I told you," snipped Carson as they all resumed their seats and the ride leveled off. "I told you that we couldn't get the kid. He'll be alright. Now what we gonna do?" he asked.

Weston seethed with anger. "I told you. We're going to get him." He looked over at Erica who was stroking Reilly's face softly. "Carson, I saw tools in the back. Get those handcuffs off of her anyway you can," he added as he nodded towards Erica's handcuffs.

"Wes, we've got to get her help," Erica pleaded.

"We will. We will. Just give me a minute," he said as he pulled the van into a vacant lot. "Go in and get us another van! They'll be looking for this one," he ordered Carson as he pointed to the Hertz car rental lot across the street. "First try to rent it…nice and calm. Then…well do what you have to," he added shaking his head. "But do it quick!"

Carson inched his large body along the seat and then thrust himself out the door with one big thud. "When I come back with the new wheels, I'll get those handcuffs off of you, missy," Carson said as he looked into the van one last time.

As he waddled away, Weston turned to Erica. "Stay here and stay down. Once Carson comes back with the vehicle grab Reilly and Pearl and get in it. If I'm not back in ten minutes, take off without me. Go to the cabin. When you get there look under the floor boards. I have a complete IV kit and information about where I've hidden evidence…you can help Reilly….and yourself."

Erica looked up like a woman worn to her soul. "Okay."

"Ten minutes," Weston shouted pointing at her watch.

She looked down and then looked at Reilly. Fear flowed out of her eyes freely unlike the tears that she held back by biting her lip. In silence she nodded.

Weston began to leave and then turned back and lunged towards her. She turned her head and his kiss landed on her ear instead of her lips. Then Weston turned and left. As he jogged back towards the building, Weston glanced back to see Carson in the Hertz office. All seemed to be going well with that venture at least.

Then he looked back at the nursing home van. Erica sat cradling Reilly…her face quivering to hold back tears. Pearl sat behind her seemingly lost to the entire situation. *Probably doesn't even know what's going on around her*, Weston thought. And for a brief moment he envied her.

Upon arriving at the Erica's office building, Weston was breathless and desperately wishing for a cigarette. Then he saw a taxi cab sitting down the road. He walked up and tapped on the driver's window. The driver, who had been lying back with his cap over his face, jolted.

"Hey, buddy, you here for a pickup?" Weston asked.

"Naw, man, I'm on break. Just sitting and chillin," he responded settling back again.

"Buddy of mine over at the Zelticor corporate building needs a ride," said Weston.

"I said, I'm on break," replied the driver as he sat upright and faced Weston.

Weston fumbled through his coat pockets and pulled out an envelope. "Well, $500.00 says that you ain't," he said.

"You messin with me?" he asked as he reached for the money.

"No," said Weston as he pulled back the envelope. "But there is a catch."

"Course," sighed the man.

"You have to go into the building and get him…go to room 312 and say you have a cab waiting for Marcus Smith."

"I know that name…is he some big shot in town?" asked the cabbie.

"Oh, something like that," said Weston. "But don't say a word to anyone else. Only in room 312…got it?"

The cab driver reached for the money again. Weston pulled it away. "When you come back, the money will be right here."

The cabbie hesitated for a moment looking Weston over. Then he looked at the building.

"Are you interested or not?" asked Weston.

The driver took a deep breath and started up his car. He drove over and parked his cab at the curb and entered the building nodding at security who eyed him and then waved him past.

Weston reached for a cigarette from his shirt pocket and lit it. He took a long drag and felt better, but then remembered how long it had been since he had eaten. *Reilly and Erica must be hungry too*, he thought. Then he looked at his watch. Pulling out keys from his jacket pocket, he approached a side delivery door of the Zelticor building and entered silently.

"Hey, who are you?" asked a clerk invoicing FedEx packages.

"Building's on fire," he said somberly.

"Get out," ordered a large woman sitting nearby as she reached for her cell phone.

Moving quickly, Weston jogged past her and turned left to the hallway where he recalled seeing a fire alarm back when he and Erica used to look for privacy during her breaks. He pulled the alarm and then returned to the delivery entrance way. "See. Told you!" he said with a smile and then raced out of the building.

People began to pour out of the building. Weston raced towards the cab where he spotted Caleb. "Follow me!" He shouted. Both men raced down a nearby alley towards where Carson waiting with the new van he had obtained. As they ran, Weston felt the envelope in his pocket. "Just a minute," he gasped out of breath. He stopped.

"What?" shouted Caleb as he slowed down and looked back at Weston.

Weston waved the money in the air as he bent over to breath. Then he straightened up and turned back. "Get in the van and meet me in just a minute ready to roll," he yelled over his shoulder.

"Hey, where'd you get that money?" Caleb asked, but Weston had already disappeared back down the alley.

Weston jogged down the alley and then spotted the cab driver getting into his vehicle cursing loudly. "Hey, buddy!" yelled Weston. Then he threw the envelope towards the cabbie and turned and ran.

Reaching the new van he saw Caleb standing at the driver's window. "I said, I'm driving," he shouted.

"Hell no!" Carson yelled back as he sat squarely in the seat. Blood veins in his forehead rose to dark ridges.

"Both of you get the hell out of the driver's seat," barked Weston. "I know where we're going."

Carson lumbered out of the driver's seat and wedged himself into the front passenger spot just as Caleb rounded the vehicle and attempted to enter the front passenger door. Scowling, Caleb flung open the side door and jumped into the middle row of seats with Erica. The van tore out of the lot spraying pebbles and dust from under its tires.

"You idiots almost got us killed. We didn't switch vans so that they could right off spot us in our new one!" Weston screamed.

"Stop yelling," cried Erica as she attempted to rock Reilly.

"Here let me help you," said Caleb as he lifted Erica's legs onto the seat and then adjusted Reilly into a better position on the seat. He moved to the edge of the seat to make more room.

"Here...there's room for us both," replied Erica as she tried to move her feet and then began another coughing fit. Then she held up her wrists. "It's all easier without handcuffs," she added as she nodded towards Carson who gave a satisfied smile.

Caleb settled into the seat and looked at Erica. "You rest. Both of you rest," he said as she laid back and closed her eyes. Then he took off his coat and wadded it up as a pillow for Erica to push between the window and her head as she rested.

"Thank you," she whispered. Holding Reilly tightly she took a deep breath and closed her eyes again. In a minute both she and Reilly were asleep, just like Pearl, whose bruised body told the story of her day.

Caleb leaned over and put his head in his hands resting his elbows on his knees. "Thanks for coming back," he mumbled to Weston.

"You were a dead man staying there," said Weston. "I'm glad you caught my hint."

"You should have seen their faces when that taxi driver said he was there for Marcus!" Caleb looked up and smiled. "Man, they were all over him...and then the fire alarm...I just ran for it."

"No handcuffs?" asked Weston.

"Guess I'm not as dangerous as Erica," he said with a chuckle.

Weston smiled briefly. Then he got quiet. "How are you feeling?" he asked somberly.

"Getting attached to me?" joked Caleb. "First you save my ass and then you ask about my health? Wow!"

"Look I don't want to kid anyone in this vehicle…one of the three ladies we're traveling with has most likely been exposed to a very powerful viral agent…and if they have, then…"

"…we have," finished Caleb.

"Yes." Weston glanced back.

"We bein' followed?" asked Carson.

"Not yet. Not yet." Sighed Weston.

"Where'd you get that money?" asked Caleb.

"Did it look familiar?" asked Weston with a slight smile.

Caleb began to riffle through his back pack. "God damn you! That money was to help us escape…you know to get food and shit like that!"

"Yes, I guess $500 would get us a hell of a lot of supplies; however, that envelope was bugged. There was a transmitter in it. Now I'm going to assume that you didn't know it was in there, but that's as much leeway as I'm giving you. Our first order of business is to help Reilly. Then if we can all get on our feet we split. That's when this little party ends."

Then Weston heard the click of a pistol being cocked. He turned to see Carson holding a gun and pointing it directly at him.

CHAPTER 37

"Something wrong, Carson," said Weston nervously as his eyes darted from Carson to the road ahead of them.

Caleb looked up from his backpack. "Whoa! Buddy, what's up?"

"Your life," Carson huffed.

Caleb looked at Weston. "What's going on? I miss something?"

Weston shook his head. "You know as much as I do on this one," he replied.

"Mr. Big Shot here…he killed my son," stated Carson as he waved the gun at Weston.

"What?" asked Weston and Caleb simultaneously.

"I ought to kill your kid. That's what I should do…killing you lets you off the hook too easily," he said as he looked over at Reilly and Erica sleeping. He began to cough and wheeze. "Now I'm sick."

"You're a chain smoker hacking up a lung. I hardly see that as his fault," said Caleb nodding towards Weston.

"No, I got a fever and chills, you smart ass," shot back Carson as he wiped his nose on his sleeve leaving a streak of mucus.

"Put down the gun," ordered Weston.

"You tell me to put down my gun? Oh, that's rich. You thinking you can tell me anything!" Carson yelled.

Erica and Pearl opened their eyes. Reilly began to fuss as Erica struggled to sit up.

"Lay down," Weston said to Erica.

"Yeah, the poison works faster that way," sneered Carson.

Erica rubbed her eyes and looked around. Half sitting, half laying, she turned back to see Pearl sleeping. When she returned her

172

gaze to the front seat and Carson she saw the gun. "What's going on?" she asked alarmed.

"I'm going to tell you," snarled Carson. "I'm going to tell all of you a few little stories about what's been going on around here and when I'm finished…I'm going to kill the good doctor here," he said.

Weston's head remained directed towards the road, but his eyes darted from it to Carson frantically.

"Ever heard of the Spanish flu?" he asked Caleb. Silently Caleb nodded his head.

"That was in 1819," whispered Erica as she attempted to clear her throat.

"Correct," replied Carson. "And how did we get the flu?"

"What?" asked Erica bewildered.

"How the hell did it get started in this country?" he yelled. "I'll tell you. There's an aspirin company I'm sure you've heard of…they held a German patent for quite a few of their little items and they were lacing their aspirin with virus."

"That's a lie," replied Weston. "There was never and I repeat never any proof of that."

Carson pushed the gun further into Weston's face. "You want to die right here, right now?" he asked. "How hard would it be for anyone to lace something with virus and then let us all die off like dogs?"

"You're crazy!" said Caleb.

The gun barrel swiftly turned to face him. "Bioterrorism has been a fact of life since the dark ages, kiddies," huffed Carson. "When the plague hit and threatened to wipe out Europe, they were using infected corpses to fling at enemies to spread the death around."

Weston shifted slightly in his seat and then ran his left arm between the seat and the door. Spotting Weston's hand, Caleb shifted his back pack with his foot so that it was directly behind Weston's seat and within reach of his fingers. Then Caleb inched his foot under his back pack to lift it slightly.

"What are you doing?" yelled Carson as he spotted Caleb looking down.

"Nothing, man. Just trying to get some leg room. So go on with your story, so you can kill this crazy man and be done with it," he said nodding towards Weston.

"I think I'll kill you too," Carson snarled and then cleared his throat. Amid a sea of coughs, sneezes and throat clearing from all of the van's occupants, Carson continued. "You know the Tuskegee Syphilis Study?"

Weston cleared his throat. "Ran from 1932 to 1972 with the government letting people believe that they were being treated, when actually..."

"...they were letting people die," added Caleb.

Everyone in the van became quiet. Carson lowered his gun to his lap and looked out the window. "They infected my son...and then they watched him die," he whispered.

"He was a part of the Tuskegee study?" asked Caleb.

"No, you dumb shit, he was infected in another study...a study five years ago of children and the pneumonia virus...bioterrorism unit, if I'm not mistaken," Carson said somberly.

"Carson, I'm not the enemy here," Weston said patronizingly.

Carson looked up at him through tears and then raised his gun. "You....you and your kind. You are the enemy, but you keep it a secret, don't you? Huh? That's what you do isn't it, Doc? You do experiments on people? What's the phrase? Oh yeah, the greater good for all. Isn't that it? Isn't that how you sleep at night...thinking you're doing a greater good?"

"I've never conducted human experiments without following proper procedure," Weston said somberly. Then he swallowed hard as he moved his left arm into his lap, covering the gun he had just taken from Caleb's back pack with his shirt.

"Then what's been going on at the nursing home, Doctor? ANSWER ME!" shouted Carson.

All eyes turned to Weston. For a moment his lips quivered. "Accident. It was an accident. Erica's mother burst into my lab. She raced out before I knew...before I realized," Weston turned slightly to look at Erica in the rearview mirror. "The next day she went to see your grandmother and...and..."

"THE NEXT DAY? DID YOU SAY THE NEXT DAY?" screamed Carson.

"Weston?" Erica said softly. "You waited?"

"No! I had no way of knowing what RCG35-98 really was yet, so I contacted my superiors. They didn't want a panic. Maybe it was nothing. Hell, she just knocked over some test tubes and was exposed for all of 60 seconds...maybe less."

"Did they pay you off, man? They buy your silence?" Caleb asked insistently.

Weston closed his lips tightly and focused intently on the road before him.

"I hear all of you talking crowding around your little cute coffee mugs...ya sit just feet away from me and talk about watching people die like the others in my shop talk about the ball game." Then Carson lowered his voice and in a sinister hissed, "Does your little woman over there know that you supervised the fiasco at Gramma's home?"

"What?" Erica stammered in shock.

Weston swerved the van throwing everyone to the left side. "You delusional son of a bitch. You don't know anything about me!" he shot back.

"Really? Cause obviously I know more than she does!" Carson shouted even more loudly. "I know what you do, Dr. Anderson. Does everyone else in this van know?"

With his defiant shout, Carson raised his pistol and fired. The bullet flew by Weston's face grazing his nose and smashing his window.

In a heartbeat, with one swift motion, Weston raised the handgun he had retrieved from Caleb's back pack and fired directly into Carson's face.

CHAPTER 38

Pearl jolted from her sleep. She looked at the wet, red splotches on her arm and very quietly began to search for a handkerchief in her pocket. With meticulous, delicate motions she began to wipe the red dots turning them into larger red streaks. Then she looked up. There were red dots everywhere in the vehicle ahead of her.

"Pull over, man!" gagged Caleb grabbing his mouth.

"Can't," replied Weston mechanically. "Can't."

"I'm gonna hurl!" gasped Caleb. He grabbed for the window, but his retching began before his hands could fully thrust it open. Vomit spewed across the side passenger door mingling with the blood that dripped silently down it.

Erica grabbed Reilly and held her close. Reilly, whose body was trembling slightly, remained silent and limp. "Weston," gasped Erica as she attempted to sit up with Reilly on her lap. "Please, god, we've got to stop this right now. Reilly needs a doctor. We can't keep traveling with...with," Erica held back her tears at the cost of her voice...only slight sobs and murmurs emerged from her lips as she stared at Carson's lifeless body.

"We're going to my cabin!" Weston barked. "We're going to get my evidence, hook Reilly up to an IV and everyone will be fine. If we stop now we're dead!"

"Look, man, just let me out. Okay? I won't tell anyone. You'll never hear from me again. I just want out," pleaded Caleb. He rocked in his seat holding his stomach trying not to look at Carson's window on which the back half of his head was splattered like a modern art piece with globs of paint streaking down it. As Caleb looked at his feet, Caleb heard an all too familiar click. He raised his head to see the barrel of his own gun pointed at him.

"No one! I repeat NO ONE leaves this little family vacation until it's done or until we're all god damn dead!" Weston yelled as he swung the gun around the interior of the vehicle.

In his rear view mirror, Weston made eye contact with Erica. In her dark green eyes he saw something he had never seen in her before—

horror directed at him. Pressing his foot harder onto the accelerator he swerved the vehicle off the road and began to blaze his own path through the forest as bushes and low hanging limbs smacked the outside of the van. "We're almost there," he whispered, but the words got lost in the air. His hands shook as he attempted to maneuver the rough terrain in the van. "Reilly's gonna live," he whispered. "Reilly's gonna live."

"Oh, my!" gasped Pearl from the very back of the van. "I've vomited all over your nice new car," she said sweetly in the same tone she might have said, "I've just spilled my tea."

Weston put the gun in his lap and wiped his forehead. "It's okay, Pearl," he said loudly, but with a gentle tone. "It's okay. We'll have the car cleaned. We're almost there."

"The body," moaned Caleb. He motioned towards Carson still attempting to avoid looking at the macabre sight. "We takin that with us?"

"Oh, uh," Weston swallowed hard. He appeared confused as if he had just then realized Carson was still there. "I uh...I uh..." he sputtered.

"We take him to the cabin and bury him out back," said Erica with a surreal clarity. "That way if someone discovers him, we know about it. Leaving him anywhere else would open us up to being caught by surprise."

Weston and Caleb stared in awe at this new side of Erica.

"We're going to get to your cabin and take care of Reilly and then the rest of us. After we've rested and are feeling better...and...and you've used your hidden evidence to get us some help, Reilly and I are leaving. We're leaving and I never want anything more to do with you. Is that understood?" Erica's voice was calm, clear and angry.

Weston nodded.

"I don't even know how we got here, but I am definitely not going any further down your road of paranoia," she concluded. "You do have some real evidence right?

Weston said nothing.

"You do have something solid to get yourself and us out of this, right?" she insisted.

"I believe I do, but I don't know precisely what they…" Weston fumbled around vaguely like a child responding poorly to a teacher.

"Just go," she said angrily. Then she sat back and wiped Reilly's face with her hand.

The occupants of the van became silent as they approached the cabin. The snapping of twigs beneath the vehicle's tires seemed amplified in the silence. Finally, behind a gathering of whispering pines, Weston slammed the gear shift into park.

"We should make sure we're not being followed," rasped Caleb as he wiped fresh vomit from his lips. Then he looked at Erica. "If you think that's a good idea…"

"Do it quickly," she ordered.

Holding his stomach, Caleb tumbled from the van. Weston sat frozen for a moment. He wanted to turn and look at Erica, but instead he silently stumbled from the van. As he did Caleb's pistol fell to the ground with a cold, hollow thump. Weston paused for a moment.

"Go," hissed Erica.

Weston did. Out of the corner of his eye he saw a hand reaching for the gun. He took a deep breath and stood as if bracing for his own execution…a bullet through the head from Erica. He took a deep breath and closed his eyes.

"Walk," Erica commanded.

Weston began to move away from the van as Erica returned to her seat with pistol in hand. Calmly she checked for bullets. Then she looked at her lifeless child.

"I'm sorry, baby," she whispered. "I am so very, very sorry." As Reilly's body struggled for each breath, Erica looked at the cabin. Was there really anything to help Reilly…to help any of them…now? For a moment Erica looked into the barrel of the gun.

"They always kill the baby first," said a voice from behind her.

Erica jumped. "What?" she asked.

Pearl placed her hand on Erica's shoulder. "They don't want to leave their babies suffering, dear," she replied morbidly.

As if in a trance Erica feverishly looked back at the gun. She began to run her finger tips along the smooth barrel. Reilly just laid there on the seat beside her... motionless. "I can't watch her suffer," she said in a hypnotic tone. "I can't watch her die." This had to end. Calmly she pointed the gun at Reilly's head. One shot. Then one shot to her own temple and this would be all over.

Pearl reached over and wiped a splatter of Carson's blood from Erica's cheek. Then she looked at the red dots on the hand holding the gun. Pearl turned, raised her coat over her face and braced...for the gun shot.

CHAPTER 39

A shot rang through the woods. Erica jolted. Pearl screamed.

Caleb raced back to the van. He opened the front driver's door and jumped into the seat. He opened his mouth to speak, but then froze as he saw Erica holding the gun pointed at Reilly. "What are you doing?" Caleb sputtered.

Erica didn't speak.

Caleb grabbed the gun and tossed it out the door. "I said what the hell are you doing?" he screamed. Then he moved between the two front seats and grabbed Erica by the shoulders. "Get away from her!" he screamed and then scooped up Reilly in his arms as he swung open the side door. He exited carrying Reilly just as Weston walked up holding a smoking riffle and a dead raccoon by the tail.

"I caught dinner," he announced morbidly. Then he saw Caleb's face.

"Stop playing Davy Crockett and let's get Reilly some help," Caleb snapped.

Erica emerged from the van sobbing.

"What happened?" Weston asked her.

"Help Reilly. Just help Reilly," she sobbed.

They walked towards the cabin and Weston threw the raccoon into a bucket in the kitchen. "Put Reilly in the first bedroom," he said to Caleb. "Erica, go get the IV kit. It's fully loaded and fresh...ready to use..."

Then Weston disappeared. He returned with a small wooden box full of papers. "I'll make a call. Then you can take her to the hospital."

"She's gonna live, right?" asked Caleb.

"She's got a heartbeat; she's still gotta chance," answered Weston as he followed Caleb to the first bedroom. "Where's Erica?" he asked impatiently.

As Caleb placed Reilly on the bed, he looked around frantically. "I'll go…"

Just then she entered the room. "Here," she said as she struggled to put the large, plastic box marked "IV SUPPLIES" on top of the dresser.

Weston grabbed the box and went to work quickly. "While I'm hooking up the IV, take off her clothes and wipe her down with cool rags."

"And then?" asked Caleb impatiently.

"And then we just need to make her comfortable and wait."

As Weston tended to the IV, Erica began removing Reilly's clothing and Caleb dashed out of the room, returning with a bowl of cool water and several rags. "This is all I could find," he said holding up some tattered Holiday Inn towels.

Erica grabbed the towels and frantically began to dip them into the cool water. Her hands shook as she sloshed water around. Reilly remained unresponsive. Then on her trembling, cold fingers, Erica felt Caleb's warm soft hands surround hers. With a firm grip, he held her hands warming them with his.

"It's going to be okay now," he whispered.

Erica surrendered for the moment to the idea that maybe things would be okay. She closed her eyes and focused on the warmth of Caleb's hands.

Weston looked up from the IV solution he was holding to see Caleb still gripping Erica's hands tenderly.

"IV is set," he said loudly startling Erica and Caleb.

Erica pulled away from Caleb and looked down at Reilly…lifeless and naked on the bed. "We need more blankets" she said as she looked up at Weston.

"I'll get them," he said as he looked into her piercing glare. "I'll get them," he repeated whispering despondently as he left the room.

"We need some Tylenol," she said to Caleb.

Silently he also exited the room leaving Erica alone with her nightmares. Then Weston returned with a several blankets. He began to wrap Reilly in them. She wiggled slightly.

"A good sign," he said trying to sound hopeful.

Erica pulled the blanket up over Reilly's body as Caleb returned. "Everything in that medicine cabinet is like 100 years old…and I didn't find anything for a kid."

"What are you looking for?" asked Weston.

"Tylenol," said Caleb.

Weston nodded towards his wooden box on the table. "Shouldn't need it now…we're gonna get help."

"From where? The Calvary?" snapped Erica.

"I'll make a call and get the other items. Then we'll be free…you'll be free at least," Weston said softly. "Anyway, I got no signal out here. It's not that far into town and I'll get the rest of the items."

"No," commanded Erica. "You can't go. You have to stay here with Reilly…that's your place…"

"I'll go," said Caleb quickly.

"You feel up to it?" asked Erica as she reached out and felt his forehead. Weston looked away.

"Yeah…just give me a minute to get my energy back," he said.

Weston walked over to the IV and tapped the fluid bag. "We should be fine here for awhile. She's getting hydrated again. We should go into the living room and let her sleep," he said somberly.

All three walked like zombies into the main room of the cabin and landed in the first open seat each encountered. "God, I'm so tired," moaned Erica.

"So am I," said Caleb as he rubbed his head. "Everything aches."

Weston reached over to the radio on the coffee table and hit the button. Then he slumped back.

"And now," said the announcer, "an update on the flu situation in the United States. Here with us is correspondent Scott Archer."

"Stay home, folks. That's the latest word from the Center for Disease Control. The Director of the Zelticor flu vaccine initiative along with the White House Chief of Staff will be holding a joint press conference in a matter of minutes, and we are told that they will be joined by the head of homeland security who is expected to announce that three Americans--a scientist, a former employee of the Zelticor Pharmaceutical, and a murder suspect—may be responsible for the current epidemic..."

CHAPTER 40

"And now I'll take you live to the Zelticor press conference…"

"Good evening, fellow Americans. I am Howard McHann, director of the Zelticor Flu Vaccine Initiative. Today we hope to accomplish three things with this press conference: 1. Update you on the our current situation; 2. advise you of the appropriate actions to be taking at this time; and 3. talk about the terrorist actions taken by three of your fellow citizens…actions that have quite possible claimed dozens…maybe hundreds of lives."

Weston, Erica, and Caleb all turned to stare at the radio. "Well, we know who the scientist is," Weston stated flatly. "And we know who the former employee is…"

"Former?" asked Erica.

Weston continued sarcastically. "The question is…who is the murder suspect? Caleb, would you like to share something with us?"

"You're an idiot," shot back Caleb.

"Perhaps…but you're also apparently a murder suspect," Weston replied.

Holding up a blood spattered sleeve of his jacket, Caleb glared at Weston. "I've got proof of who's a murderer right here…do you?"

"Shut up, both of you!" commanded Erica. She reached over and turned up the radio.

"The number of fatal cases of the flu are growing far above the average number for the United States at this point in the flu season. A nursing home not far from here has reported the deaths of every resident of its east wing. We are currently researching the possibility of bioterrorism via the release of a potentially deadly virus. Our current recommendation is for you to stay home. Many schools and businesses are being temporarily shut closed. We urge you to get the current vaccine because this will help you build up your immunity even if it does not directly address this new strain. "

"No it won't," announced Weston. "Not if it's too late and

you've already been exposed."

"Shut up, Weston," snapped Erica.

"Now," announced McHann. "I will turn things over to the head of Homeland Security."

"Good evening," said a somber voice. "I come to you tonight with shocking news of terrorism from one of our own citizens. Dr. Weston Anderson, a world renowned scientist who has played a pivotal role in the World Health Organization's preparations for many viruses including the H5N1, is being charged with treason for terrorist acts against the American people. Dr. Anderson had been employed by Zelticor to create a vaccine for the American people...instead he developed a new virus and then went into hiding offering it to the highest bidder. Undercover agents also discovered that Dr. Anderson tampered with vaccines, so that many arriving in clinics are completely ineffective..."

"Bullshit!" shouted Weston. "That's a lie!"

Erica glared at Weston. Wiping the sweat from her forehead with her hand, she rubbed her hands on her jeans and walked into the kitchen. A moment later she returned with several glasses of water, offering them to Caleb and Weston. "So, you were...involved?" she asked hesitantly.

Weston bit his lip and looked out the window. "Yes," he replied somberly. "Yes."

Caleb slammed down the cup he was drinking from and said, "You were on the payroll of a company playing with people's lives? Tell me, Dr. Anderson, how much of a monster are you?"

Weston turned away from Caleb, who then grabbed the older man's shoulder and shoved him.

"Come on, Dr. Anderson! I've come this far through the looking glass with you. Goddamn it! Answer me...answer Erica. Are you killing her baby like you killed her friend? Are you killing her grandmother also?"

Weston turned and with all of his force slugged Caleb and sent him to the floor. "It's not like that at all!" he shouted.

"Where's grandma?" asked Erica suddenly realizing that she was not present.

"I...I haven't seen her...." Weston began.

"...since we got out of the car..." Caleb finished slowly. He rubbed his jaw and painstakingly stood up. Weston and Erica immediately headed out the door towards the van with Caleb following.

Inside the van Pearl sat rocking and softly singing "Bye bye baby...bye bye baby..." Like the soundtrack for a horror movie, her frail voice constantly repeated the words.

"Grandma!" shouted Erica. "Grandma!"

Pearl's glazed eyes continued to stare forward and her song played on.

"Granny! Hey, Granny!" yelled Caleb. "Let's take you inside." As he reached for her he saw the blood spatters across her arm. "...and let's get you cleaned up." Then he looked at her mouth. "You got it on your face too? Oh, God, we really gotta get you cleaned up..."

"That's not Carson's blood," gasped Erica.

Pearl began coughing again and blood splattered the across her hand.

"Get her inside," ordered Weston. "I don't know what I've got to help her....but get her inside."

Erica and Caleb began to ease Pearl from the van. Like a bizarre game of Twister they stretched and struggled to move her from the back seat. As she reached the door she fell onto Caleb who lost his footing and the two landed on the damp ground.

"Grandma!" shrieked Erica. Weston rushed over to lift Pearl off of Caleb.

"Is she okay?" asked Caleb as he struggled to his feet.

Weston picked up Pearl. Surprised by how easily he lifted her frail body, he almost flung her over his shoulder. "It's okay, Pearl. We're going to get you inside and get you some sleep."

He carried her into the bedroom across from Reilly followed closely by Caleb. "What have you got to help her?" Caleb asked.

"Nothing," Weston answered morbidly. Pursing his lips together he remained silent as he pulled a blanket to cover her up. Dust flew everywhere as he spread the blanket. "Bring her some juice or water...or something," he ordered and then left the room without looking back.

Caleb rushed to the kitchen stifling his own coughing. Opening the refrigerator he spotted a wooden box. Quietly he looked around then very carefully lifted its lid. In the box he spotted a vile half filled with clear liquid. Confused he very gently returned the lid and then picked up the pitcher of ice water that Erica had placed in earlier and poured Pearl a glass. He returned to Pearl's room with the image of the half full vile burned into his head. Erica sat by the bed washing Pearl's arms and face. When Pearl began a coughing fit, Erica quickly handed her the towels for coughing the blood into something besides her hands.

"Go lay down," Caleb said to Erica. "You need rest."

"I wish...I wish there was something more we could do," whispered Erica.

"Go rest," repeated Caleb. Then he reached into his pocket. "I found some adult Tylenol in my backpack you're welcome to use."

Erica stood up and stepped into the hallway and then stopped and grabbed Caleb's arm. "Something happened. Beeman, Weston's assistant, he showed up at our house with flu vaccine."

Erica and Caleb stood staring at one another silently.

"It's okay. Everything is going to be okay," reassured Caleb. But there was not one syllable that rang with confidence. He turned to walk away, but as he moved beyond Erica's grasp she stepped towards him and touched his shoulder.

"I don't know Weston. I thought I did. I do know this cabin...it's where we conceived Reilly. I actually thought I knew him then for a brief moment, but the truth is I've been chasing this illusion...this imaginary man who I thought would take one look into Reilly's eyes and become Dad of the year and sweep me off my feet. I was wrong."

"Go to sleep," said Caleb. "I'll keep watch. You go to sleep."

Erica entered Reilly's room, closed the door behind her, and then curled up with her baby…drifting to sleep with tears racing from her eyes to the sweat soaked curls on Reilly's head. Softly Erica prayed. "God, just this one thing…let this one thing be real from Weston. Let him save Reilly."

Caleb stood in the hallway listening to the prayer and then he slowly walked to the living room and stared out the window at Weston burying Carson. Taking one last drink of water, Caleb laid down on the couch waiting for the Tylenol to take effect. He would need his strength to rescue everyone from this man who now sat at the edge of a make shift grave a shovel on his lap, a riffle in one hand and a pint of whiskey in the other.

"Tomorrow you die," Caleb whispered and then closed his eyes falling asleep to the voice on the radio describing Weston's activities for the past week…and adding Caleb and Erica as the deadly assistants to one of the most unthinkable acts of terrorism on U.S. soil…

CHAPTER 41

"Hey! Hey! Wake up!" sputtered Weston into Caleb's face.

Startled Caleb shoved Weston aside and scrambled to his feet. "What the hell?" Caleb shouted.

"Your turn to take watch," Weston said wiping the whiskey from his mouth.

Yawning, Caleb rubbed his eyes and looked at Weston in the glow of the fireplace as he sprawled across the floor with a rifle in one hand and a bottle in the other. "Are you drunk?" asked Caleb.

"I need some sleep. Come on be a pal," Weston sputtered as he grabbed a cushion from a nearby chair and pulled it down to the floor.

"What am I watching for?" asked Caleb.

"*Them*...and check on Erica, Reilly and Pearl...oh, and watch out for *them*," Weston said as he closed his eyes.

Caleb stared at Weston and repeated, "Them?"

Briefly Weston opened his eyes and appeared lucid for a fleeting moment as he said, "Them. The angels of light...who bring darkness." Then his eyes closed again and he rolled over with one loud groan.

Caleb slowly removed the rifle from Weston's arms and walked over to the fireplace and leaned the riffle against the wall next to it. Throwing on a few logs, he sat down and stared into the flames. Hearing a whimper from the other room, he fumbled around towards the hallway, running his hands along the wall to find the switch in the darkness.

Once he had the hall light on, Caleb peered into the rooms. On his right lay Pearl, a feverish pile of bones. On his left he saw Erica asleep and looking peaceful in a way that he had never seen on her face before. Then he spotted something else he had never seen before— Reilly's blue eyes. The little girl looked up at Caleb quietly.

"Mama" she said.

Caleb smiled and then put his index finger to his lips. "Shhhhh. I'll be right back."

He returned a few minutes later with a baby bottle he had found in Erica's purse and then filled with juice, but Reilly had fallen back to sleep. Quietly he put the bottle on the nightstand and kissed her forehead. Then he returned to the living room, grabbed the riffle and then took the quilt away from Weston who was still curled on the floor.

"Brrrr," he whispered as he wrapped the quilt around himself and sat down with the rifle pointed at Weston's head. Staring out the large picture window, Caleb watched the unmoving darkness. Then he saw her. Wearing her favorite pink t-shirt and torn jeans, she was right there. "Sandra?" he asked as he stood up in disbelief. Frantically he felt around for the flashlight. "Sandra? Sandra! Wait!" he whispered.

Unable to find the flashlight, he groped his way to the door. He twisted the doorknob in a rush to go outside. The bitter air stung his face and arms, but still he moved forward into the dark. "Sandra!" he yelled. Then he turned and there she was standing with the wind to her back and her short, brown hair wiggling in the breeze.

"I'm sorry," he sobbed. "I'm so so sorry. I thought…I thought I was…it's…I'm going to kill him. He's going to pay…I'm so sorry…Sandra!"

Suddenly a bright light surrounded the figure. Growing stronger and stronger like an apocalyptic explosion all around the woman, it engulfed her. Caleb tried to scream, but only emptiness emerged. Blinded by the sun piercing his eyelids, Caleb tried to focus. He looked around to see the sunrise over the musty cabin with the cliché log furnishings that made up Weston's rural retreat.

Caleb took a moment to rub his still tear-filled eyes and with a renewed emptiness he returned to the cabin. Then he looked at the floor. Weston was gone. Frantically Caleb moved around the quilt and the couch throws and pillows.

"Looking for this?" asked a voice from behind.

Caleb snapped around to face Weston who held up the rifle. "Yeah. Yeah, I am old man."

Weston took a bite out of an apple and pulled the gun away just as Caleb reached for it. "Don't think so, Junior," he retorted. "Have a seat," he said waving at the chair nearby. "Oh, come on…I figured you'd like a chance to play the good news/bad news game."

Caleb sat down while glaring into Weston's eyes. Then his eyes darted to the rifle.

"Oh, I'm not going to shoot you," Weston said with an eerie chuckle that sent shivers down Caleb's spine. "No, I suppose that the people who have now surrounded our cabin will do that…see that's the bad news."

"And what's the good?"

"That you got a full night's sleep, you lazy little shit. You didn't watch outside at all did you?"

Caleb stood up. "Someone's out there?"

"You think I'm just paranoid, don't you?"

"Yes. Yes, I do," replied Caleb with confidence.

"Having someone point a rifle at you while you're trying to sleep will do that to you. What were your words? Oh, yeah, 'tomorrow you're dead'."

"I was tired and angry," replied Caleb. "I'm not a murderer."

"Does Sandra agree with you?" shot back Weston.

Caleb swung a punch, but Weston moved out of his way and then raised the rifle. "Sit down, Junior."

Caleb remained standing and stepped forward into Weston's face. "Okay, crazy man. Let's say you're not paranoid. Tell me who's out to get you. The boogie man?"

"Close," said Weston in the songlike tone of a man on the edge of sanity. "Try the Director of Homeland Security…Oh, and let's not forget his pals the Secretary of Defense, the Vice President and maybe even the President himself."

"Wow! All those people out to get a useless drunk…our country is in real trouble if you've been able to outsmart the whole administration. Good for you, Weston. Good for you."

"Shut up and sit down," he snapped. "I know something about their little pharmaceutical company that has been making them millions."

"Of course you do," replied Caleb in a patronizing tone. For a moment he walked away from Weston towards the window and looked out into the still of the morning. Then he turned back. "And what about Erica? Is she out to get you? Is she one of *them*?"

Weston sat down on the couch and laid down the gun. Then he sighed and looked down. "She wasn't supposed to be a part of any of this," he said as he wiped away the last of the whiskey from his mouth.

"Well where does she fit into this now?" Caleb asked as he too sat down.

"My grandfather...he was a scientist," Weston began. "Only he really believed the idea that the few should sacrifice for the many and he didn't bother himself with too many ethics committees when he wanted to do research. As a kid I thought that man was the whole world. He was a genius who made Einstein look stupid. I loved to visit him in the lab...to walk around the room...to see him working. That's why I became a scientist."

"How sweet," replied Caleb sarcastically.

"When I was in grad school, some of my grandfather's activities began to catch up to him. I mean he was making some incredible discoveries that ultimately would save many many lives, but people wanted to know how. I wanted to know how. He told me he used research from the Nazis..."

"As in Hitler?" asked Caleb with interest.

"Yes, sir. As in Hitler. You see Hitler had some horrific experiments going on...and my grandfather...well, he thought they could be useful."

"Great," replied Caleb sarcastically.

"Look I don't justify him, but when a scientist crosses the line and still comes up with something useful....well...let's just say maybe...just maybe they become discoveries that people like you use every day!" snapped Weston startling Caleb.

"Excuse me?" shot back Caleb indignant.

"Ever take an aspirin? Well, some of its early, most well-known producers made pretty good use of 'unauthorized' research, but we never take a moment to think about that," snarled Weston.

Caleb rolled his eyes. "Okay. Point made. So old gramps was using Nazi research…go on," said Caleb impatiently.

"He was also doing all new horrific experiments…on children. One day I went to meet him for lunch at his lab…he was getting older and forgetful. He wasn't there and he hadn't locked up his desk. I found his notes…lists of names…I…I couldn't believe it. So I grabbed everything I could and ran before he returned. He thought there'd been a break-in and the truth would finally come out. Right there at his desk he committed suicide waiting for me to arrive for lunch. I quit my own work that I was doing at the time…some of it was based on work from my grandfather and I just couldn't stomach using it…"

"Cancer," said Caleb as he took a deep breath.

"What?"

"You were working on cancer treatments…for pancreatic cancer."

"I…uh…yeah, I…how did you know that?"

"There was a drug…"

"Stregbuitan."

"You stopped clinical trials of it…you stopped a useful drug that people needed all because of your grandfather?"

"A minute ago you were appalled at the horrific experiments on human subjects, now you think it's okay because…because… let me guess Sandra? Well, listen, buddy, there was never any conclusive evidence and I needed to find out about where the data had come from. I needed to know because the drug would have never have gone forward without verification. It wasn't just my ethics!"

Caleb looked away from Weston, but the emotion in his voice told the story in his eyes. "You let people die."

"No, you just want to believe that I did."

"So what about Erica…was she one of your subjects? Is that

how she relates to all of this?"

Now it was Weston's turn to look away. He stood up and walked towards the window. Taking deep breaths he focused on an elm six feet from the porch.

"Answer the question," said Erica from the entrance to the hallway.

Startled Weston and Caleb both turned.

"Was I a lab experiment of yours?" she asked with controlled anger.

Weston focused on her deep green eyes for a moment. "Not mine..." he replied somberly. "...my grandfather's."

CHAPTER 42

Erica stood silently staring. Weston's eyes locked onto hers. Caleb looked back and forth between the two and then looked down.

Neither spoke. Neither moved. "Well, I guess I'll leave you two alone," Caleb mumbled, but remained silently seated.

Weston cleared his throat. "I've tried to set things right. I looked for everyone on my grandfather's list to help them…make them aware of what had happened to them…or at least that's how it started," replied Weston.

"You never warned me," Erica said in a tone that betrayed her anger which was still controlled but growing stronger.

"I wasn't sure I had the right person at first and then…you…we had that night…"

"…here at the cabin," she added.

"Yes, and I didn't know how to tell you. I mean what did you want me to say? 'I'm falling in love with you and oh, my grandfather used you in unethical experiments?'"

"Yes!" screamed Erica. Her explosion of anger startled both men. "Yes, you bastard! This was my life!" Erica stopped for a moment as realization swept across her face. "My heart problems? I had heart problems as a child," she whispered as her mind wandered briefly. "Do you have any idea what it's like to be told that you may be dying when you're only eight-years-old? That's what doctors told my parents, that I had heart problems. They said I'd never lead a normal life as an adult and I spent most of my childhood on the living room couch." A tear streaked her face as her expression darkened. "Was all of that because of your grandfather?"

Weston took a step towards Erica, but she pulled away. "The experiment began with your mother," he said softly. "He gave her drugs during her pregnancy….she was told they were for morning sickness, but actually he wanted to explore fetal heart development. There were several pregnant women used at the time…most of them lost their babies. You…you were lucky…the damage was minimal."

"Minimal?" Erica gasped. "My whole life changed and you say it was minimal?" For a moment she stared deeply into his eyes. "And Reilly? Is there anything wrong with Reilly?"

"No...she's fine. You were fine...you outgrew the effects. I planned to tell you, but...things got complicated."

"Complicated? Is that why you cut me off? One day we're getting married and the next you just disappear from my life? First you don't show up for the ultra sound and then you call off the wedding."

"I should have been at the ultra sound," Weston blurted. "Your mother was right to come to tell me off. I was afraid...afraid to find out something was wrong with our baby."

"You weren't even man enough to come and find out," Erica cried and then cupped her hand over her mouth. "Our plans and dreams."

"I was at her birth! I was going to marry you, Erica! But you always want so badly to live the fairy tale and it has never existed! We didn't meet across some crowded room on a starlit night. I looked you up after finding your name in my grandfather's notes. My family arranged for you to get that scholarship to the university to make amends. Then...then you ended up in one of my classes,"

"How beautiful," Caleb said sarcastically. "You were a lab experiment, Erica!"

The words echoed and then hung in the air. They were frozen in the middle of the room with nothing to remove them. Erica choked on her tears. Weston gasped for air.

"Oh god! I am so sorry," Weston said reaching out to her.

Erica pulled away and stared with anger and hatred in her eyes. Finally, Caleb stood. The rustling of his coat seemed amplified, but still the words remained. Erica rushed out of the room with her hands covering her face.

"So now what?" asked Caleb coolly.

"Now?" asked Weston in horror like a man whose last straw of sanity had been torched. "Now?" he whispered. "Well, my dear boy, I made a deal with the devil. Cliché I know, but isn't that what all mad scientists like myself do?" Weston walked over to the window and stared out. He thought he saw the bushes rustling despite the absence of wind and he hung his head. "Now I'm trying to stop the monster I created, a monster that others want to live."

"Weston, you had better come clean with me right now. Totally and completely," Caleb said with urgency.

"I was asked to develop a more accurate method of anticipating flu mutations and make vaccine production more efficient and instead I created a new virus strain that the Homeland Security was saying had potential to be used..."

"...potential..." Caleb repeated harshly.

"Yes, potential for a weapon or defense...oh who knows!" responded Weston. "I swear I stayed focused on my job. I wanted to help people, but then I discovered everyone was more interested in my new strain virus than in saving the world."

"I'm not following you," said Caleb.

"I didn't stop working on my assigned task voluntarily."

"You were told to stop?" asked Caleb.

"Yes," replied Weston.

Just then Erica returned to the room wiping her eyes with a tissue. "And my mother? What was her role in this?"

Weston avoided Erica's glare. "I told you already. In layman's terms she burst into my lab, broke test tubes and got exposed. Then she carried the virus to the nursing home when she went to visit your grandmother...only your grandmother already had a cold so she was not allowed visitors that week. It took awhile for her to finally get infected when the quarantine of those suffering from RCG3598 got botched at the home."

Caleb looked at Erica and Weston with a puzzled expression. Shaking his head he asked, "So ultimately you're to blame?" Stepping away from Weston, Caleb looked out the window trying to gain composure. Then he spotted the rustling bushes. He looked at Erica and reached out his hand. "Erica, we need to get out of here and turn him in."

Weston rushed between Caleb and Erica. Staring in Erica's eyes, he pleaded, "Wait! Please, Erica, wait! My error was in not going above my department about the lab breach and the exposure, but I already knew things were in motion and I thought if Beeman and I could contain it…" his voice trailed off as he stared at her.

"You're saying someone else is running the show over there," she said coldly.

"Yes, and that's why we're in hiding."

"What does Reilly have to do with any of this? Why take her?" insisted Erica.

"And why return her?" interjected Caleb.

"I said they were using her to silence me," insisted Weston. "And possibly to observe if she had been exposed to the virus she would be their youngest test subject to date."

"Then why do we have her back?" shouted Caleb.

"I don't know…"

"Erica, tell him!" Caleb said harshly.

Erica stared in horror.

"Tell me what?"

"Tell him!" Caleb's voice grew louder.

"Beeman came and gave Reilly a flu shot," she gasp hanging her head. "He gave her an injection."

Weston's mouth fell open and he slumped down into the chair behind him. For a moment he simply ran his hands through his hair over and over and over. Finally, he spoke. "You let him give our child an injection?"

"He said you asked him to do it," Erica said softly with her lips quivering. She approached Weston and knelt down beside him. "I would never do anything to hurt Reilly. I thought...I honestly thought..."

Weston embraced Erica and for a moment the parents held one another tightly.

"I need to get Beeman here," Weston said with resolve. "I'm going to make at least one thing right. I promise you, Erica."

"How?" asked Caleb. "Exactly how are you getting Beeman out here?"

"Don't worry about that," Weston declared. "I can do this."

"Hold it! I'm still not clear here," said Caleb.

"Listen, kid, bioterrorism is a reality. No one is supposed to be doing it, but....there are people who believe since it exists we need to be a part of it or die," Weston sighed as he rubbed the back of his neck.

"So our country is engaged in bioterrorism?" asked Caleb astonished.

Weston shook his head vehemently. "Whoa! I didn't say that. You don't get it do you, kid? This is a wakeup call. We'll use this as a test run, get findings set up programs."

"And all the while it becomes big business for someone," Erica blurted.

"Okay, so why are we not turning in this guy because quite frankly I don't care about all this smoke and mirrors crap?" Caleb asked as he turned to Erica.

Erica took a deep breath and brushed the hair from her face. Then she said, "They need a fall guy."

"Fall guy? Give me a break, Erica. There's still a simple answer to the question of who started this epidemic," sniped Caleb.

"I tried to contain it," Weston's words grew soft. "They took advantage of my attempts to avoid a panic."

Caleb and Erica stared at Weston.

"Okay, the truth is," Weston confessed slowly, "the truth is that this probably would have happened anyway. It just shouldn't have come from my lab. I am to blame."

Caleb rolled his eyes.

"It really doesn't matter at this point," responded Erica. "Caleb, until we have leverage, we can't just walk into their hands. You're heard the news. Weston isn't the only one in this room being labeled as a terrorist as far as they're concerned."

"You let those people die in the nursing home," Caleb shouted at Weston.

Weston turned silently towards the fireplace. "I can save Reilly. Maybe I can straighten out all of this, but I need time."

"We need to expose whoever is controlling it now," stated Erica. "If we can do that, we can get out of this, right?"

"Possibly," replied Weston. "In town…a safe deposit box. I've got evidence. I swear," said Weston. "That's what will bring Beeman here and maybe we can get some other answers."

"I'll go and get it," said Erica. As Weston opened his mouth to object she blurted, "Obviously you can't go. Your face is everywhere as a terrorist."

"Are you sure you feel up to it?" asked Weston.

"No, no I don't, but that's why I need it," answered Erica as she shivered slightly. Then she looked from Weston to Caleb, both trembling with their fevers. "That's why we all need it."

"I'll go too," said Caleb.

Erica paused and looked at Weston. "Can you…are you up to…"

"I can take care of my own daughter," he stated. Then they heard a low wail coming from Pearl's room. "You should…you should say goodbye to her because….just because," Weston's words trailed off as he motioned to the room from which the moaning seeped through the cracks in the door.

CHAPTER 43

Erica silently entered Pearl's room. Caleb followed her leaving Weston to sit and stare out the window and nurse yet another bottle of whiskey.

"Grandma?" whispered Erica.

Pearl rocked back and forth in the bed slowly.

"Grandma? Can you hear me?" asked Erica.

"We should do something…we need to help her," said Caleb into Erica's ear as he stood behind her. "Weston is a mad man," he added.

Erica turned and looked at Caleb. Tears streamed down her face in graceful silence. She rubbed her nose across her the sleeve of her shirt and then walked to the window.

Caleb followed her. "You're going to let your grandmother die because of this lunatic? We need to get help. What if he's lying?" Caleb whispered. "What if he is a terrorist?"

"I don't know about that, but I do know we need to get help," said Erica. Then she nodded towards Pearl. "Unless it's too late. The problem, Caleb, is that I think it may be. At least for her. Let's give her some Tylenol and juice and then we have to get help, help for us all."

"Then let's go," Caleb replied.

Erica put her hand on his arm. "I won't excuse anything he's done, but none of us are getting help until we get ourselves out of this madness."

"So you trust, Weston?" Caleb asked.

"Hey, I didn't say I trust him," she shot back. "I've learned that the hard way, but I don't trust you either," she said matter of factly. "I've known Weston for years. I've known you less than a week. Now I've just got to go with my gut."

They both looked at the elderly woman rocking in the bed, her body so thin that each movement looked like it might snap a limb off from her frail frame. Sweaty and bloodied, the body rocked and moaned.

Caleb quietly left and then returned with a pill and some juice. He and Erica struggled to get anything down Pearl's throat.

"Go get some rags and let's wash her up," said Erica as she wiped her own juice covered hands on her jeans.

After Caleb walked out Erica leaned in towards Pearl. "I'm sorry, Grandma. I'm so very, very sorry."

Pearl's eyes looked up into Erica's. They were tiny gray mirrors in the midst of an otherwise vacant stare, mirrors with one tiny little spark still visible.

"Bring me my baby," Pearl begged. "He shouldn't die alone…without his mamma. No one should take a baby away from his mamma when he's dying," she pleaded.

Caleb returned and began to wipe Pearl's face and arms.

Erica and Caleb looked at one another. Then Erica looked around the room. Going over to Reilly's diaper bag, Erica pulled out a rag doll and brought it over to Pearl. Tenderly she placed it in her grandmother's arms.

"Here. Here's your baby," Erica said softly. "And he's not dying. He's right here for you to take care of," she whispered.

Pearl's eyes never left Erica's as she spoke. For one moment Pearl became lucid again. "Why?" she rasped. "Why doesn't anyone ever investigate when an old person dies?" she asked. "At the home people died. No one ever asked 'Why?'"

More tears filled Erica's eyes. "I'm going to ask why," she said. "I promise. Right now you rest. I'll be back soon with help. Just hold on."

Pearl grasped the rag doll and began to choke out a lullaby. Then she paused. "Where's Paulser?" she asked.

Caleb looked at Erica. "He's coming," Erica replied compassionately. "He's coming, Grandma."

Caleb moved quietly to the hallway and stood with his head

bowed as he listened to Pearl's haunting whispers.

"I knew my husband wouldn't leave me alone with a dying baby. I knew he'd be here. We'll have a very nice funeral…I love my babies," Pearl whispered and began to cry.

"I know you love your babies," reassured Erica. "Paulser will be here soon and it will all be okay." She leaned over and kissed her grandmother's feverish forehead.

Then with amazing clarity, Pearl swallowed hard, looked Erica in the eyes, and said, "That man killed Ann. He pushed her down the stairs when they were yelling about God."

"No, Grandma," Erica said gently. "Ann died in a car accident. She was my mother. You and I sat at the funeral together. Remember?"

"Ann fell down stairs and the other man pulled out a wood box and gave her a shot." Pearl said in a chilling tone as she nodded towards the doorway where Caleb stood now joined by Weston.

CHAPTER 44

Erica turned to look at the two men.

"What's wrong?" asked Caleb as he took a few steps into the room.

"I don't know," said Erica puzzled.

Weston leaned in nervously. "She's just rambling." He said.

Erica looked Weston with concern as she began smoothing the blankets. "I love you, Grandma," she whispered leaning over the frail woman. "Now you get some sleep."

Erica's body tensed as she stood up and approached the doorway passing silently by Caleb and Weston.

"Are you ready to go?" asked Weston following Erica into the hallway.

She said nothing, but stepped quickly to the living room. Stopping near the fireplace she reached for the poker and began to jab at the obviously dying flames.

Caleb and Weston exchanged glances before following Erica. Both stopped just inside the room and stood silently watching her. After a minute Weston cleared his throat and broke the silence. "Erica? I know you're upset about your grandmother, but we need to pull things together. Remember the plan?"

"When my mother came to see you, did you give her a shot?" Erica asked pointedly.

"A shot?" asked Weston dumbfounded. "No, why would I give her a shot?"

"My grandmother said..."

"Your grandmother wasn't with your mother at my lab," blurted Weston quickly.

"And besides she's not exactly coherent right now," added Caleb quickly. "Why what did she tell you?"

204

"What do you care?" asked Erica staring at Caleb. "Why would you be in the least bit concerned what she'd have to say?"

"I...I don't," sputtered Caleb.

"Is there something you wanted to say?" asked Weston staring intently at Erica. He stopped for a moment as he began to cough uncontrollably.

Erica looked at the speckles of blood on his hand that had come from his mouth and she cringed. Quickly her eyes darted away. "No. No, nothing. Let's go," she said to Caleb.

Caleb also turned and pretended to be looking at dried skin on his fingers. He could feel the urge to cough inside of himself, but swallowed it down for fear that he also was going to spew blood. "Let's go," he said softly to Erica in a voice laced with despair.

Erica's body was shaking slightly. She tried to control it, so that the others wouldn't see. Then she pulled on her coat.

"You sure?" asked Caleb. With the question the coughing escaped from his lungs. He turned and coughed violently into his hands. Gasping for breath, Caleb's body wretched horrifically.

"Caleb? Caleb?" asked Erica frantically. "Caleb?"

"It's time to go. Go. Go now," commanded Weston.

Caleb's cough began to subside and he sat down trying to catch his breath. He immediately shoved his hands into his pockets and then into the leather gloves that were in them. Never once did he dare to look for fear that he would see his own blood splattered across his palms.

"So where are we going?" Erica asked Weston.

Quietly Weston handed her a piece of paper from his pocket. "Don't speak to anyone. Just hand them this at the lock shop," he whispered. "And whatever you do, don't get caught. If you do, you'll go down and we'll all die."

"What?" whispered Caleb confused.

"Just do it right," insisted Weston with a hint of frustration.

Silently Caleb and Erica walked towards the door. Erica hesitated and looked at Reilly's room.

"Go now. I'll take care of her…I promise," Weston said softly as he nodded his head. Then he looked at Caleb. "And when you both return, I'll turn myself in. You two can go and get away. Just this last thing…I need you to do this so we can ensure that at least you two can get out of this and save Reilly."

With his final words he looked directly into Erica's eyes. For a moment he thought he saw a spark of caring in Erica's eyes. Then she turned away and nodded silently as she and Caleb left through the front door of the cabin.

Weston stumbled onto the couch. His jaw throbbed and the rest of his body had begun to shake violently from chills. He could feel another coughing fit coming on, but he tried to stop it by grabbing a bottle of Vodka. Instead he spewed Vodka and blood back into the bottle and down the sides of it.

He never saw the bushes begin to rustle again. Nor did he see the dark figures emerge as they watched Erica and Caleb head towards town and exit from view.

CHAPTER 45

Wobbling slightly Weston strained to focus in the dimly lit room.

"Ann?" he asked as he leaned forward towards the shadows. "Ann?"

For a moment she was there, in front of him. She was holding the small picture. "This is your child!" she screamed waving it around. "Some great father you're going to be! Couldn't even make to the ultra sound. You're just like Erica's worthless father. With all of Erica's education, she couldn't even find a better person than a loser like you!"

Clutching the Vodka bottle tightly, he wiped at the sweat dribbling down the wrinkles on his forehead into his eyes. "Ann! Ann!" he rasped. "I'm so sorry!"

"A little late now, isn't it, Dr. Anderson?" asked a deep voice.

Startled Weston fell off of his chair onto the floor as he jerked his head around to look up. "Beeman?" he asked finally.

"Weston, you're a mess. You don't even make a good terrorist. You're just an alcohol soaked loser." As Beeman spoke he looked around the room and removed his gloves. Walking over to the fireplace he reached for the poker and jabbed at the cold embers and sighed. "I really thought you'd go out like some super techno geek. You know, give us all a real run for our money."

Weston rubbed his head and then pulled himself back onto the chair as he attempted to straighten his sweat soaked shirt. "What do you want from me?" he hissed finally.

Beeman smiled. "From you? Nothing." Then the smile disappeared. "Your child, is it still alive?"

"What did you give her?" said Weston finding the first real strength he had felt in days. Standing up he towered over Beeman.

"What?"

Weston took an imposing step forward and grabbed Beeman's

collar. "Erica said you gave her a shot. What did you give her?"

Beeman pulled back and broke free sending Weston staggering backwards. "The baby? Here's something funny," said Beeman as a devilish grin spread across his face. "I actually gave her a vaccine that is showing quite a bit of promise for your little creation…you know that virus that is so quickly spreading and leaving bodies in its wake."

"I didn't create a vaccine for it yet," shouted Weston.

Beeman rolled his eyes. "Oh, and the great Dr. Weston is the only one who could do it?"

Weston staggered to his feet again, but this time Beeman's fist met his right cheekbone just beneath the eye. "What the hell?" shouted Weston as he hit the ground.

"Shut up and just listen for once. Will you?" Beeman snapped. "Your little brat is only alive right now because I gave her that shot. According to our research so far no one under the age of two whose been infected has survived this virus. They die in less than five days," he said somberly.

Remaining on the floor, Weston straightened up slightly as he rubbed his cheek. "So why? Why give it to Reilly?"

"That's the funny part really," smirked Beeman. "I went there to plant evidence of you killing that woman in the stairwell. Only I got there and your little girlfriend said you never come around anymore. So it was highly unlikely that she or anyone else would believe you left something there."

"I didn't kill her," Weston insisted. "You were there. You know it."

"I was there, indeed," said Beeman with a hint of anger. "I cleaned up your mess. She threatened to tell everyone about what we were doing. She was going to ruin it all. Your career and mine. Mine because I so foolishly let you talk me into covering up the virus exposure."

Weston lumbered to his feet and stood for a moment glaring at Beeman. "She was alive? She talked to you?" he said in astonishment.

"Temporarily, yes."

A look of horror swept over Weston's face. "You? You killed her?"

Beeman sucked in his cheeks for a moment and then rolled his head from side to side as if to remove a cramp. "I injected her with poison. The same poison that you'll now find in your refrigerator. The same poison that I do believe your new friend Caleb Phillips has already discovered."

Weston's lips began to form the word "why" but it never passed into sound.

Beeman smiled slightly at the sight and walked over to the window. With his back to Weston he replied, "I needed leverage. In case we got caught. I needed a way to say it was all your fault."

"I was the department head, so yes I take responsibility, and have taken it throughout, but I have video to the contrary. I told you that day to call the authorities and you told me that it was done. People showed up at that nursing home that I thought were the CDC and other government officials. But they weren't, were they?" Weston's voice now rang of pent up anger. "Six days of you telling me everyone had been notified while I was up to my elbows in elderly people dying faster than I could help them."

"Future initiatives," said Beeman.

"What?" shouted Weston as he approached Beeman and then grabbed him by the shoulder.

Beeman whirled around to face Weston. "The Department of Future Initiatives at Astrium International. They're a department who handles, well, items that might be significant to powerful people for future development."

"So why Ann?"

"Bad enough that she burst into your lab, but then when she insisted on seeing old granny at the nursing home and then spotted you working there, well, she couldn't leave alive. You shoving her downstairs made it perfect."

209

"I didn't shove her. She fell. We were standing in the stairwell, she was demanding to know what was happening and then she fell. She shoved me and then lost her balance and fell on her own. I tried to help her…"

Beeman pulled a .45 caliber pistol from his pocket and pointed it at Weston. "Stop being an idiot. She had to die. We both knew it!" Beeman screamed.

Reilly began to cry in the other room. Both men turned to look at the hallway leading to her room.

"She needs to come with me," hissed Beeman. "We need to know why the vaccine worked on her."

"You'll have to kill me first!" screamed Weston.

"If you insist!" shouted Beeman. Then a shot rang out.

CHAPTER 46

"I don't think that stealing a car is a way to keep out of the spotlight," whispered Erica as she followed Caleb down a trail to a series of cabins. Erica swatted at flies and mosquitoes as she shuffled down the dirt path that lead away from Weston's cabin.

"I saw it when we passed by here earlier. No one is home," he said. Then reaching the vehicle he turned to Erica and smiled. "Completely unlocked...maybe they wanted us to have it," Caleb whispered halfheartedly joked. "Besides, I don't know if Dr. Anderson is paranoid or living out a nightmare, but I just thought..."

Erica put a finger to her lips to indicate the need for silence. Quickly they got into the black Ford Explorer and Caleb flipped down the visor. Keys smacked his forehead.

"Damn!" he blurted.

"Shhhh!" said Erica.

Caleb started the car and they peeled out of the driveway and headed towards the main road to town.

"Oh, don't get me wrong," said Erica as she looked behind them. "It did seem the smart thing to dodge out through the trees and find a car they won't associate with us...I just don't think we're outsmarting anyone who really wants to watch us and now we've added the possibility of local law enforcement."

They drove along the narrow, dirt road in silence. Erica closed her eyes and tried to breath in the smell of the pine trees they were passing, but her nose was too clogged. Still she remembered driving this road so many times with Weston, laughing and talking.

"I think I've forgotten my birth control pills," she told Weston that last time they came out to the cabin.

"We'll pick something up in town," he told her. "Besides, you probably put them in your suitcase and just forgot."

He always had an answer, a solution. That's what Erica had liked about him. There was nothing tragic or beyond his powers...at least back then. "I didn't even see this coming," she whispered.

"What?" asked Caleb startling her.

"Oh, nothing," she sighed realizing she had said it aloud. Then she touched her hair, matted and frizzy. "Oh, god, I must look a mess!" she said.

Caleb smiled at her and then looked out at the road again. "Well, for someone one the run, you actually look pretty good," he replied.

Erica smiled back. "Oh, and you're an expert on being on the run?" she joked.

Suddenly Caleb's smile vanished and he stared ahead intently. "What does the paper say?"

"What?"

"The paper! The one Weston gave you. What does it say?" he snipped angrily.

"Relax," Erica shot back startled by his mood change. She began to search for the paper among the pile of tissues she had strewn across the seat.

"Relax? Relax? Sure! Why the hell not? After all, it's not my kid back there with the lunatic!" he snapped.

Erica looked up abruptly. Then she sat up straight and moved ever so slightly towards the door. "Excuse me?" she asked coldly.

"I'm sorry. Just give me the directions. I feel like shit. We should be seeing doctors!"

"Yeah, we all feel like shit. So let's get this job done and all go home!" Erica replied. "But that's not what set you off just now. Who are you anyway? I know why I'm here, but I have yet to understand you."

"You heard it all earlier. Weston he...he killed my..." Caleb sputtered out the words.

"Wife? You're trying to say the study he stopped makes him

responsible for your wife's death?" Erica asked softly. "So let's see. You decided to be the hero and come and kill Weston?"

Caleb focused on the road. "What I have decided doesn't matter," he mumbled.

"Well apparently it does because you're out here with me. And I know you're working for someone...I heard you."

"Yes," he replied hoarsely, then paused. "I was...a senator who hung me out to dry. His re-election campaign must be doing better. Does any of that matter now?" he shot back.

"Why do the police think that you killed your wife?" Erica shouted.

Caleb swerved to the side of the road almost hitting a tree. Tissues and paper scattered across the seats and the floor and Erica's head snapped back against the window.

"You really want to know?" he shouted as he slammed the gear shift into park. "I'll tell you why! Because the most beautiful, brave woman I had ever known was turning into a skeleton in front of my eyes. Do you know that on September 11th she was in Tower 2? She was there trying to get a new account. We lived in New York back then. She was on her way out when it all started. Instead of just leaving, when all the chaos started, she went back to the office she had just been in. She went back 'cause there was this woman back in that office on crutches. Sandra went back and told everyone to leave and then she helped this woman out. She didn't have to."

Caleb put his head against the steering wheel. "I was so proud of her. I was so god damn pissed too. She could have died. But then maybe that would have been better."

"I don't follow you," Erica said softly.

"She had breathing problems after that day...she just wasn't right. Then they told her that she had cancer...among other problems..." Caleb kept his head pushed against the steering wheel as he shook it. Tears dropped onto his khaki pants. "But there was hope...there was hope and then there wasn't hope."

Caleb looked up, his eyes were red and rimmed with tears. Like a child waking from a night terror, Caleb stared at Erica. He blew his nose on a tissue nearby and then cleared his throat. "I began to suspect that nothing was being done. That she was simply a guinea pig because of all the things they tried on her..."

"Maybe they just didn't know. Maybe what she experienced in all that debris hadn't been charted before," said Erica.

"She asked me to be brave. She asked me to be brave like her." Caleb's voice broke up as he spoke. "Every moment was pain...pain...that's all it was. So I took her home from the hospital. I made her a great meal, not that she could eat it and what she did swallow came right back up. Then I kissed her and we looked at old photos. She rarely slept, but that night she smiled at me and dozed off." Caleb bowed his head and his words began to trail off softly. "Then I... I set her free. I made her free from the pain."

Erica stared in disbelief. "I'm so sorry," she sputtered. "I'm really so very sorry."

Caleb took a deep breath, cleared his throat and then lifted his head. He started the car and began to drive. "My father and Senator Harris were college roommates. The Senator agreed to help us out. Suddenly it became a suicide and I was granted my own freedom."

"No you weren't," replied Erica as she rubbed the back of her head.

"You're right. I couldn't be free...not without Sandra."

"...and then there's Harris...Harris..." added Erica. "and Harris wanted a favor.".

"Yes," Caleb said softly.

They drove for several miles down the curving roads. Caleb kept an eye on the rear view mirror for any vehicles that seemed to be behind them too long. Nothing eventful happened and for a brief moment they were just two people in the beautiful wooded countryside.

"What did Harris want from you?" Erica asked finally. "It may be important to us understanding what's going on here."

Caleb looked over at Erica. Then he stared forward in silence for another minute. "He wanted to find out if there was going to be a potential scandal with one of his political cronies. The upcoming election is pretty important to his party and there were whispers of a certain lobbyist and a member of the administration making some big bucks off something questionable at a pharmaceutical company."

"Bigger than usual?" asked Erica.

"Yeah. In fact, it was a huge profit. But the real problem was that the UN and WHO were asking questions. You see, certain...uh...scientists, I guess that's what you'd call them, anyway they were employed by Zelticor and were really hyping up this whole H5N1 virus. In some countries there were panicked people rioting at clinics."

"Then the question came up of why were there so few cases in this country," Erica stated, "questions of why the U.S. was seemingly exempt."

"So you know the story?"

"I work for the Zelticor's parent company, Astrium International. My employer makes sure to monitor these things and I know Homeland Security was all over us...two weeks ago we were accused of inaccurate reporting. Marcus was going to head a new task force to consider re-vamping the vaccine development."

"Marcus make any particularly large purchases lately?" asked Caleb.

"Turn left here," said Erica as she looked at the map. "Yes. Yes, indeed. In fact, Marcus was usually strapped for cash, because he really liked to spend Friday nights at the casino. Then about a month ago he suddenly had money to burn. We all joked that his casino time had finally paid off."

They began to approach the town and Caleb slowed down near a tourist site. "Horse rental," he read on the large sign. "Okay, so maybe we didn't need to steal a car."

"Sure. We could have stolen a horse" said Erica dryly. Then she turned to him. "But I still don't understand. Why you?"

"I was puttering around doing cyber security. Investigating

Weston seemed to Harris like a good fit for paying back the favor I owed him."

Erica unbuckled her seatbelt and turned to face Caleb. "But why not pick us up? Huh? They could have had us a million times...they could have had Weston and completely ignored us. Is this all really going on...outside of Weston's head?"

"Well, we're definitely missing a piece of the puzzle."

"Maybe you should..."

"Call Senator Harris..." Caleb reached for his cell phone and began to dial.

Erica flipped down the visor and looked into the mirror. She began to try to play with her hair. "There must be something else...something we're missing."

Caleb stopped dialing. He froze. Staring at Erica, his mouth slowly opened. "Get a horse. It's the fastest way back to the cabin and you can get off road. Get back to the cabin right away. I know what they're after...you have to get back there before it's too late."

"Too late for what?" asked Erica.

"I said go!" shouted Caleb. "You need to get back there and a horse is your best bet."

"But I haven't ridden a horse since high school!" protested Erica as she unbuckled, flung open the door and jumped out of the vehicle. She said nothing as she paused once more to look at Caleb. Then she headed for the stable.

Caleb turned his attention back to the cell phone. "Hello? Senator Harris? It's all coming together now," he said while smiling wryly. Looking up he watched Erica disappear on a horse into the woods. He waited to see if anyone had noticed she took the horse, but the area remained still and silent as a light rain began to fall.

"I think you know where I am right now. Get here. NOW!" Caleb barked. "You'll have everything you've been waiting for." Then he hit the off button and dropped the cell phone.

CHAPTER 47

For a moment, Caleb continued to stare. Feverish and exhausted, he had no more strength. *Time to sleep*, he whispered as he slumped over into the passenger's seat. *Time to sleep.*

"Caleb, go!" a shrill voice rang in his ears. "Caleb, go!"

"Sandra?" Caleb gasped. His mouth was so dry he felt like he was choking, Caleb struggled to respond. He looked up at the driver's side window and saw a figure. "Sandra? Oh, god!" he sobbed. "I'm so tired..." he gagged as he struggled to swallow. He began to twist in an effort to remove his coat while still laying in the seat, then he saw the figure again. "A gun? Sandra?" he gasped. Then everything went dark.

"Hello, Sleeping Beauty," rasped a voice.

Caleb opened his eyes. Blurred figures danced all around him. He began to cough.

"Throw some water on him," came a voice from one of the blurs.

"Water, water..." Caleb mumbled.

"Open your eyes," barked the voice.

Caleb's body shivered slightly as it fought the fever. He wiped his eyes and saw a glass of water near him. Reaching for it, Caleb's hand shook. *Water! Water!* His sweaty hand shook violently resisting his attempts to bring it to his lips.

"Goddamn it! Someone help the idiot...least we can do for a dying man," the voice replied.

Then the water reached his lips. Caleb choked and gagged as the wonderful liquid reached him. He sat back and took a deep breath that sent him into a coughing fit. As his body convulsed he heard the words in his head...*a dying man*. The coughing subsided and he wiped his eyes and his face with his crusty sleeve.

"Okay, Sleeping Beauty," said the voice again.

Caleb focused. "Senator?" he gasped.

"Who were you expecting, Caleb? Your poor wife who you put a bullet through after a night of drinking?"

Caleb struggled to sit upright. Then he looked around the room at the various goons Harris had brought. Finally, his eyes came to rest on Harris' face. Managing a nod, Caleb replied coldly, "Go to hell, Senator. I'm sure you'll be right at home."

"Well, listen to that," replied Harris sarcastically. He made a broad sweeping motion with his arm around the barren banquet room. "Isn't he something? We drag him into the backroom of this dump of a diner and he acts like he's the queen of England. You and your friends will be dead by dinner time, but I promise to tell everyone what a gracious host you were right to the end," he added dryly.

"You're going to kill them?" asked a nearby figure.

Caleb looked up at one of the men leaning against a pile of stacked chairs. The smell of mold and dust cloaked every breath he inhaled.

Harris turned violently and glared with fierce anger as he tightened his lips. "Shut up, idiot. You're here to hold the gun and be a witness that I did nothing wrong. So shut up!"

"Yeah, he's not killing anyone. We're going to die all by ourselves," snapped Caleb. "You just plan to supervise the autopsy, right Harris?"

Harris chuckled manically. "Well, you are smarter than I thought. Too bad it took you so long to catch on."

Caleb labored to clear his throat. "Let me see if I've got this all straight. You didn't send me to find out about Dr. Anderson's work at all. You sent me and Erica and her baby into the virus infested nightmare so you could watch us die. And then what? Uh, you sell the virus to the highest bidder?"

Harris smiled and laughed as he drank the remaining water from Caleb's glass. He looked up and saw the stares of disbelief on the faces around him. Then he chuckled. "Virus, vaccine, who knows? Both will fetch an amazing price. I've got it. You don't..."

"No..." Caleb's words got lost among the razors blades that

218

seemed to be sliding down his throat.

"Yes, you idiot. I've got a vaccine that none of you have. Oh, and you've got a few things wrong in your story. First of all, I did send you to find out about Dr. Anderson. But then you stumbled onto something better. You and your little girlfriend there walked right into an experiment being conducted by....well let's just say parties truly interested in national security."

"What?" asked Caleb incredulously.

"I came to see that simply knowing whether or not Dr. Anderson was going to spill the beans about some of my colleagues wasn't an issue anymore. There was some money to be made."

"And what about your constituents?" snapped Caleb.

"What about them? They see me in church every Sunday singing as loud as I can and all is right in their worlds!" Then Harris began to chuckle. "Anyway, America needs to protect itself and let's face it, someone needs to do the research studies that the general public just doesn't have the stomach for..." Harris paused and looked at Caleb's face. "Come on! Ultimately even you benefit...we all do. We just don't like to admit it."

"And the good Reverend Lewis?"

Harris laughed. "You're kidding, right?"

Caleb closed his eyes. Then he tried to steal a look at his watch without Harris noticing. Unfortunately the numbers escaped his focus and he looked up again. "I need some water," he said flatly.

Harris nodded at one of the men nearby who left the room and returned with a pitcher of water and more glasses. As he poured the water Caleb's shaking hand extended, ready to grab the minute the glass was filled.

"I don't need to tell you that Reverend Lewis has the money to accomplish anything he wants and right now what he wants is a safer America."

Caleb gulped down the water and then stopped for a moment. "You're sick," he blurted.

"I didn't say I believed any of Lewis' shit and quite frankly I'd be real surprised if Reverend Lewis himself believes it and he's the head of the whole shebang. But he does believe that there is an element in the United States out to get the faithful...and without his flock there's no radio show, no book sales, no seminars, no political clout." Harris laughed. "Son, it's all about being on the winning team. Reverend Lewis' followers—who I might say total a pretty hefty number in this country—want to know they're safe and if someone keeps telling them they are, then they are. So they pony up the money without even knowing it, to help us keep medical science advancing. Funny thing is, most of them think their dime is going to fight stem cell research."

Caleb looked up confused.

"You still don't get it, do you?" asked Harris as he leaned in towards Caleb. "This medical research is messy, but necessary. You'd be amazed at how much of what you currently take for granted came about in not so nice ways. But when you need that life saving surgery or that pill to get you through the night, well maybe you just don't care." Then Harris laughed. "But God save the embryos! Keep people fighting shadows and they get too tired to throw punches where they're needed."

Caleb tried to stand up. The room rocked slightly as he gripped the table to steady himself.

"Don't leave now....you haven't heard the best part," said Harris.

Unable to leave, Caleb dropped back into his seat.

"You deserve to know the truth before you die...I owe your father that much," he said. Then he took a long drink of water, set the glass on the table and smiled again. "My concern really isn't Lewis or medical research. I care about keeping America safe and we can do that now."

"Bioterrorism?"

"Son, the goal is to control bioterrorism and that we are doing. After all if we have it, they won't use it on us!" snapped Harris.

"Sort of like a pre-emptive war?" retorted Caleb.

Harris picked up his glass of water and hurled it across the floor.

All the men in suits jumped to their feet as it shattered. "You are such a waste of my energy!" Harris shouted as he stood up.

A waitress appeared in the doorway. "Is everything okay?" she asked nervously.

"We're just fine in here!" shouted Harris.

One of the nameless men moved towards the waitress ominously and pulled the door closed after she quickly exited.

Harris leaned in towards Caleb. "You walked right into it, asshole. A full fledged bioterrorism drill..."

"On old people," said Caleb who found the strength to stand up and took a swing.

The men in the suits were on him instantly. One threw a wild punch to Caleb's gut. He tried to double over in pain, but the men jerked him upright to face Harris.

"I came late to this party, but trust me, the people involved watched and followed you every step of the way. You see, the doctors wondered how stress affected the virus...how different age groups were affected...how quickly it could be spread. Thank you, Mr. Phillips. Thank you. Initially I hired you for info. Then I needed you to preoccupy Dr. Anderson while we secured his work," Harris stopped and smiled, "Which by the way we did. Now he's a waste of time too. No wait. Having him on the front pages has been truly convenient for keeping everybody busy."

Caleb spit on Harris, who then reached out and smacked Caleb across the face. "You little puke. You're a terrorist...I can lock you up...I can lock all of you up and no one can stop me." Harris stood up and smoothed out his tie. "You really should be more careful about who you keep company with..." he said grinning.

Then the emergency exit door swung open. At first it simply swung in the strong winds. Everyone turned. Harris nodded towards the door and three of the men in suits walked over to it and exited. After a moment of silence, Harris nodded towards the door again. His aide walked over to it and carefully peered out. Then he exited.

For several minutes Harris and Caleb sat in puzzled silence.

221

Four shots were heard. Then Harris pulled out his gun and stood up. A dark figure appeared in the doorway. Caleb hit the floor as a series of pops blistered the air. A moment later, Harris lay in a bloody pool near Caleb on the floor.

"Here!" a gruff voice shouted.

Caleb looked up to see a frail man with a pistol holding out a wooden box. The man looked strangely familiar to Caleb. The stranger lowered his eyes, but stepped closer. His hand shook as he extended the box.

"I'm sorry," he said with a quivering voice that seemed oddly out of place coming from the large figure that held the pistol.

"What?" asked Caleb as he carefully stood up.

"Tell him...tell him I'm sorry. I could have stopped all of this 20 years ago with one bullet." The man paused as he looked up at the ceiling while struggling to maintain his composure. "One bullet...maybe my son wouldn't have...wouldn't have taken this war over...one bullet and that bastard would never have had access to my son."

Caleb wiped his hands on his pants and glanced at Harris. Then his eyes came to rest on the shaking figure before him. "I don't understand. If Weston harmed your son, why are you helping him?"

The man thrust the gun into his waistband and then wiped his eyes with his coat sleeve. "Weston didn't harm my son. He is my son." Then the man pointed at the box. "Take this to Weston. Tell him that his old man...that I...I still believe in him and I'm sorry for what I let his grandfather do..." his words became jumbled as he turned away from Caleb.

The man stomped towards the door, looked out and then turned back to Caleb. "Death to the tyrant!" he said in a hypnotic tone. Then he pulled out his gun, placed it to his temple and pulled the trigger.

CHAPTER 48

Erica's vomit drizzled down the mane of the chestnut quarter horse as she gripped the horse's neck and waited to be able to breathe again. Orange fluid with chunks of the eggs she had choked down at breakfast spewed from her mouth.

"Oh, God!" Erica sobbed. Each wretch promised to be the last, but then her body would convulse again and again. The horse impatiently stomped its hooves as its rider continued to hang off the saddle pulling back on the reins.

After several minutes Erica sat up to the best of her ability. Brushing aside tangles of hair matted that kept falling into her face, she looked around. She had planned to stay off the main road, but her only hope of finding the cabin quickly now was to continue on it. Weakly she pushed her heels into the sides of the horse and tapped the reins on its neck directing it back to the road. "Go," she coughed. The vomiting was about to begin again, but this time Erica did not stop or even slow her ride. "I've got to get Reilly. I'm going to get her and go home…or out of state to a hospital," she explained to the horse.

Trees and shrubs seemed to whirl by like a carnival ride she desperately wanted to leave as Erica grabbed the horse's neck for another round of vomiting. She hated the horse. She hated the woods. She hated Weston. "No more," she whispered. "No more. I'm just going to leave with Reilly and Grandma. We're just leaving and that's all. We're just leaving and that's all," she repeated her new mantra with each statement being louder than the last.

Then in the distance off the road, she saw the cabin. She jerked the reins to stop the animal, but pulled too hard and it rose to its hind legs. With no strength left, Erica tumbled off with a devastated thud to the ground.

Half crawling, half walking she headed for the cabin and her family. "Weston!" she gurgled softly as the scream in her head drowned in a new wave of vomiting. "Weston!" Seeing Reilly's diaper bag by the door gave her renewed strength. "Reilly!"

Erica surged towards the door, but lost her footing and fell into the darkness of the cabin. For a moment she laid on the floor with no strength to move. The darkness felt good. "Just a minute to sleep," she thought. "Just one minute." She stretched her hands out on the floor and let them play in the cool liquid beneath them for a moment. She could hear the rain outside as it grew heavier and the sky became darker. Closing her eyes she began to dream of a stream slowly carrying her body away. Her fingers splashed in the water.

Then there was a sudden clap of thunder and a moan. Startled, Erica opened her eyes and clumsily sat up. She held up her hand in the darkness. There was no water on her fingers. This was thicker and...and...slightly sticky. It was drying on her fingers. With the next flash of lightening, Erica gulped in huge breath when she saw the dark stains that covered her hands. Then she heard the moan again.

"Erica..."

Her body shivered with fever as she struggled to her feet. With shaking hands, Erica fumbled for a lamp; however, it was her feet that discovered one. She tumbled over the lamp, but in a frantic sweeping of her hands she was able to grab it. Her world crashed into pieces with the tiny click that revealed the disheveled room around her, the bloody floor beneath her, and the bloodied body besides her.

"Oh, God! Weston!" she cried. Erica knelt down beside him and cradled his head in her arms. In disbelief she looked into his eyes. "Wes, it's going to be okay. I promise," she whispered as tears streamed down her face.

"No," he gasped. "I promised you. I promised Reilly..."

As Weston's blood soaked into her shirt Erica began to choke on her tears. "Where is Reilly?" She whispered.

"I'm sorry," Weston mumbled and then waved a hand towards the doorway.

Erica gently laid him down and stood to her feet. Initially her voice was inaudible as she cried out. "Reilly!" she sobbed as she rushed down the hallway.

She returned to the living room in panic. "Where is my baby?" she cried. Kneeling besides Weston again, Erica tried to turn his face towards her. "Please, Wes. Please!" She begged.

"Time...time...no more time," he wheezed. "Flash drive...all notes scanned onto it and a video of Beeman...of Beeman," he wheezed coughing up red liquid with each labored word.

"What flash drive? What notes?" she asked frantically. "Where is our baby?"

"She was beautiful," gasped Weston. "Our baby...she was beautiful!"

Erica froze in horror. She looked at the flash drive and stood up. "Where is Reilly?" Erica begged.

Then, putting a blood stained hand to her mouth she began to gag. More vomit flew from her mouth. Making every effort to choke it down her throat, Erica dropped the flash drive and ran to the back of the cabin. In each room she frantically overturned blankets and pillows. Lamps were thrown against walls as were pictures.

Finally she reached Pearl's room. Grabbing the elderly woman's body, Erica began shaking it. "Grandma! Where is Reilly? Grandma!" she sobbed.

Erica ran out of Pearl's room and down the hall. She returned to Weston.

Weston lay gasping in the pool of his blood. "I'm sorry," he whispered trying to raise his head. "This is all my..."

"Wes, where's Reilly!" she cried hysterically.

"I tried to protect her...she's...she's...she's," Weston's thudded to the floor as he gasped for breath.

For a moment Erica knelt beside Weston in a state of confusion. The world around her was not real. She was a cut-out doll on a stage of horror.

Then without another word or thought, in shock she wandered outside into the rain.

CHAPTER 49

Caleb looked at the box and then at the body of the stranger who had handed it to him. He tucked the box under his coat and headed for Main Street. However, the closer he got to the center of town, the more surreal the world around him became. The area was full of people old, young, coughing, crying all walking towards the only health clinic in town.

Caleb saw the crying children. Every baby in his mind became Reilly…suffering…sobbing. Some were limp and lifeless, others screeching through mucus filled lungs.

There were elderly people as well who shuffled along coughing and moaning. They reached out bony hands as they were jostled by the other bodies moving mindlessly towards the small brick building marked "CLINIC."

As he passed by the line, people who assumed he had come from the clinic itself began to reach out to him.

"Sir, please, my baby is sick! How much longer before we can get in there?" asked a woman who grabbed his arm.

Stunned, Caleb stood silent.

"She's only two-years-old. She's a baby…all we've got. Please!" She begged.

Caleb turned away. Toward the end of the line he saw an elderly woman fall. No one stopped. The lone figure in the orange shawl became just a lump in the scenery. As more people headed in the direction of the clinic, they stepped over the body. Caleb's eyes remained fixated on the site. He could not speak. He could not move. He simply watched even as hands grabbed at him and the man with the small child raised his voice. Finally, one little girl who was walking with her mother, paused and reached out to the lump. Carefully, the small child pulled the shawl up over the old woman's frozen stare. Then the mother jerked the girl's arm and together they found a place in line.

Just then a thin man in a white coat came out and looked out at the crowd.

"What's going on here?" asked Caleb looking into the man's dark tired eyes.

The man rubbed his eyes as he surveyed the line and adjusted his stethoscope around his neck. "The hospital in town closed five years back," he said wearily. "Flu's hit the community pretty hard just in the past few days. Started with an elderly woman who came here to live with her daughter after leaving some nursing home in Atlanta I think...I don't know. I've just never seen anything like this before."

"There must be someone who can help," insisted Caleb.

"I keep calling for help, but..." his voice trailed off in despair. "Did you see those horrifying images of Hurricane Katrina? Well, look around you. Same nightmare different night," he said softly. "I don't think there's any help coming and the hospital is more than an hour away."

Caleb remembered the television pictures from Hurricane Katrina...the bodies in the streets. The elderly in the wheel chairs left for dead. Death everywhere and no help coming.

Shaking Caleb clutched the box tighter and began to walk towards his car. Then a man spotted him. "Mister, what's in the box? Is it medicine? Hey, mister! Come on! My kid's sick!"

Suddenly the words medicine rippled through the crowd. More voice began shouting, begging for help. Then the crowd shifted from a line to a mass pressing against him and yelling so neither his voice or the doctor's could be heard. The people pushed Caleb backward causing him to trip over the step and fall onto the floor. As he fell, his pistol thudded to the ground near him. Quickly he grabbed for it and began to swing it around. No one saw. At this point the panic had overtaken them and bodies were simply pushing forward into a pile on him as people screamed for his help.

Fighting for breath on the bottom of the pile, Caleb prepared to simply fire the gun into the bodies above him. Then he saw the face of a small child. She blinked her soft brown eyes, tears streamed out from these circles of horror, reflecting the immense terror in her mind. Then the gun slipped from his fingers.

BAM!

A gun shot ripped through all of the confusion and for one brief moment all was quiet. *Did I fire?* His mind raced through the proceeding seconds. *Where is that little girl? Where is the little girl?* Then he felt the weight come off from him. Bodies began moving away and he could breathe again. People began standing and walking away.

Caleb scanned for the little girl with an overwhelming urge to comfort her. She was nowhere in sight. The box lay in pieces on the floor revealing torn newspapers and a wad of bubble wrap. Quickly Caleb lunged for the tiny object and clutched it to his chest.

Barely breathing, he struggled to his feet and began to run avoiding the faces, avoiding the tears. *Enough! Enough death!* He sobbed. He swallowed hard as he passed the lump covered by the orange shawl. It was time for him to leave…to find his own place to die.

"How can someone let all those people die?" Sandra had asked him as they sat watching Hurricane Katrina on the news in 2005.

"No one saw it coming," he said bitterly to himself as he walked down the dirt path remembering Sandra's question. "No one saw it coming."

Then his cell phone rang. Glancing at it, his first impulse was to toss it in the park, but then he remembered Erica.

"Hello?" he said somberly.

"Help me," sobbed Erica. "Please help me…Reilly's dead."

CHAPTER 50

"What?" he shouted, but the connection was already broken.

Still running, he reached the car he had stolen earlier and jumped into it banging his head against the roof. Then he slammed the door and drove like a demon trying to find his way out of hell. As the cabin came into view he wiped his eyes with the back of his hand. "As good a place to die as any," he declared.

He entered the front room numb and shaking. Pausing briefly at pool of blood in the living room, Caleb began to yell. "Erica?" he shouted hoarsely. "Erica?"

He walked past Reilly's room, dark, empty and silent. Then he saw Pearl's door slightly ajar "Pearl?" he whispered softly as he entered.

The silence in her room was oddly peaceful. He entered and sat on the edge of her bed. Despite already knowing the truth in his gut, Caleb reached for Pearl's wrist to check for a pulse. He laid it back down carefully. "You were going to tell me about your babies...your husband...you were going to tell me about the yellow and red bands..." he added softly as he fingered the plastic band still on her wrist from the nursing home.

In her other arm she clutched a rag doll. Embracing it tenderly and careful not to roll onto it, Pearl had found her final moments of comfort in that small child's toy.

"I didn't really know you, but, uh, well, I'm I'm sorry...I'm just sorry," he whispered. Then he grabbed the quilt from the end of the bed and pulled it up over her, stopping for one brief moment at her face. "You didn't kill your babies...you didn't." Then he kissed her forehead and pulled it up over her.

For several minutes he sat in silence trying desperately to drink in the peace. Although church was a far distant memory for him, he indulged himself for a moment picturing Pearl in some sort of heaven with her babies and her husband.

"Caleb?" Erica's voice sliced the silence and jarred Caleb.

"Yeah," he said as he exited the room and joined Erica in the kitchen.

"Here," said Erica holding out a box with a trembling arm. "There's a syringe in here."

"I know. I saw it earlier. Just like Pearl described, but that doesn't mean anything."

Caleb held up the bubble wrap.

"What is it?" asked Erica.

"It better be our salvation," said Caleb as he unwrapped it. Dropping the plastic wrapper Caleb held up a flash drive.

"Weston said something about this," she whispered reaching for it.

Caleb surrendered it to her and then he pulled her close.

She pushed away from him. "Are you an idiot?" she asked. "We've gotta get out of here. We have to get this into the right hands before they kill us too."

"Oh, please," said Caleb. "We're already dead anyway. What does it matter?"

As Erica blew her nose on a tissue, she motioned towards the refrigerator. "There's juice and some vitamin C tablets. We'll rest for just few minutes," she moaned. "I just can't go on yet." She began to wipe her eyes as she added, "Would you please...move Weston's body? I can't handle seeing it again."

"Body?" asked Caleb.

"Yeah," said Erica. "It's in the living room. You had to have seen it when you walked in."

Caleb shook his head. "There was blood all over the floor, but there was no body there."

Erica cautiously walked towards the living room. Taking Caleb's hand, she entered to see the bloody floor, but no Weston.

"I don't understand! He was here!" She insisted. "He was right here!"

"What can I say? He's not now," replied Caleb.

Erica put her hands over her face and began to sob. Caleb reached out and touched her shoulder. "You're tired," he said softly. "Lay down on the couch. Let's get some rest."

Caleb turned on the radio and then tossed Erica a quilt. He wrapped himself in a chair cover and sat in the large recliner. They drifted to sleep listening to the voices from the radio....listening until they heard their names.

"Okay, folks, so what about these people....uh Caleb Phillips and Erica Schmidt? The administration says that they are trying to sabotage the flu vaccine supply....apparently they've already killed the scientist they were working with who started this whole epidemic and apparently murdered Ms. Schmidt's baby daughter. I'm taking callers, let's find out what you think," declared the voice.

Caleb stirred. Erica's eyes opened and she sat up. "How do they know about Weston and Reilly?" she asked.

Wiping the sleep from his eyes, Caleb turned to look at the radio. "I don't know. I don't know."

"Where the hell is the phone?" Erica asked as she stood and looked around the room.

"The phone? Why?" asked Caleb.

Erica grabbed Caleb's backpack and began to rummage through it frantically.

"Hey!" he shouted.

"Get that number," she commanded nodding towards the radio and ignoring his shout.

Caleb turned it up loudly and began yanking open drawers in the nearby desk.

"That number again is 555-9000," repeated the voice.

"None of these pens work!" said Caleb as he scribbled.

Erica began to press the buttons on the cell phone she pulled out of Caleb's bag. He reached up and put his hand on the phone. "It's probably tapped."

"I'm counting on it," Erica replied and then stepped away from Caleb.

"Hello? Hello? Oh, yes, this is Erica Schmidt. I'd like to talk to…hello?"

"You're on the air with Jim O' Flannagan."

"Hello, this is Erica Schmidt."

"Ms. Schmidt, if this really is you, a lot of my listeners would like to see you dead right now."

"Things are not what they seem. Zelticor has some answering to do…and so do some very powerful people in this country….maybe as high up as the White House," Erica said slowly calculating each word.

"The White House? Look, lady, I'm one of the first to criticize this administration, but I don't see how you stealing a virus to foreign countries or murdering the American Scientist who created them is the fault of the White House."

"I didn't kill anyone or steal anything, but you need to look again at the Military Commissions Act. It not only allows detainment without due process, but there's a little something in it that makes a lot of room for medical experimentation. I didn't kill anyone, but I have plenty of proof of what I'm saying….memos, names, dates... Hello? Hello?" Erica looked at Caleb and smiled. "Signal's been cut off."

CHAPTER 51

Just outside in the shadows of the trees a figure emerged looking up at the cabin. He stood silently watching. Alone in his thoughts, he stood completely unaware that he was not truly alone.

"Mr. Beeman?" hissed a voice behind him sending chills through his soul. Startled, Beeman dropped his cell phone and turned.

"Oh!" he sighed with relief. "Jameson!"

Jameson's face was drawn tightly. His hands remained in his pockets. "Mr. Beeman, it's over."

The wind danced through the tree softly as Beeman studied the man who faced him. "Michael, what are you talking about?"

Slowly Michael Jameson pulled his right hand out of his coat pocket to reveal a gun. "Where is the child?"

"What?"

Without flinching Jameson lowered the gun slightly and pulled the trigger. "I said where is the child?"

Beeman doubled over in pain and fell to the ground. "Oh, god! Oh, god! What's the matter with you? We're on the same team!" he screamed. The leg of his black suit shimmered slightly when the sun hit the blood seeping through.

"I don't think so," Jameson replied coldly. "The board has decided that you have become a liability now. The election is tomorrow and that woman has evidence that could bring down the whole party...starting with the Vice President." Then without another word or a change in his expression, Jameson took careful aim and fired into Beeman's other thigh.

"Oh, god! Please! Please! Please don't kill me!" Beeman begged as he rolled around the ground. "The kid is gone. I sent her off about half an hour ago."

"With?"

"With them!" he screamed in pain as he continued to roll around

233

holding his legs. "With our security team…the team took her."

"They haven't been responding. Why?" shouted Jameson.

"I don't know. Oh, god! I don't know!"

Jameson raised his gun and aimed it directly at Beeman's head.

"Text them. Text the word 'dolphin'. That's our emergency word. Help me! Please, Michael! Help me."

Jameson fired his gun again. Then there was silence.

CHAPTER 52

"Did you hear gun shots?" asked Erica nervously. She grabbed Caleb's arm and dashed down the hallway away from all windows. "They're out there!"

"Of course they are!" yelled Caleb with new found energy. "Are you insane making that phone call? Why don't you just string up a banner that says 'kill us'?"

"They've killed my child…I have nothing left to live for," she shot back.

"So suicide by cop? That's a solution?"

"Do you trust me?" Erica asked. She wiped a wisp of sweat matted hair from her face and bit her bottom lip as she stared at Caleb.

Caleb nodded silently. Carefully Erica walked down the hallway to the door to the linen closet and began pulling out sheets and tossing them onto the floor. Once the shelves were cleared, she easily pulled out the three middles ones and tossed them aside.

Caleb tapped her on the shoulder and began to whisper the words, "What the hell?"

Erica glanced at him briefly and then turned back to the closet and pushed on the back of the it. Nothing happened. She began to feel around. Still nothing. Then running her hand along the edges she found a small switch. With one flick, the back slide to the left revealing a narrow stairway.

Erica began to climb the stairway. Caleb followed but then Erica stopped. "Hit the switch on the wall to close the panel," she whispered.

Caleb stepped down to the bottom and ran his hand along the wall. Finding the switch he flicked it.

They continued to climb the small, winding metal stairs. Caleb paused. "Not claustrophobic are you?" whispered Erica.

Caleb remained silent in the narrow stairway. For a moment he tried to turn and look back at the bottom of the stairwell, but then he felt the drywall against his cheek and realized that there was no room.

Finally, they reached the top and entered a small room with wooden panels on the floor, all four walls and the ceiling. With a soft click, the sole light bulb in the ceiling came on and illuminated the coffin-like room.

"Yes," Caleb replied.

"Yes, what?" asked Erica.

"I really hate close spaces and by really...I MEAN REALLY."

"Look, this is our only shot," she insisted.

"I can't breathe!"

"Yes, you can."

Erica crawled to the far side away from the door so that Caleb could sit. She sat down with her knees against her chest and surveyed the barren room.

Caleb knelt and on his knees he edged into the small room. "Can't even stand up in this...this box! What the hell is this place?" asked Caleb.

"It was his 'safe place'. He had it build exactly ten feet by six feet and three feet to the ceiling," she replied with a shaking smile as she remembered the last time she had been in this place.

"Why?"

Erica shrugged to keep herself from breaking down with tears. Finally she took a deep breath and tried to speak. "Weston was always cloak and dagger. He had this room built with a bunch of electronic security so that no one could bug this room or detect it without coming up here physically."

"Really? No one can hear us up here?"

"Hell if I know. I think this is where we conceived Reilly though."

"Thanks for that little visual aide of you and old gramps there.

Now I'm really not sure I can breathe," Caleb replied.

As he felt around in the shadows, he bumped into Weston's laptop case. Moving to allow the dim light to shine on it, he spotted Weston's leather briefcase. "Hey, what's this?"

"That's Weston's laptop case," she said stunned.

"I never saw him carrying anything," said Caleb as Erica reached for it.

"The night before his lab was trashed he came out here to the cabin. He mentioned that to me on the phone that morning. Said it made him think of us," Erica said softly. After a bit of fumbling, she unzipped several sections and began to rifle through them. Then she pulled out a brown box.

Caleb reached for it and then held it up to the light. "It's addressed to you," he said.

Erica opened it and found a flash drive and a note. For several minutes she read the note, then very carefully folded it up and push it into her pocket.

"Does it say what this flash drive has that the one I found doesn't?"

Erica shook her head. Caleb wanted to ask her about the contents of the note, but her trembling lips and the tears now streaming freely down her face told him all he needed to know.

Erica stared at the flash drive in astonishment for several seconds. Finally she thrust it into her sock and reached for Caleb's hand

"Reilly would be proud of you," he whispered.

Erica tried to speak, but couldn't find her voice. Caleb reached out and embraced her. For several moments they held onto one another tightly. Finally Erica pulled back and smiled. "You know you look like the guy in that ad for jeans. The one where the guy has no shirt on and is tossing a Frisbee."

"I get that all the time," he said finally allowing a smile.

As they sat in silence their smiles gave way to fatigue and they laid down staring up at the lone light bulb. "I'm going to expose these bastards," Erica replied with an eerie calm. "They've probably already planned our deaths…if we're lucky it's just quick gun shots. If we're not they'll put us in a hospital somewhere and 'observe' us," she said making quote marks in the air with her hands. "The Patriot Act…remember that? There's a clause in it that states that while the government is not officially allowed to experiment, agents of the government may incarcerate anyone believed to be carrying a deadly virus in the name of national security."

"What do you mean incarcerate? Don't you mean hospitalize? Where are you getting this stuff from?"

"Remember that story about the Tuskegee Syphilis Study? That was government sponsored…and that was during a time of relative peace…now we're fighting terrorists."

"The war is over," whispered Caleb.

Erica sat up. "Is it? Maybe Weston was a casualty of war," Erica said, her voice trailing off as she closed her eyes.

"Maybe we're all casualties of war," Caleb mumbled.

"Maybe we are," repeated Erica. "You know, I once saw a war documentary where they were throwing the bodies of babies into the back of a truck. That's the face of war," she whispered.

"I saw 9-11 up close and personal," Caleb whispered back. "The end of any kind of innocence that the post-Vietnam generations could have known."

Erica turned away. With one trembling hand she dabbed at her eyes with the sleeve of her shirt. "Innocence?" Erica squeaked out between tears. "Forget innocence. This is a battle involving people who believe they have unlimited power. For the past few days I've thought I could walk away at any time…now I see that I couldn't."

"So now?"

"Now we stop running and start fighting. I've got so much proof that we're probably going to be dead the second we so much as look outside this cabin," replied Erica. Then she sat silent for a few moments staring at the pine panels on the wall. "My mother didn't die in a car accident," she announced.

Caleb reached out and rubbed her shoulder. "I'm sorry. Your mom...uh how did she..."

Erica took a deep breath. "She called Weston from my grandma's nursing home. Said she and Grandma were sick. He went to meet her and presumably some nursing home officials," Erica began to sob. She stopped for several seconds. "They argued in a stairwell. My mother shoved Weston and lost her balance. She fell down the stairs. Beeman arrived and told Weston to start containment of the place and he would take care of my mother. The next thing Weston knew it was being reported that my mom died in a car accident. Apparently Beeman set that up so that no one would walk into what was happening at the nursing home." Erica pulled the note from her pocket and waved it silently.

Caleb embraced Erica. For several minutes he held her in his arms as she cried.

"But your grandmother lived for quite a few weeks after the exposure," comforted Caleb. "Weston must have been doing something good for her."

Catching her breath, she wiped away tears and nodded. "When Weston met me I was an experiment, but changed. He said it changed. I think he did love me."

"Yeah," Caleb said trying to sound comforting.

Erica wiped away a few more tears and then took a deep breath. "This flash drive you got....Weston said it has memos...very recent ones...give names, dates. The Vice President's chief of staff is clearly talking on some of the audio," she added. "It was his idea to take over the nursing home from Weston, but yet not go 'on the record' and get them real help."

Caleb started to speak, but Erica held up her hand to silence him.

"I think initially it started out simply as an investment....maybe even legal and harmless at first. Then things developed unexpectedly and before long people had their hands in a deadly cookie jar with no good way out."

"So everybody wins if no body squeals," replied Caleb

sarcastically. "I get it now. Harris hired me to see if Weston was going to play ball with the whole scam, but…"

"But then the game changed."

"And Harris lost interest in me because I wasn't needed for that purpose anymore."

For several minutes they sat in silence. "Two tracks," whispered Caleb finally.

"What?" asked Erica.

"There were two fresh tire tracks when I pulled up. Two vehicles."

"Yes, so there were two cars full of them."

"Why take Weston's body, but leave Pearl's body behind? Wouldn't they need both for the study? And how did everyone find out so quickly that Reilly was dead. It just happened and yet that talk radio guy talked like it was old news."

"Is there another player? Someone we don't know about yet?" asked Caleb excitedly. He wiped the sweat from his forehead and unzipped his jacket. "Like someone who could help us?"

Erica nodded. "If they had this info in their hands tonight, tomorrow's election would be a whole different ballgame," replied Erica excitedly. "This might be our ticket out."

"What about turning all of this over to that group of scientists Weston talked about…"

"Can we get a hold of them?" asked Caleb. "Before we get killed?"

CHAPTER 53

"I'll turn myself in," announced Erica as she pulled back away from Caleb.

"Excuse me? I thought you said fight?" he asked bumping his head on the low ceiling. "God damn it!" He began to rub his head.

"Move," said Erica. "Let's get out of here. It all starts with me appearing to give up." Erica grabbed for the papers in Weston's laptop case.

"And then?" asked Caleb.

Erica motioned towards the door and the narrow stairway that led down. Confused, Caleb moved towards the door and then looked back one more time. Erica motioned impatiently towards the door. Carefully, Caleb crawled out and onto the stairway. Then he began another fit of coughing and covered his mouth with his hands. He swallowed hard and continued his descent. As he reached for the railing his hand slipped slightly and he stumbled.

"What's wrong?" asked Erica.

Caleb looked down at the blood on his hand and froze. "Uh, nothing," he replied quickly wiping his hand on his jeans and then continuing.

At the bottom of the stairs, Caleb stretched. As Erica emerged, she embraced him again and whispered, "Let's go to the bedroom."

Still disoriented from the room upstairs, Caleb wobbled slightly as he followed her. She went over to the dresser and pulled out a sweatshirt that had belonged to Weston. Tossing it to Caleb, she returned to the drawers and began rummaging through them. She turned back holding a roll of medical tape.

Caleb mouthed the word "What?"

Then Erica bent over and pulled the flash drive out of her sock and held it. Erica looked at the drive for a moment as if she had never seen one before. She grabbed the medical tape and tossed both items to Caleb.

"Find a secure place on your body to tape the flash drive," she whispered softly. "Then go back upstairs until I'm gone. They'll take me away and after a quick search here, they'll leave. You'll be free to find Weston's contacts. I'm sure his papers or the flash drive must give some information for them."

Caleb raised the new sweatshirt he had just put on and began to tape the flash drive to his chest. Erica walked over and ripped it from his body.

"OUCH! He shouted.

Shaking her head, Erica pointed to his pants and then to her inner thigh.

"A safe hiding place," she whispered.

Caleb rolled his eyes. He motioned for her to turn around.

"Oh, please!" she sighed as she turned.

"Hey, not until you buy me dinner," he replied smiling briefly.

Erica turned to face the door.

"Are you sure you want to turn yourself in?" Caleb asked quietly as he reached out to her.

Erica paused as she spotted a pacifier on the floor. "Yes," she replied with determination. "Head for town. I think Weston's group will find you, but if not get a ride back into Atlanta and...and I guess try Weston's apartment. His office. They've got to know what's going on."

"So in other words, go save the world," he whispered and smiled.

"Yep...but make sure to save yourself also ..." her voice trailed off as she turned back around to look at him. Briefly she smiled and then marched into the main room of the cabin. "I'm giving myself up and I have all the notes and everything," she announced loudly.

In the light of the living room Erica glanced at the papers she had just taken out of Weston's laptop case. A yellow sticky note on the top of one bundle said, "Scanned onto flash drive." Tearing up the note, she held up the papers and waved them over her head in full view of the large picture window.

The room remained quiet. She shivered slightly. Then she looked down the hall at Caleb. She mouthed the words "good luck" to Caleb and then walked out the front door holding papers high in the air.

One lone, black car sat on the dirt road in front of the cabin. Jameson stood leaning against the car. His black overcoat fluttered slightly in the wind. Cigarette smoke floated effortlessly from under the brim of his black hat tipped down slightly to cover his face.

"You?" asked Erica in surprise.

"Me," Jameson said dryly.

"And this is it?" asked Erica loudly. "No sirens or SWATT team?"

The Jameson offered a crooked smile as he grabbed for the papers. "You've watched too many movies," he replied.

"I'll turn them over when I arrive someplace safe," Erica snapped as she thrust the papers into her suede coat and zipped it up the rest of the way.

For a moment Jameson snarled, his fat cheeks jiggling slightly. Then with confident, measured strides, he walked around to the back passenger side door and opened it for Erica. She stopped a moment and looked at the open door. Then she looked back at the cabin. Not so long ago it had been her romantic refuge with Weston, now it was her nightmare.

"Wear this," he said coldly as he tossed a face mask to her.

Erica stared at it.

"You're contagious and I'm not getting sick over you," he replied as his voice cut through the crisp air. "Where's your friend?"

"What?" asked Erica, startled.

"Mr. Phillips," he said abruptly.

"I don't know. I guess Caleb's gone…Weston is dead."

Suddenly the man's frozen expression altered dramatically. "What do you mean gone?"

"I mean he's gone. He left last night."

Quickly the man dodged away from the car as he swiftly pulled out his cell phone. Erica moved towards him, but he walked away at a rapid pace. Then he turned and narrowed his eyes as he looked at Erica with a scowl. "You're both dying. Tell me where he is so that I can take you both to a hospital. You're carrying a very serious virus." He began to raise his voice sharply as he spoke.

"I don't know where he is," she responded defiantly tossing aside the face mask and getting into the front seat.

"No one was seen coming or going from this cabin since you arrived yesterday," he snapped.

"You've been watching all night. So why not come in and get us sooner."

"Your friend will be dead by this time tomorrow. We'll find him one way or another," he hissed and got into the car. Rolling down the window he kept his face turned towards it and the fresh air during the thirty-five minute ride. Erica sat back and closed her eyes, drifting to sleep momentarily as she listened to the hum of the road.

Then the passenger door swung open.

"Wake up!" said a woman's voice.

Erica felt a hand grab her and she tumbled halfway out of the car tangled in her still buckled seatbelt. "Huh? What?" she stuttered.

Erica struggled to get back into the seat and unbuckle. Her body felt numb and her fingers were awkward devices. Finally, the woman leaned in and clicked the seat belt open. She extended a hand with a rubber glove on it. "You're wanted in the main conference room," she said sharply and pointed to the building.

Erica looked around and rubbed her eyes. "Is this the hospital?"

"No," replied a young, thin man wearing a medical mask and gloves who briskly walked up from behind her. "Please come with me." He then marched ahead of her into the building.

"Where are we?"

"Would you like something to drink?" he asked as they entered a room with a large table.

"No…I mean, yes. Yes, I'd really like some water," she replied.

The man disappeared. In a moment he returned with a large plastic cup full of water. Silently he sat it down and then left like a wind-up soldier ready to continue his route. Erica sat alone gulping water from the cup.

"Good afternoon, Ms. Schmidt," said a voice from behind.

Erica turned quickly to see a distinguished looking middle aged man enter the room.

"I'm Mark Rousseau."

"Mr. Rousseau, what is going on here? I was told I was going to the hospital!" Erica said.

"You are going to the hospital, but first we need to chat," he said sharply as he dropped a manila folder on the table. Unbuttoning his suit jacket, he sat down at the far end of the table several feet from Erica and straightened his tie. Then he opened the folder and began to read it silently. "A very busy lady these past few days," he said finally. "Quite a body count."

"Did you say you had questions for me?" Erica snapped as she rubbed her forehead.

Rousseau looked up over his glasses. "Yes," he replied sternly. "Were you aware that Dr. Anderson was creating new strains of virus that he unleashed on an elderly population or that he was altering life saving vaccines?"

"I don't know what Weston was doing. I wasn't involved at all," answered Erica as she raised the cup to her mouth for the last drop of water.

The man shuffled his papers and then paused as he looked up at her. "I understand you have papers? Notes from Dr. Anderson?"

Erica nodded and then unzipped her coat. She reached into her

245

pocket and pulled out a bundle of wadded papers. "Here. This is what I have. Now I want to go to the hospital."

Staring at her cynically, he reached for the papers. Clearing his throat, Rousseau said, "To whom have you shown these?"

"No one," she replied.

"Oh, come on now," he shot back.

Erica stood up and began coughing. When she stopped she took a deep breath and shouted, "Listen! You've been watching me for days. Have you seen me give them to anyone?" Then she slammed her hand down on the table. "You've watched. You've listened. Now you have his notes. I want to leave," she said. Then she zipped up her coat and walked over to the door.

"You are the guest of the United States government, Ms. Schmidt, I suggest that you sit back down," he said.

Erica grabbed the door knob and flung open the door. Two men in suits stood in the doorway.

"You can't hold me," insisted Erica. "I haven't done anything."

"You haven't done anything? Good God! There's bodies every which way and you're currently suspected of treason. This isn't a game, Ms. Schmidt. And you look very much like a terrorist at this point. So you are going nowhere."

"I want an attorney," she insisted.

"I don't think so. Not right now," replied Rousseau as he looked back down at the paperwork.

"You can't do this in America!" she shouted.

"No, Ms. Schmidt, YOU can't do this! We will not allow terrorists to just waltz in here and take advantage of our country…harm our citizens…kill our people. NO MORE!" he shouted. Then he stood up. "Scientists and medical professionals are among the most trusted in our country. When they lose their commitment to human life and to the country to which they have sworn their allegiance, then they are the worst type of scum."

"I need medical attention," Erica said somberly.

"Like you provided for your daughter?"

"The truth." Erica responded flatly.

"What?" askcd Rousseau annoyed.

"I have the truth and it's going to be released."

Rousseau closed the folder and stood up. "You don't know the game you're playing. Do you ever want to see your child again?"

CHAPTER 54

Waiting in the sweltering heat of the small wooden room, Caleb took off his shirt and laid down. He briefly heard the soft buzz of inaudible voices. His stomach tightened. Something was wrong. With one shaking hand he wiped his forehead.

Caleb heard the shelves below the room rattling. Someone was there, exploring…looking for him. He crawled further back into the room. With his back pressed firmly against the far wall, he closed his eyes and held his breath as if somehow that would keep them from spotting him. The rattling grew louder. They had found the room! Caleb froze in position. Only the sweat rolling off his neck and face dared to move.

Then the rattling stopped. There was nothing. He was still alone in this casket that Weston called his safe place. All alone. Finally, he rolled over…into darkness. Reaching out his hands, he felt a smooth wooden wall. There were now walls on all sides of him as he laid in the darkness. Then with one frantic burst of energy, he kicked the door panel and saw the light from a lamp in the hallway.

For a moment he lay panting feeling the air hit his face.

There were no voices. Everything was lifeless below in the hallway. *Breath. Breath. Breath.* His mind began to calm. He had no sense of time, but darkness now permeated the hallway as he moved down the stairs. Reaching the bottom he shook himself and looked at his hands. Then he went into the bathroom to wash them and grab a shirt from the closet. Erica was gone. Now it was time for him to move. Silently and quickly. Time to fulfill his pledge.

Unsure of whether the house was still being watched, Caleb opted to go through the window in Pearl's room. Without turning on lights, he passed her body, still there under the blanket with the small rag doll protruding slightly. He pulled on his coat, which he had found where he left it on the door hook, and opened the window. As the cold air rushed in, he turned and looked one last time at Pearl. "Goodbye," he whispered and then thrust himself through the opening and tumbled onto the ground below.

He stayed pressed against the cabin wall for a moment, scanning the area under the full moon. No movement.

Then he dodged among the trees trying to find his way out of the woods. He pulled his coat up around his neck and watched his breath form white wisps in the night air.

He stopped and looked around the darkness.

"Mr. Phillips," a voice cut through the stillness.

"Huh?" Startled Caleb turned around. He saw no one.

"You have something for me," said the voice.

"Who are you? Where are you?" shouted Caleb.

Then he saw a shadow move. Caleb took a step backward and fell over a branch. "Damn it!" he shouted. Then he looked up and saw a hand inches from his face.

"I'm here to help you," replied the figure.

"Help me? Who the hell are you?" asked Caleb.

The figure said nothing, but stood with a hand extended. Caleb looked around and then cautiously reached up for the hand. Gripping him firmly, the stranger pulled Caleb to his feet with one powerful heave.

"Thank you," said Caleb as he wiped off the patches of wet mud from his pants.

The figure turned silently and began to move away.

Caleb grabbed it and attempted to pull it towards him. "Where are you going?" he snapped.

Then a fist met his jaw sending him back against a tree, and Caleb staggered almost to the ground. "Don't ever touch me again," boomed the voice. Then as Caleb rubbed his jaw a hand grabbed his neck and thrust him back against the tree again. "You think you know the game is being played, but you don't. You only know the surface of what's going on. You saw the people...the people in town suffering," said the man. "There's more to come."

Caleb labored to breath. Clawing at the hand around his throat, he broke free. "Who are you? That's a simple enough question. Answer it!"

"You mean am I one of the good guys?" he said patronizingly.

"Yeah, something like that. I'm not giving anything to some nut case lurking in the woods. Who are you?"

"Reilly is alive," said the man.

"I know that."

"No you don't. You just guessed at it. Hoped for it. I was Dr. Anderson's confidante. He was trying to give me something, but could never do it because he was always being followed. He kept meeting with me...pretending to give it to me hoping that they would make a move and we could expose them, but he never did give it to me because he believed that as long as he had something valuable his loved ones would be safe...he was wrong. He was very very wrong and it was this thinking that almost got all of you killed at various points during the past few days."

"Look, I just want out of this....alive. I don't give a damn about any of this. I was just a hired gun of sorts and now I'm not needed."

"But you do care. You care because you can't let Sandra go and you can't let Ms. Schmidt go and you can't let Reilly go. You think that all that matters is your little corner of the world. Well, there's more going on and if you're going to survive...if any of you are going to survive in a world worth living in, you had better care deeply about all of this. Now give me the flash drive and then crawl into your little world again."

Caleb turned and using all of his force he slammed his right fist into the man's jaw. "And what about Erica? What about Reilly? Huh? I give you the flash drive and what about them?"

Then Caleb heard the voices in the distance. A gunshot ripped apart the night. Hitting the ground, Caleb lay quietly for a moment near the man he had just slugged. "My name is Jameson," announced. "I worked with Weston and Erica. I know who killed Erica's mother and I know every move you've made today."

The voices grew louder. As Caleb caught his breath he heard

shouts…directions. He heard Jameson's name.

"They're here! Give me the flash if you want to live," hissed Jameson.

Caleb quickly unbuttoned his jeans and reached to his thigh for the drive that was tapped to his leg. With a quick jerk he pulled the tape off. "Here," he whispered. "Here. Take it and get it away from me."

As the man reached for the drive, Caleb's other hand grabbed him. "But by tomorrow morning, all three of us had better be free and alive."

The man wrestled his arm free of Caleb's grip. "You will be. You will be," he said and then disappeared into the night.

Caleb lay back on the ground knowing that he had just given away his only bargaining chip to an unknown man in a forest. Then a light blinded his eyes.

"Hello, Mr. Phillips. Nice night for a walk, isn't it?" snarled the voice and then a fist slammed into his jaw.

CHAPTER 55

Slowly Caleb opened his eyes. For a moment he didn't move. There were voices and figures all around him, sitting close. Whispers fluttered through the air; whispers that stopped as Caleb's eyelids opened.

He intensely rubbed his head wishing he could wipe away the pain that seemed to literally be cracking open his skull. He felt himself being dragged, then shoved into a car. For a moment he fell over devoid of strength and purpose.

"Hello, Mr. Phillips. Rough day?" asked a man's voice.

Caleb sat up and his eyes began to focus he realized he was in the back of a limo. He saw several men in suits and dark overcoats…nameless, formless…dark shadows without distinction like the man who hit him. All except one, who wore small, round glasses with gold trim. His wrinkled face was void of all expression as he looked from the folder in his lap to Caleb.

Though unable to focus enough to take a meaningful shot, Caleb lunged at the man anyway. The simple move required all of his remaining energy, but yet he only moved inches before he was effortlessly pushed back into his seat by hands on both sides of him.

"You're not in any condition to take on me or anyone else in this car," replied the man as he adjusted his suit and glared at Caleb.

"Where are we?" asked Caleb. The words fought their way through what felt like bundles of cotton on his tongue. He struggled to swallow, but his dry mouth refused.

"Obviously, I said we're in a car," replied the man.

"I mean where are we going, idiot!" snapped back Caleb.

The man cocked his head and narrowed his eyes. "We've already searched you…very thoroughly while you were unconscious," the man said somberly. Then he looked back down at his paperwork. "We won't hesitate to do it again, but this time you'll be awake and I guarantee that it won't be pleasant…no, no, no." He began to write something with a gold pen.

For a moment Caleb got lost in the movements of the shiny gold. Then he shook himself as his vision began to clear. "Look I'm done with all of this. I was hired to follow Weston Anderson. That's all. He's dead now, as I'm sure you know. I just want to go home." Caleb stared intently at the man.

For a moment, the elderly man's face was sweep with emotion. First his lips turned up slightly and then a harsh chuckle escaped from his lips. "Oh, please, Mr. Phillips. I know that you're still a bit disoriented. Tired, de-hydrated, and God knows what Anderson drugged you with, but c'mon. We're both adults here. Either you think I'm a fool or you're one and I tend to believe the latter. After all you've been through and all of your contact with Dr. Anderson, do you honestly believe that we're going to take your word that you have nothing damaging against us? You think you're just going to waltz away without any questions being asked? Oh, wait. I forgot that's what you did after you pulled the trigger to the gun against your wife's head, wasn't it?"

Rage surged through Caleb's brain. The two silent, large men, seated on either side of him grabbed his arms as he impulsively lunged forward again. "Let me go!" he shouted struggling for freedom. "I said let me out of here!" He continued to struggle as the man across from him smirked. "I did not kill her. Sandra had cancer. Sandra was sick," he shouted as tears covered his face.

"Really? Because the records that Senator Harris has say that she didn't. You killed her the night. She died at your hand!" The man nodded at the people holding Caleb's arms and suddenly he was free, free to slump over into his lap and sob.

"No...no...no...no, she was sick. Sandra was pregnant during 9-11, she came out sick and no one would help us!" Caleb screamed. "The baby was stillborn and then Sandra never....she never felt good again and...and..." Then he looked up through his tears.

"We just want the information that Dr. Anderson gave you...oh, and your eternal silence."

"I don't have information. I don't have anything," Caleb whispered as if in a horrified trance.

"Mr. Phillips, where is it? We know that Dr. Anderson kept secret files. Hell, he knew that we knew. That's why he kept us chasing red herrings. Smart man. Too bad he just didn't see the war on terror the way we do. After tomorrow's election, we'll be able to focus and get back on track." The right side of the man's mouth curled upwards as he shook his head. "People just don't have the guts...but obviously you do. Willing to go to the mat for Anderson and he was probably screwing you just like Harris." The man wore a chilling smile on his face for a moment as he slowly said the last four words of his sentence.

"I honestly don't have it. I just don't," Caleb muttered.

"Perhaps Ms. Schmidt will be of more help," shot back the man bitterly. Then he picked up the phone near him. "Driver," he said into it. "We'll be dropping Mr. Phillips off in the custody of the appropriate authorities."

At the mention of Erica's name, Caleb shook himself. He pictured Reilly sleeping in that bed in the cabin. "Where is Erica?"

"That's really none of your business."

"I want to talk to my lawyer."

"You're a prisoner of war who is suspected of terrorism. You don't have any rights."

"I get an attorney," said Caleb as his head began to clear.

"No. No, you don't. Not until I say you do and that's not right now."

"You can't hold me!"

The man leaned forward. "Hell, yes, I can. And I'm certainly not giving you a chance to say so much as 'boo' until after tomorrow's election."

"Is that what this is all about? The election?"

The man nodded to the goon on Caleb's left who soundly thrust his fist into Caleb's stomach.

"Ooooph!" Caleb doubled over.

Just then the phone rang again.

"Hello? Yes, Mr. Secretary. Um...yes, are you sure?

They…they have all the notes? Everything of Anderson's? They have it all? Are you sure it's the real thing? You know we've been fooled before…yes, I understand. Did they say what they were going to do with it? Well, of course, yes, you have to work with them because if this gets exposed with the election tomorrow... I understand…but what about…release? But…okay…well, I think this is a huge mistake. Yes, I understand," the man said into the phone. Then he hung up and stared at Caleb with an angry glare. For a moment he was eerily motionless. Then he reached for the phone again. "Driver, pull over. Anywhere. Just pull over!"

For several minutes the man stared blankly out the window leaving all of Caleb's continuing questions dying in the air. Then the car turned and began to slow down. After a few minutes the car stopped. Silence permeated the car. Even as Caleb looked around, the man across from him still did not move or acknowledge the world around him.

Finally, the man said slowly, "You're not much of an American, Mr. Phillips…"

Caleb glared in silence.

Then the door opened. The two men next to Caleb exited the car.

Erica entered followed by two men in suits, dark and silent. Younger than the man who sat across from Caleb, they both nodded, but remained silent.

"Erica!" gasped Caleb. He reached out and fumbled a hug as she tumbled in and landed on Caleb's left side. "Are you okay?"

She nodded and gripped his arm. "Reilly's alive," she whispered in his ear. They embraced.

"Mr. Phillips, all of this has been a huge mistake," said one of the men who had entered with Erica. "Dr. Anderson suffered from delusions and this whole thing has been in his mind."

Caleb turned quickly. "In his mind? Hey, Chuckles over here was just telling me to wake up and realize that *something* is going on," he said as he pointed at the elderly man across from him. "He was saying that something was in our veins!"

"Well, obviously he was mistaken. There is nothing going on

and if you and Ms. Schmidt would like to leave you are both free to do so. In fact, there's a limo parked to the right of this vehicle and it will take you both to the hospital of your choice and, of course, you may pick up Ms. Schmidt's child who is recovering nicely at St. Mary's Children's Hospital about half an hour from here."

"We're ready to leave," said Erica instantly.

Caleb looked around puzzled. "What about…"

Erica tightened her grip on his arm. Shaking her head as she spoke, she softly stated "Weston was paranoid. It was a game and we played it. Time to go."

Their eyes met. Caleb could see the intensity on her face. Taking her hand in his he caressed it for a moment. "But …"

"The door is open, Mr. Phillips. I suggest you leave."

Erica opened the door with a shaking hand and then stepped out, alone in the breeze. Caleb remained seated. He looked around quickly in disbelief and started to speak, but the words never left the cotton balls in his mouth. Finally, he turned and looked out at Erica. Suddenly a hand grabbed his arm.

"Mr. Phillips, I assume it goes without saying that since nothing happened here, there is no story to tell."

"Yeah, sure," he mumbled then, as if in a dream, he tumbled out of the car.

The door closed behind him and the vehicle sped away. Erica stood for a moment looking up at the cold drizzle coming down from the sky.

"God, I never thought this nightmare would end," she gasped.

Caleb looked up at the clouds and allowed the rain to dot his face. "Sandra!" he whispered into the air.

Then he turned and looked at Erica. Taking her hands he said, "…that night I woke up and saw my wife in the living room with a gun. She was so very sick...," he said with frightening calm. "She was holding the gun and looked up...I tried to...I grabbed the gun...it went off...I couldn't tell you before....I blamed Weston....I just...I just don't know…." Caleb stammered as he wiped his eyes.

Erica embraced him. "It's okay. It's okay." For several minutes they stood in the rain looking into the clouds for answers.

Finally Erica moved. "Let's go get Reilly," Erica said softly as she led him to the limo.

"Did the good guys win?" he asked quietly against the backdrop of the limo's soft hum.

"I'm not sure," she said hesitantly. "What I do know is that the upcoming election saved us…"

"Is anything at all better because we did this?" asked Caleb.

"I hope so," she said somberly. "I hope so."

Erica entered the car and Caleb flopped in next to her exhausted. "We're free and Reilly is alive. For today that's enough," she said as she buckled her seatbelt and closed her eyes.

Caleb sat up for a moment. "How many times have we said 'good enough for today'? Did all of our 'good enoughs' add up to what happened to us?" Caleb questioned.

"I don't know," Erica said softly.

Caleb leaned forward and turned on the television set positioned in the console in front of him. As a news program droned on, Caleb leaned back to sleep.

"And now let's return to the breaking news story. Dr. Weston Anderson, accused of bioterrorism in the U.S., was shot and killed by FBI agents in a gun battle earlier today. But in another development, a video posted to the Internet earlier today by a group claiming to be supporters of Dr. Anderson, showed him taking the blame for RCG35-98, but stating it was no longer in his possession."

Erica and Caleb both opened their eyes. Erica sat up.

The reporter continued, "There also were claims that Anderson had video tapped proof that the current administration may have been involved with decisions made at Zelticor. We will now take you to a press conference by Roger Thompkins, deputy director of Homeland

Security."

"Oh, my god! Weston's message made it!" Erica said with joy.

On the screen Thompkins was standing at a podium clearing his throat. "Dr. Weston Anderson was a brilliant man who had much to offer his country. Unfortunately, Sadly, he made unfortunate decision. We have examined all of the evidence and must now conclude that this taped message was merely yet another rouse by Dr. Anderson in an effort to make himself look innocent. His life can simply be summed up as someone with great potential who succumbed to forces and was a part of an attempted bioterrorist plot against the United States citizens..."

Erica collapsed into the seat as Caleb hit the power button on the television. "The good guys...they didn't...."

"This is just round one," said Caleb stroking Erica's hand. "The truth is out there. The people who know are out there."

Erica rested her head on his shoulder meanwhile at St. Mary's Hospital in the pediatric ward a man leaned over Reilly's crib. "Daddy's just begun to fight, Princess. You wait and see."

ABOUT THE AUTHOR

Ms. Smelser is an accomplished freelance writer. Her writing has been published in *Newsweek Magazine*, *Education Digest*, and *The Journal of Literacy and Technology*. Aside from these national venues, her work has appeared in many local publications throughout her 17 years of work as a freelance writer. She holds a Ph.D. from Michigan State University in Composition Studies, a master's degree in professional writing from Eastern Michigan University, and a bachelor's degree in English from Calvin College. In addition, she is a mother of two daughters and an educational consultant.

18717189R00142

Made in the USA
Lexington, KY
20 November 2012